IRISH FAIRY TALES

THE·GOLDEN·BIRD
FLIES·AWAY·WITH·THE
·APPLE·

from the story of 'The Greek Princess'

Irish Fairy Tales

Selected by Jennifer Chandler
of The Folklore Society
from *Celtic Tales* and *More Celtic Tales*
collected and annotated by Joseph Jacobs

Illustrated by
JOHN D. BATTEN

WORDSWORTH CLASSICS

In loving memory of
MICHAEL TRAYLER
the founder of Wordsworth Editions

8

Readers who are interested in other titles from
Wordsworth Editions are invited to visit our website at
www.wordsworth-editions.com

For our latest list and a full mail-order service contact
Bibliophile Books, 5 Thomas Road, London E14 7BN
TEL: +44 (0)20 7515 9222 FAX: +44 (0)20 7538 4115
E-MAIL: orders@bibliophilebooks.com

Originally published as
Celtic Fairy Tales 1892 and *More Celtic Fairy Tales* 1894
This edition published 2001 by Wordsworth Editions Limited
8B East Street, Ware, Hertfordshire SG12 9HJ

ISBN 978-1-8402-2434-4

Typeset in Great Britain by Antony Gray
Printed and bound by Clays Ltd, St Ives plc

Contents

Full-page illustrations

Connla and the Fairy Maiden

Connla of the Fiery Hair was son of Conn of the Hundred Fights. One day as he stood by the side of his father on the height of Usna, he saw a maiden clad in strange attire coming towards him.

'Whence comest thou, maiden?' said Connla.

'I come from the Plains of the Ever Living,' she said, 'there where there is neither death nor sin. There we keep holiday always, nor need we help from any in our joy. And in all our pleasure we have no strife. And because we have our homes in the round green hills, men call us the Hill Folk.'

The king and all with him wondered much to hear a voice when they saw no one. For save Connla alone, none saw the fairy maiden.

'To whom art thou talking, my son?' said Conn the king.

Then the maiden answered, 'Connla speaks to a young, fair maid, whom neither death nor old age awaits. I love Connla, and now I call him away to the plain of pleasure, Moy Mell, where Boadag is king for aye, nor has there been complaint or sorrow in that land since he has held the kingship. Oh, come with me, Connla of the Fiery Hair, ruddy as the dawn with thy tawny skin. A fairy crown awaits thee to grace thy comely face and royal form. Come, and never shall thy comeliness fade, nor thy youth, till the last awful day of judgment.'

The king in fear at what the maiden said, which he heard though he could not see her, called aloud to his druid, Coran by name.

'Oh, Coran of the many spells,' he said, 'and of the cunning magic, I call upon thy aid. A task is upon me too great for all my skill and wit, greater than any laid upon me since I seized the kingship. A maiden unseen has met us, and by her power would take from me my dear, my comely son. If thou help not, he will be taken from thy king by woman's wiles and witchery.'

Then Coran the druid stood forth and chanted his spells towards the spot where the maiden's voice had been heard. And none heard her voice again, nor could Connla see her longer. Only as she vanished before the druid's mighty spell, she threw an apple to Connla.

For a whole month from that day Connla would take nothing, either to eat or to drink, save only from that apple. But as he ate it grew again and always kept whole. And all the while there grew within him a mighty yearning and longing after the maiden he had seen.

But when the last day of the month of waiting came, Connla stood by the side of the king his father on the plain of Arcomin, and again he saw the maiden come towards him, and again she spoke to him.

' 'Tis a glorious place, forsooth; that Connla holds among short-lived mortals awaiting the day of death. But now the folk of life, the ever-living ones, beg and bid thee come to Moy Mell, the plain of pleasure, for they have learnt to know thee, seeing thee in thy home among thy dear ones.'

When Conn the king heard the maiden's voice he called to his men aloud and said, 'Summon swift my druid Coran, for I see she has again this day the power of speech.'

Then the maiden said: 'Oh, mighty Conn, fighter of a hundred fights, the druid's power is little loved; it has little honour in the mighty land, peopled with so many of the upright. When the Law will come, it will do away with the druid's magic spells that come from the lips of the false black demon.'

Then Conn the king observed that since the maiden came Connla his son spoke to none that spake to him. So Conn of the hundred fights said to him, 'Is it to thy mind what the woman says, my son?'

' 'Tis hard upon me,' then said Connla; 'I love my own folk above all things; but yet, but yet a longing seizes me for the maiden.'

When the maiden heard this, she answered and said, 'The ocean is not so strong as the waves of thy longing. Come with me in my curragh, the gleaming, straight-gliding crystal canoe. Soon

CONNLA AND THE FAIRY MAIDEN

we can reach Boadag's realm. I see the bright sun sink, yet far as it is, we can reach it before dark. There is, too, another land worthy of thy journey, a land joyous to all that seek it. Only wives and maidens dwell there. If thou wilt, we can seek it and live there alone together in joy.'

When the maiden ceased to speak, Connla of the Fiery Hair rushed away from them and sprang into the curragh, the gleaming straight-gliding crystal canoe. And then they all, king and court, saw it glide away over the bright sea towards the setting sun. Away and away, till eye could see it no longer, and Connla and the fairy maiden went their way on the sea, and were no more seen, nor did any know where they came.

Guleesh

There was once a boy in the County Mayo; Guleesh was his name. There was the finest rath a little way off from the gable of the house, and he was often in the habit of seating himself on the fine grass bank that was running round it. One night he stood, half leaning against the gable of the house, and looking up into the sky, and watching the beautiful white moon over his head. After he had been standing that way for a couple of hours, he said to himself, 'My bitter grief that I am not gone away out of this place altogether. I'd sooner be any place in the world than here. Och, it's well for you, white moon,' says he, 'that's turning round, turning round, as you please yourself, and no man can put you back. I wish I was the same as you.'

Hardly was the word out of his mouth when he heard a great noise coming like the sound of many people running together, and talking, and laughing, and making sport, and the sound went by him like a whirl of wind, and he was listening to it going into the rath. 'Musha, by my soul,' says he, 'but ye're merry enough, and I'll follow ye.'

What was in it but the fairy host, though he did not know at first that it was they who were in it, but he followed them into the rath. It's there he heard the *fulparnee*, and the *folpornee*, the *rap-lay-hoota*, *and* the *roolya-boolya*, that they had there, and every man of them crying out as loud as he could, 'My horse, and bridle, and saddle! My horse, and bridle, and saddle!'

'By my hand,' said Guleesh, 'my boy, that's not bad. I'll imitate ye,' and he cried out as well as they, 'My horse, and bridle, and saddle! My horse, and bridle, and saddle!' And on the moment there was a fine horse with a bridle of gold, and a saddle of silver standing before him. He leaped up on it, and the moment he was on its back he saw clearly that the rath was full of horses, and of little people going riding on them.

Said a man of them to him, 'Are you coming with us tonight, Guleesh?'

'I am surely,' said Guleesh.

'If you are, come along,' said the little man, and out they went all together, riding like the wind, faster than the fastest horse ever you saw a-hunting, and faster than the fox and the hounds at his tail.

The cold winter's wind that was before them, they overtook her, and the cold winter's wind that was behind them, she did not overtake them. And stop nor stay of that full race, did they make none, until they came to the brink of the sea.

Then every one of them said, 'Hie over cap! Hie over cap!' and that moment they were up in the air, and before Guleesh had time to remember where he was, they were down on dry land again, and were going like the wind.

At last they stood still, and a man of them said to Guleesh, 'Guleesh, do you know where you are now?'

'Not a know,' says Guleesh.

'You're in France, Guleesh,' said he. 'The daughter of the king of France is to be married tonight, the handsomest woman that the sun ever saw, and we must do our best to bring her with us, if we're only able to carry her off; and you must come with us that we may be able to put the young girl up behind you on the horse, when we'll be bringing her away, for it's not lawful for us to put her sitting behind ourselves. But you're flesh and blood, and she can take a good grip of you, so that she won't fall off the horse. Are you satisfied, Guleesh, and will you do what we're telling you?'

'Why shouldn't I be satisfied?' said Guleesh. 'I'm satisfied, surely, and anything that ye will tell me to do I'll do it without doubt.'

They got off their horses there, and a man of them said a word that Guleesh did not understand, and on the moment they were lifted up, and Guleesh found himself and his companions in the palace. There was a great feast going on there, and there was not a nobleman or a gentleman in the kingdom but was gathered there, dressed in silk and satin, and gold and silver, and the night was as bright as the day with all the lamps and candles that were lit, and Guleesh had to shut his two eyes at the brightness. When he opened them again and looked from him, he thought he never saw anything as fine as all he saw there. There were a hundred tables spread out, and their fill of meat and drink on each table of them, flesh-meat, and cakes and sweetmeats, and wine and ale, and every drink that ever a man saw. The musicians were at the two ends of the hall, and they were playing the sweetest music that ever a man's ear heard, and there were young women and fine youths in the middle of the hall, dancing and turning, and going round so quickly and so lightly, that it put a *soorawn* in Guleesh's head to be looking at them. There were more there playing tricks, and more making fun and laughing, for such a feast as there was that day had not been in France for twenty years, because the old king had no children alive but only the one daughter, and she was to be married to the son of another king that night. Three days the feast was going on, and the third night she was to be married, and that was the night that Guleesh and the sheehogues came, hoping, if they could, to carry off with them the king's young daughter.

Guleesh and his companions were standing together at the head of the hall, where there was a fine altar dressed up, and two bishops behind it waiting to marry the girl, as soon as the right time should come. Now nobody could see the sheehogues, for they said a word as they came in, that made them all invisible, as if they had not been in it at all.

'Tell me which of them is the king's daughter,' said Guleesh, when he was becoming a little used to the noise and the light.

'Don't you see her there away from you?' said the little man that he was talking to.

Guleesh looked where the little man was pointing with his finger, and there he saw the loveliest woman that was, he thought, upon the ridge of the world. The rose and the lily were fighting together in her face, and one could not tell which of them got the victory. Her arms and hands were like the lime, her mouth as red as a strawberry when it is ripe, her foot was as small and as light as another one's hand, her form was smooth and slender, and her hair was falling down from her head in buckles of gold. Her garments and dress were woven with gold and silver, and the bright stone that was in the ring on her hand was as shining as the sun.

Guleesh was nearly blinded with all the loveliness and beauty that was in her; but when he looked again, he saw that she was crying, and that there was the trace of tears in her eyes. 'It can't be,' said Guleesh, 'that there's grief on her, when everybody round her is so full of sport and merriment.'

'Musha, then, she is grieved,' said the little man; 'for it's against her own will she's marrying, and she has no love for the husband she is to marry. The king was going to give her to him three years ago, when she was only fifteen, but she said she was too young, and requested him to leave her as she was yet. The king gave her a year's grace, and when that year was up he gave her another year's grace, and then another; but a week or a day he would not give her longer, and she is eighteen years old tonight, and it's time for her to marry; but, indeed,' says he, and he crooked his mouth in an ugly way – 'indeed, it's no king's son she'll marry, if I can help it.'

Guleesh pitied the handsome young lady greatly when he heard that, and he was heartbroken to think that it would be necessary for her to marry a man she did not like, or, what was worse, to take a nasty sheehogue for a husband. However, he did not say a word, though he could not help giving many a curse to the ill-luck that was laid out for himself, to be helping the people that were to snatch her away from her home and from her father.

He began thinking, then, what it was he ought to do to save her, but he could think of nothing. 'Oh! If I could only give her some help and relief,' said he, 'I wouldn't care whether I were alive or dead; but I see nothing that I can do for her.'

He was looking on when the king's son came up to her and asked her for a kiss, but she turned her head away from him. Guleesh had double pity for her then, when he saw the lad taking her by the soft white hand, and drawing her out to dance. They went round in the dance near where Guleesh was, and he could plainly see that there were tears in her eyes.

When the dancing was over, the old king, her father, and her mother the queen, came up and said that this was the right time to marry her, that the bishop was ready, and it was time to put the wedding ring on her and give her to her husband.

The king took the youth by the hand, and the queen took her daughter, and they went up together to the altar, with the lords and great people following them.

When they came near the altar, and were no more than about four yards from it, the little sheehogue stretched out his foot before the girl, and she fell. Before she was able to rise again he threw something that was in his hand upon her, said a couple of words, and upon the moment the maiden was gone from amongst them. Nobody could see her, for that word made her invisible. The little man*een* seized her and raised her up behind Guleesh, and the king nor no one else saw them, but out with them through the hall till they came to the door.

Oro! Dear Mary! It's there the pity was, and the trouble, and the crying, and the wonder, and the searching, and the *rookawn*, when that lady disappeared from their eyes and without their seeing what did it. Out of the door of the palace they went, without being stopped or hindered, for nobody saw them, and, 'My horse, my bridle, and saddle!' says every man of them. 'My horse, my bridle, and saddle!' says Guleesh; and on the moment the horse was standing ready caparisoned before him. 'Now, jump up, Guleesh,' said the little man, 'and put the lady behind you, and we will be going; the morning is not far off from us now.'

Guleesh raised her up on the horse's back, and leaped up himself before her, and, 'Rise, horse,' said he; and his horse, and the other horses with him, went in a full race until they came to the sea.

'Hie over cap!' said every man of them.

'Hie over cap!' said Guleesh; and on the moment the horse rose under him, and cut a leap in the clouds, and came down in Erin.

They did not stop there, but went of a race to the place where was Guleesh's house and the rath. And when they came as far as that, Guleesh turned and caught the young girl in his two arms, and leaped off the horse.

'I call and cross you to myself, in the name of God!' said he; and on the spot, before the word was out of his mouth, the horse fell down, and what was in it but the beam of a plough, of which they had made a horse; and every other horse they had, it was that way they made it. Some of them were riding on an old besom, and some on a broken stick, and more on a bohalawn or a hemlock-stalk.

The good people called out together when they heard what Guleesh said, 'Oh! Guleesh, you clown, you thief, that no good may happen you, why did you play that trick on us?'

But they had no power at all to carry off the girl, after Guleesh had consecrated her to himself.

'Oh! Guleesh, isn't that a nice turn you did us, and we so kind to you? What good have we now out of our journey to France. Never mind yet, you clown, but you'll pay us another time for this. Believe us, you'll repent it.'

'He'll have no good to get out of the young girl,' said the little man that was talking to him in the palace before that, and as he said the word he moved over to her and struck her a slap on the side of the head. 'Now,' says he, 'she'll be without talk any more; now, Guleesh, what good will she be to you when she'll be dumb? It's time for us to go – but you'll remember us, Guleesh!'

When he said that he stretched out his two hands, and before Guleesh was able to give an answer, he and the rest of them were gone into the rath out of his sight, and he saw them no more.

He turned to the young woman and said to her, 'Thanks be to God, they're gone. Would you not sooner stay with me than with them?' She gave him no answer. 'There's trouble and grief on her yet,' said Guleesh in his own mind, and he spoke to her again, 'I am afraid that you must spend this night in my father's house, lady, and if there is anything that I can do for you, tell me, and I'll be your servant.'

The beautiful girl remained silent, but there were tears in her eyes, and her face was white and red after each other.

'Lady,' said Guleesh, 'tell me what you would like me to do now. I never belonged at all to that lot of sheehogues who carried you away with them. I am the son of an honest farmer, and I went with them without knowing it. If I'll be able to send you back to

your father I'll do it, and I pray you make any use of me now that
you may wish.'

He looked into her face, and he saw the mouth moving as if she
was going to speak, but there came no word from it.

'It cannot be,' said Guleesh, 'that you are dumb. Did I not hear
you speaking to the king's son in the palace tonight? Or has that
devil made you really dumb, when he struck his nasty hand on
your jaw?'

The girl raised her white smooth hand, and laid her finger on
her tongue, to show him that she had lost her voice and power of
speech, and the tears ran out of her two eyes like streams, and
Guleesh's own eyes were not dry, for as rough as he was on the
outside he had a soft heart, and could not stand the sight of the
young girl, and she in that unhappy plight.

He began thinking with himself what he ought to do, and he did
not like to bring her home with himself to his father's house, for
he knew well that they would not believe him, that he had been in

France and brought back with him the king of France's daughter, and he was afraid they might make a mock of the young lady or insult her.

As he was doubting what he ought to do, and hesitating, he chanced to remember the priest. 'Glory be to God,' said he, 'I know now what I'll do; I'll bring her to the priest's house, and he won't refuse me to keep the lady and care her.' He turned to the lady again and told her that he was loth to take her to his father's house, but that there was an excellent priest very friendly to himself, who would take good care of her, if she wished to remain in his house; but that if there was any other place she would rather go, he said he would bring her to it.

She bent her head, to show him she was obliged, and gave him to understand that she was ready to follow him any place he was going. 'We will go to the priest's house, then,' said he; 'he is under an obligation to me, and will do anything I ask him.'

They went together accordingly to the priest's house, and the sun was just rising when they came to the door. Guleesh beat it hard, and as early as it was the priest was up, and opened the door himself. He wondered when he saw Guleesh and the girl, for he was certain that it was coming wanting to be married they were.

'Guleesh, Guleesh, isn't it the nice boy you are that you can't wait till ten o'clock or till twelve, but that you must be coming to me at this hour, looking for marriage, you and your sweetheart? You ought to know that I can't marry you at such a time, or, at all events, can't marry you lawfully. But ubbubboo!' said he, suddenly, as he looked again at the young girl, 'in the name of God, who have you here? Who is she, or how did you get her?'

'Father,' said Guleesh, 'you can marry me, or anybody else, if you wish; but it's not looking for marriage I came to you now, but to ask you, if you please, to give a lodging in your house to this young lady.'

The priest looked at him as though he had ten heads on him; but without putting any other question to him, he desired him to come in, himself and the maiden, and when they came in, he shut the door, brought them into the parlour, and put them sitting.

'Now, Guleesh,' said he, 'tell me truly who is this young lady, and whether you're out of your senses really, or are only making a joke of me.'

'I'm not telling a word of lie, nor making a joke of you,' said Guleesh; 'but it was from the palace of the king of France I carried off this lady, and she is the daughter of the king of France.'

He began his story then, and told the whole to the priest, and the priest was so much surprised that he could not help calling out at times, or clapping his hands together.

When Guleesh said from what he saw he thought the girl was not satisfied with the marriage that was going to take place in the palace before he and the sheehogues broke it up, there came a red blush into the girl's cheek, and he was more certain than ever that she had sooner be as she was – badly as she was – than be the married wife of the man she hated. When Guleesh said that he would be very thankful to the priest if he would keep her in his own house, the kind man said he would do that as long as Guleesh pleased, but that he did not know what they ought to do with her, because they had no means of sending her back to her father again.

Guleesh answered that he was uneasy about the same thing, and that he saw nothing to do but to keep quiet until they should find some opportunity of doing something better. They made it up then between themselves that the priest should let on that it was his brother's daughter he had, who was come on a visit to him from another county, and that he should tell everybody that she was dumb, and do his best to keep everyone away from her. They told the young girl what it was they intended to do, and she showed by her eyes that she was obliged to them.

Guleesh went home then, and when his people asked him where he had been, he said that he had been asleep at the foot of the ditch, and had passed the night there.

There was great wonderment on the priest's neighbours at the girl who came so suddenly to his house without anyone knowing where she was from, or what business she had there. Some of the people said that everything was not as it ought to be, and others, that Guleesh was not like the same man that was in it before, and that it was a great story, how he was drawing every day to the priest's house, and that the priest had a wish and a respect for him, a thing they could not clear up at all.

That was true for them, indeed, for it was seldom the day went by but Guleesh would go to the priest's house and have a talk with him, and as often as he would come he used to hope to find the young lady well again, and with leave to speak; but, alas, she remained dumb and silent, without relief or cure. Since she had no other means of talking, she carried on a sort of conversation between herself and himself, by moving her hand and fingers, winking her eyes, opening and shutting her mouth, laughing or smiling, and a thousand other signs, so that it was not long until they understood each other very well. Guleesh was always thinking how he should send her back to her father; but there was no one to go with her, and he himself did not know what road to go, for he had never been out of his own country before the night he brought her away with him. Nor had the priest any better knowledge than he; but when Guleesh asked him, he wrote three or four letters to the king of France, and gave them to buyers and sellers of wares, who used to be going from place to place across the sea; but they all went astray, and never a one came to the king's hand.

This was the way they were for many months, and Guleesh was falling deeper and deeper in love with her every day, and it was plain to himself and the priest that she liked him. The boy feared greatly at last, lest the king should really hear where his daughter was, and take her back from himself, and he besought the priest to write no more, but to leave the matter to God.

So they passed the time for a year, until there came a day when Guleesh was lying by himself on the grass, on the last day of the last month in autumn, and he was thinking over again in his own mind of everything that happened to him from the day that he went with the sheehogues across the sea. He remember then, suddenly, that it was one November night that he was standing at the gable of the house, when the whirlwind came, and the sheehogues in it, and he said to himself, 'We have November night again today, and I'll stand in the same place I was last year, until I see if the good people come again. Perhaps I might see or hear something that would be useful to me, and might bring back her talk again to Mary' – that was the name himself and the priest called the king's daughter, for neither of them knew her right name. He told his intention to the priest, and the priest gave him his blessing.

Guleesh accordingly went to the old rath when the night was darkening, and he stood with his bent elbow leaning on a grey old flag, waiting till the middle of the night should come. The moon rose slowly, and it was like a knob of fire behind him; and there was a white fog which was raised up over the fields of grass and all damp places, through the coolness of the night after a great heat in the day. The night was calm as is a lake when there is not a breath of wind to move a wave on it, and there was no sound to be heard but the *cronawn* of the insects that would go by from time to time, or the hoarse sudden scream of the wild geese, as they passed from lake to lake, half a mile up in the air over his head; or the sharp whistle of the golden and green plover, rising and lying, lying and rising, as they do on a calm night. There were a thousand thousand bright stars shining over his head, and there was a little frost out, which left the grass under his foot white and crisp.

He stood there for an hour, for two hours, for three hours, and the frost increased greatly, so that he heard the breaking of the *traneens* under his foot as often as he moved. He was thinking, in his own mind, at last, that the sheehogues would not come that night, and that it was as good for him to return back again, when he heard a sound far away from him, coming towards him, and he recognised what it was at the first moment. The sound increased, and at first it was like the beating of waves on a stony shore, and then it was like the falling of a great waterfall, and at last it was like a loud storm in the tops of the trees, and then the whirlwind burst into the rath of one rout, and the sheehogues were in it.

It all went by him so suddenly that he lost his breath with it, but he came to himself on the spot, and put an ear on himself, listening to what they would say.

Scarcely had they gathered into the rath till they all began shouting, and screaming, and talking amongst themselves; and then each one of them cried out, 'My horse and bridle, and saddle!

My horse, and bridle, and saddle!' and Guleesh took courage, and
called out as loudly as any of them, 'My horse, and bridle, and
saddle! My horse and bridle, and saddle!' But before the word was
well out of his mouth, another man cried out, 'Ora! Guleesh, my
boy, are you here with us again? How art you getting on with your
woman? There's no use in your calling for your horse tonight. I'll
go bail you won't play such a trick on us again. It was a good trick
you played on us last year?'

'It was,' said another man; 'he won't do it again.'

'Isn't he a prime lad, the same lad! To take a woman with him
that never said as much to him as, "How do you do?" since this
time last year!' says the third man.

'Perhaps he likes to be looking at her,' said another voice.

'And if the *omadawn* only knew that there's an herb growing up
by his own door, and if he were to boil it and give it to her, she'd
be well,' said another voice.

'That's true for you.'

'He is an omadawn.'

'Don't bother your head with him; we'll be going.'

'We'll leave the *bodach* as he is.'

And with that they rose up into the air, and out with them with
one *roolya-boolya* the way they came; and they left poor Guleesh
standing where they found him, and the two eyes going out of his
head, looking after them and wondering.

He did not stand long till he returned back, and he thinking in
his own mind on all he saw and heard, and wondering whether
there was really a herb at his own door that would bring back the
talk to the king's daughter. 'It can't be,' says he to himself, 'that
they would tell it to me, if there was any virtue in it; but perhaps
the sheehogue didn't observe himself when he let the word slip
out of his mouth. I'll search well as soon as the sun rises, whether
there's any plant growing beside the house except thistles and
dockings.'

He went home, and as tired as he was he did not sleep a wink
until the sun rose on the morrow. He got up then, and it was the
first thing he did to go out and search well through the grass
round about the house, trying could he get any herb that he did

not recognise. And, indeed, he was not long searching till he observed a large strange herb that was growing up just by the gable of the house.

He went over to it, and observed it closely, and saw that there were seven little branches coming out of the stalk, and seven leaves growing on every branch*een* of them; and that there was a white sap in the leaves. 'It's very wonderful,' said be to himself, 'that I never noticed this herb before. If there's any virtue in a herb at all, it ought to be in such a strange one as this.'

He drew out his knife, cut the plant, and carried it into his own house; stripped the leaves off it and cut up the stalk; and there came a thick, white juice out of it, as there comes out of the sow-thistle when it is bruised, except that the juice was more like oil.

He put it in a little pot and a little water in it, and laid it on the fire until the water was boiling, and then he took a cup, filled it half up with the juice, and put it to his own mouth. It came into his head then that perhaps it was poison that was in it, and that the good people were only tempting him that he might kill himself with that trick, or put the girl to death without meaning it. He put down the cup again, raised a couple of drops on the top of his finger, and put it to his mouth. It was not bitter, and, indeed, had a sweet, agreeable taste. He grew bolder then, and drank the full of a thimble of it, and then as much again, and he never stopped till he had half the cup drunk. He fell asleep after that, and did not wake till it was night, and there was great hunger and great thirst on him.

He had to wait, then, till the day rose; but he determined, as soon as he should wake in the morning, that he would go to the king's daughter and give her a drink of the juice of the herb.

As soon as he got up in the morning, he went over to the priest's house with the drink in his hand, and he never felt himself so bold and valiant, and spirted and light, as he was that day, and he was quite certain that it was the drink he drank which made him so hearty.

When he came to the house, he found the priest and the young lady within, and they were wondering greatly why he had not visited them for two days.

He told them all his news, and said that he was certain that there was great power in that herb, and that it would do the lady no hurt, for he tried it himself and got good from it, and then he made her taste it, for he vowed and swore that there was no harm in it.

Guleesh handed her the cup, and she drank half of it, and then fell back on her bed and a heavy sleep came on her, and she never woke out of that sleep till the day on the morrow.

Guleesh and the priest sat up the entire night with her, waiting till she should awake, and they between hope and unhope, between expectation of saving her and fear of hurting her.

She awoke at last when the sun had gone half its way through the heavens. She rubbed her eyes and looked like a person who did not know where she was. She was like one astonished when she saw Guleesh and the priest in the same room with her, and she sat up doing her best to collect her thoughts.

The two men were in great anxiety waiting to see would she speak, or would she not speak, and when they remained silent for a couple of minutes, the priest said to her, 'Did you sleep well, Mary?'

And she answered him, 'I slept, thank you.'

No sooner did Guleesh hear her talking than he put a shout of joy out of him, and ran over to her and fell on his two knees, and said, 'A thousand thanks to God, who has given you back the talk; lady of my heart, speak again to me.'

The lady answered him that she understood it was he who boiled that drink for her, and gave it to her; that she was obliged to him from her heart for all the kindness he showed her since the day she first came to Ireland, and that he might be certain that she never would forget it.

Guleesh was ready to die with satisfaction and delight. Then they brought her food, and she ate with a good appetite, and was merry and joyous, and never left off talking with the priest while she was eating.

After that Guleesh went home to his house, and stretched himself on the bed and fell asleep again, for the force of the herb was not all spent, and he passed another day and a night sleeping. When he woke up he went back to the priest's house, and found that the young lady was in the same state, and that she was asleep almost since the time that he left the house.

He went into her chamber with the priest, and they remained watching beside her till she awoke the second time, and she had her talk as well as ever, and Guleesh was greatly rejoiced. The priest put food on the table again, and they ate together, and Guleesh used after that to come to the house from day to day, and the friendship that was between him and the king's daughter increased, because she had no one to speak to except Guleesh and the priest, and she liked Guleesh best.

So they married one another, and that was the fine wedding they had, and if I were to be there then, I would not be here now; but I heard it from a birdeen that there was neither cark nor care, sickness nor sorrow, mishap nor misfortune on them till the hour of their death, and may the same be with me, and with us all!

The Field of Boliauns

One fine day in harvest – it was indeed Ladyday in harvest, that everybody knows to be one of the great holidays in the year – Tom Fitzpatrick was taking a ramble through the ground, and went along the sunny side of a hedge; when all of a sudden he heard a clacking sort of noise a little before him in the hedge. 'Dear me,' said Tom, 'but isn't it surprising to hear the stone-chatters singing so late in the season?' So Tom stole on, going on the tops of his toes to try if he could get a sight of what was making the noise, to see if he was right in his guess. The noise stopped; but as Tom looked sharply through the bushes, what should he see in a nook of the hedge but a brown pitcher, that might hold about a gallon and a half of liquor; and by and by a little wee teeny tiny bit of an old man, with a little *motty* of a cocked hat stuck upon the top of his head, a deeshy daushy leather apron hanging before him, pulled out a little wooden stool, and stood up upon it, and dipped a little piggin into the pitcher, and took out the full of it, and put it beside the stool, and then sat down under the pitcher, and began to work at putting a heel-piece on a bit of a brogue just fit for himself. 'Well, by the powers,' said Tom to himself, 'I often heard tell of the Lepracauns, and, to tell God's truth, I never rightly believed in them – but here's one of them in real earnest. If I go knowingly to work, I'm a made man. They say a body must never take their eyes off them, or they'll escape.'

Tom now stole on a little farther, with his eye fixed on the little man just as a cat does with a mouse. So when he got up quite close to him, 'God bless your work, neighbour,' said Tom.

The little man raised up his head and, 'Thank you kindly,' said he.

'I wonder you'd be working on the holiday!' said Tom.

'That's my own business, not yours,' was the reply.

'Well, maybe you'd be civil enough to tell us what you've got in the pitcher there?' said Tom.

'That I will, with pleasure,' said he; 'it's good beer.'

'Beer!' said Tom. 'Thunder and fire! Where did you get it?'

'Where did I get it, is it? Why, I made it. And what do you think I made it of?'

'Devil a one of me knows,' said Tom; 'but of malt, I suppose, what else?'

'There you're out. I made it of heath.'

'Of heath!' said Tom, bursting out laughing. 'Sure you don't think me to be such a fool as to believe that?'

'Do as you please,' said he, 'but what I tell you is the truth. Did you never hear tell of the Danes.'

'Well, what about *them?*' said Tom.

'Why, all the about them there is, is that when they were here they taught us to make beer out of the heath, and the secret's in my family ever since.'

'Will you give a body a taste of your beer?' said Tom.

'I'll tell you what it is, young man, it would be fitter for you to be looking after your father's property than to be bothering decent quiet people with your foolish questions. There now, while you're idling away your time here, there's the cows have broke into the oats, and are knocking the corn all about.'

Tom was taken so by surprise with this that he was just on the very point of turning round when he recollected himself; so, afraid that the like might happen again, he made a grab at the Lepracaun, and caught him up in his hand; but in his hurry he overset the pitcher, and spilt all the beer, so that he could not get a taste of it to tell what sort it was. He then swore that he would kill him if he did not show him where his money was. Tom looked so wicked and so bloody-minded that the little man was quite frightened; so says he, 'Come along with me a couple of fields off; and I'll show you a crock of gold.'

So they went, and Tom held the Lepracaun fast in his hand, and never took his eyes from off him, though they had to cross hedges and ditches, and a crooked bit of bog, till at last they came to a great field all full of boliauns, and the Lepracaun pointed to a big boliaun, and says he, 'Dig under that boliaun, and you'll get the great crock all full of guineas.'

Tom in his hurry had never thought of bringing a spade with him, so he made up his mind to run home and fetch one; and that he might know the place again he took oft one of his red garters, and tied it round the boliaun.

Then he said to the Lepracaun, 'Swear ye'll not take that garter away from that boliaun.' And the Lepracaun swore right away not to touch it.

'I suppose,' said the Lepracaun, very civilly, 'you have no further occasion for me?'

'No,' says Tom; 'you may go away now, if you please, and God speed you, and may good luck attend you wherever you go.'

'Well, goodbye to you, Tom Fitzpatrick,' said the Lepracaun; 'and much good may it do you when you get it.'

So Tom ran for dear life, till he came home and got a spade, and then away with him, as hard as he could go, back to the field of boliauns; but when he got there, lo and behold! Not a boliaun in the field but had a red garter, the very model of his own, tied about it; and as to digging up the whole field, that was all nonsense, for there were more than forty good Irish acres in it. So Tom came home again with his spade on his shoulder, a little cooler than he went, and many's the hearty curse he gave the Lepracaun every time he thought of the neat turn he had served him.

The Horned Women

A rich woman sat up late one night carding and preparing wool, while all the family and servants were asleep. Suddenly a knock was given at the door, and a voice called, 'Open! Open!'

'Who is there?' said the woman of the house.

'I am the Witch of one Horn,' was answered.

The mistress, supposing that one of her neighbours had called and required assistance, opened the door, and a woman entered, having in her hand a pair of wool-carders, and bearing a horn on her forehead, as if growing there. She sat down by the fire in silence, and began to card the wool with violent haste. Suddenly she paused, and said aloud, 'Where are the women? They delay too long.'

Then a second knock came to the door, and a voice called as before, 'Open! Open!'

The mistress felt herself obliged to rise and open to the call, and immediately a second witch entered, having two horns on her forehead and in her hand a wheel for spinning wool.

'Give me place,' she said; 'I am the Witch of the two Horns,' and she began to spin as quick as lightning.

And so the knocks went on, and the call was heard and the witches entered, until at last twelve women sat round the fire – the first with one horn, the last with twelve horns.

And they carded the thread, and turned their spinning wheels, and wound and wove, all singing together an ancient rhyme, but no word did they speak to the mistress of the house. Strange to hear, and frightful to look upon, were these twelve women, with their horns and their wheels; and the mistress felt near to death, and she tried to rise that she might call for help, but she could not move, nor could she utter a word or a cry, for the spell of the witches was upon her.

Then one of them called to her in Irish, and said, 'Rise, woman, and make us a cake.'

Then the mistress searched for a vessel to bring water from the well that she might mix the meal and make the cake, but she could find none.

And they said to her, 'Take a sieve and bring water in it.'

And she took the sieve and went to the well; but the water poured from it, and she could fetch none for the cake, and she sat down by the well and wept.

Then a voice came by her and said, 'Take yellow clay and moss, and bind them together, and plaster the sieve so that it will hold.'

This she did, and the sieve held the water for the cake; and the voice said again, 'Return, and when thou comest to the north angle of the house, cry aloud three times and say, "The mountain of the Fenian women and the sky over it is all on fire." '

And she did so.

When the witches inside heard the call, a great and terrible cry broke from their lips, and they rushed forth with wild lamentations and shrieks, and fled away to Slievenamon, where was their chief abode. But the Spirit of the Well bade the mistress of the house to enter and prepare her home against the enchantments of the witches if they returned again.

And first, to break their spells, she sprinkled the water in which she had washed her child's feet, the feet-water, outside the door on the threshold; secondly, she took the cake which in her absence the witches had made of meal mixed with the blood drawn from the sleeping family, and she broke the cake in bits, and placed a bit in the mouth of each sleeper, and they were restored; and she took the cloth they had woven, and placed it half in and half out of the chest with the padlock; and lastly, she secured the door with a great crossbeam fastened in the jambs, so that the witches could not enter, and having done these things she waited.

Not long were the witches in coming back, and they raged and called for vengeance.

'Open! Open!' they screamed. 'Open, feet-water!'

'I cannot,' said the feet-water; 'I am scattered on the ground, and my path is down to the lough.'

'Open, open, wood and trees and beam!' they cried to the door.

'I cannot,' said the door, 'for the beam is fixed in the jambs and I have no power to move.'

'Open, open, cake that we have made and mingled with blood!' they cried again.

'I cannot,' said the cake, 'for I am broken and bruised, and my blood is on the lips of the sleeping children.'

Then the witches rushed through the air with great cries, and fled back to Slievenamon, uttering strange curses on the Spirit of the Well, who had wished their ruin; but the woman and the house were left in peace, and a mantle dropped by one of the witches in her flight was kept hung up by the mistress in memory of that night; and this mantle was kept by the same family from generation to generation for five hundred years after.

Hudden and Dudden and
Donald O'Neary

There was once upon a time two farmers, and their names were Hudden and Dudden. They had poultry in their yards, sheep on the uplands, and scores of cattle in the meadow-land alongside the river. But for all that they weren't happy. For just between their two farms there lived a poor man by the name of Donald O'Neary. He had a hovel over his head and a strip of grass that was barely enough to keep his one cow, Daisy, from starving, and, though she did her best, it was but seldom that Donald got a drink of milk or a roll of butter from Daisy. You would think there was little here to make Hudden and Dudden jealous, but so it is, the more one has the more one wants, and Donald's neighbours lay awake of nights scheming how they might get hold of his little strip of grassland. Daisy, poor thing, they never thought of; she was just a bag of bones.

One day Hudden met Dudden, and they were soon grumbling

as usual, and all to the tune of, 'If only we could get that vagabond Donald O'Neary out of the country.'

'Let's kill Daisy,' said Hudden at last; 'if that doesn't make him clear out, nothing will.'

No sooner said than agreed, and it wasn't dark before Hudden and Dudden crept up to the little shed where lay poor Daisy trying her best to chew the cud, though she hadn't had as much grass in the day as would cover your hand. And when Donald came to see if Daisy was all snug for the night, the poor beast had only time to lick his hand once before she died.

Well, Donald was a shrewd fellow, and downhearted though he was, began to think if he could get any good out of Daisy's death. He thought and he thought, and the next day you could have seen him trudging off early to the fair, Daisy's hide over his shoulder, every penny he had jingling in his pockets. Just before he got to the fair, he made several slits in the hide, put a penny in each slit, walked into the best inn of the town as bold as if it belonged to him, and, hanging the hide up to a nail in the wall, sat down.

'Some of your best whiskey,' says he to the landlord. But the landlord didn't like his looks. 'Is it fearing I won't pay you, you are?' says Donald. 'Why I have a hide here that gives me all the money I want.' And with that he hit it a whack with his stick and out hopped a penny. The landlord opened his eyes, as you may fancy.

'What'll you take for that hide?'

'It's not for sale, my good man.'

'Will you take a gold piece?'

'It's not for sale, I tell you. Hasn't it kept me and mine for years?' and with that Donald hit the hide another whack and out jumped a second penny.

Well, the long and the short of it was that Donald let the hide go, and, that very evening, who but he should walk up to Hudden's door?

'Good-evening, Hudden. Will you lend me your best pair of scales?'

Hudden stared and Hudden scratched his head, but he lent the scales.

When Donald was safe at home, he pulled out his pocketful of bright gold and began to weigh each piece in the scales. But Hudden had put a lump of butter at the bottom, and so the last piece of gold stuck fast to the scales when he took them back to Hudden.

If Hudden had stared before, he stared ten times more now, and no sooner was Donald's back turned, than he was off as hard as he could pelt to Dudden's.

'Good-evening, Dudden. That vagabond, bad luck to him – '

'You mean Donald O'Neary?'

'And who else should I mean? He's back here weighing out sackfuls of gold.'

'How do you know that?'

'Here are my scales that he borrowed, and here's a gold piece still sticking to them.'

Off they went together, and they came to Donald's door. Donald had finished making the last pile of ten gold pieces. And he couldn't finish because a piece had stuck to the scales.

In they walked without an 'If you please' or 'By your leave'.

'Well, I never!' That was all *they* could say.

'Good-evening, Hudden; good-evening, Dudden. Ah! You thought you had played me a fine trick, but you never did me a better turn in all your lives. When I found poor Daisy dead, I thought to myself, "Well, her hide may fetch something"; and it did. Hides are worth their weight in gold in the market just now.'

Hudden nudged Dudden, and Dudden winked at Hudden.

'Good-evening, Donald O'Neary.'

'Good-evening, kind friends.'

The next day there wasn't a cow or a calf that belonged to Hudden or Dudden but her hide was going to the fair in Hudden's biggest cart drawn by Dudden's strongest pair of horses.

When they came to the fair, each one took a hide over his arm, and there they were walking through the fair, bawling out at the top of their voices, 'Hides to sell! Hides to sell!'

Out came the tanner.

'How much for your hides, my good men?'

'Their weight in gold.'

'It's early in the day to come out of the tavern.' That was all the tanner said, and back he went to his yard.

'Hides to sell! Fine fresh hides to sell!'

Out came the cobbler.

'How much for your hides, my men?'

'Their weight in gold.'

'Is it making game of me you are! Take that for your pains,' and the cobbler dealt Hudden a blow that made him stagger.

Up the people came running from one end of the fair to the other. 'What's the matter? What's the matter?' cried they.

'Here are a couple of vagabonds selling hides at their weight in gold,' said the cobbler.

'Hold 'em fast; hold 'em fast!' bawled the innkeeper, who was the last to come up, he was so fat. 'I'll wager it's one of the rogues who tricked me out of thirty gold pieces yesterday for a wretched hide.'

It was more kicks than halfpence that Hudden and Dudden got before they were well on their way home again, and they didn't run the slower because all the dogs of the town were at their heels.

Well, as you may fancy, if they loved Donald little before, they loved him less now.

'What's the matter, friends?' said be, as he saw them tearing along, their hats knocked in, and their coats torn off, and their faces black and blue. 'Is it fighting you've been? Or mayhap you met the police, in luck to them?'

'We'll police you, you vagabond. It's mighty smart you thought yourself, deluding us with your lying tales.'

'Who deluded you? Didn't you see the gold with your own two eyes?'

But it was no use talking. Pay for it he must, and should. There was a meal-sack handy, and into it Hudden and Dudden popped Donald O'Neary, tied him up tight, ran a pole through the knot, and off they started for the Brown Lake of the Bog, each with a pole-end on his shoulder, and Donald O'Neary between.

But the Brown Lake was far, the road was dusty, Hudden and Dudden were sore and weary, and parched with thirst. There was an inn by the roadside.

'Let's go in,' said Hudden; 'I'm dead beat. It's heavy he is for the little he had to eat.'

If Hudden was willing, so was Dudden. As for Donald, you may be sure his leave wasn't asked, but he was lumped down at the inn door for all the world as if he had been a sack of potatoes.

'Sit still, you vagabond,' said Dudden; 'if we don't mind waiting, you needn't.'

Donald held his peace, but after a while he heard the glasses clink, and Hudden singing away at the top of his voice.

'I won't have her, I tell you; I won't have her!' said Donald. But nobody heeded what he said.

'I won't have her, I tell you; I won't have her!' said Donald, and this time he said it louder; but nobody heeded what he said.

'I won't have her, I tell you; I won't have her!' said Donald; and this time he said it as loud as he could.

'And who won't you have, may I be so bold as to ask?' said a farmer, who had just come up with a drove of cattle and was turning in for a glass.

'It's the king's daughter. They are bothering the life out of me to marry her.'

'You're the lucky fellow. I'd give something to be in your shoes.'

'Do you see that now! Wouldn't it be a fine thing for a farmer to be marrying a princess, all dressed in gold and jewels?'

'Jewels, do you say? Ah, now, couldn't you take me with you?'

'Well, you're an honest fellow, and as I don't care for the king's daughter, though she's as beautiful as the day, and is covered with jewels from top to toe, you shall have her. Just undo the cord, and let me out; they tied me up tight, as they knew I'd run away from her.'

Out crawled Donald, in crept the farmer.

'Now lie still, and don't mind the shaking; it's only rumbling over the palace steps you'll be. And maybe they'll abuse you for a vagabond, who won't have the king's daughter; but you needn't mind that. Ah! It's a deal I'm giving up for you, sure as it is that I don't care for the princess.'

'Take my cattle in exchange,' said the farmer; and you may guess it wasn't long before Donald was at their tails driving them homewards.

Out came Hudden and Dudden, and the one took one end of the pole, and the other the other.

'I'm thinking he's heavier,' said Hudden.

'Ah, never mind,' said Dudden; 'it's only a step now to the Brown Lake.'

'I'll have her now! I'll have her now!' bawled the farmer, from inside the sack.

'By my faith, and you shall though,' said Hudden, and he laid his stick across the sack.

'I'll have her! I'll have her!' bawled the farmer, louder than ever.

'Well, here you are,' said Dudden, for they were now come to the Brown Lake, and, unslinging the sack, they pitched it plump into the lake.

'You'll not be playing your tricks on us any longer,' said Hudden.

'True for you,' said Dudden. 'Ah, Donald, my boy, it was an ill day when you borrowed my scales.'

Off they went, with a light step and an easy heart, but when they were near home, who should they see but Donald O'Neary, and all around him the cows were grazing, and the calves were kicking up their heels and butting their heads together.

'Is it you, Donald?' said Dudden. 'Faith, you've been quicker than we have.'

'True for you, Dudden, and let me thank you kindly; the turn was good, if the will was ill. You'll have heard, like me, that the Brown Lake leads to the Land of Promise. I always put it down as lies, but it is just as true as my word. Look at the cattle.'

Hudden stared, and Dudden gaped; but they couldn't get over the cattle; fine fat cattle they were too.

'It's only the worst I could bring up with me,' said Donald O'Neary; 'the others were so fat, there was no driving them. Faith, too, it's little wonder they didn't care to leave, with grass as far as you could see, and as sweet and juicy as fresh butter.'

'Ah, now, Donald, we haven't always been friends,' said Dudden, 'but, as I was just saying, you were ever a decent lad, and you'll show us the way, won't you?'

'I don't see that I'm called upon to do that; there is a power more cattle down there. Why shouldn't I have them all to myself?'

'Faith, they may well say, the richer you get, the harder the heart. You always were a neighbourly lad, Donald. You wouldn't wish to keep the luck all to yourself?'

'True for you, Hudden, though 'tis a bad example you set me. But I'll not be thinking of old times. There is plenty for all there, so come along with me.'

Off they trudged, with a light heart and an eager step. When they came to the Brown Lake, the sky was full of little white clouds, and, if the sky was full, the lake was as full.

'Ah now! Look, there they are,' cried Donald, as he pointed to the clouds in the lake.

'Where? Where?' cried Hudden and, 'Don't be greedy!' cried Dudden, as he jumped his hardest to be up first with the fat cattle. But if he jumped first, Hudden wasn't long behind.

They never came back. Maybe they got too fat, like the cattle. As for Donald O'Neary, he had cattle and sheep all his days to his heart's content.

The Story of Deirdre

There was a man in Ireland once who was called Malcolm Harper. The man was a right good man, and he had a goodly share of this world's goods. He had a wife, but no family. What did Malcolm hear but that a soothsayer had come home to the place, and as the man was a right good man, he wished that the soothsayer might come near them. Whether it was that he was invited or that he came of himself, the soothsayer came to the house of Malcolm.

'Are you doing any soothsaying?' says Malcolm.

'Yes, I am doing a little. Are you in need of soothsaying?'

'Well, I do not mind taking soothsaying from you, if you had soothsaying for me, and you would be willing to do it.'

'Well, I will do soothsaying for you. What kind of soothsaying do you want?'

'Well, the soothsaying I wanted was that you would tell me my lot or what will happen to me, if you can give me knowledge of it.'

'Well, I am going out, and when I return, I will tell you.'

And the soothsayer went forth out of the house and he was not long outside when he returned.

'Well,' said the soothsayer, 'I saw in my second sight that it is on account of a daughter of yours that the greatest amount of blood shall be shed that has ever been shed in Erin since time and race began. And the three most famous heroes that ever were found will lose their heads on her account.'

After a time, a daughter was born to Malcolm; he did not allow a living being to come to his house, only himself and the nurse. He asked this woman, 'Will you yourself bring up the child to keep her in hiding far away where eye will not see a sight of her nor ear hear a word about her?'

The woman said she would, so Malcolm got three men, and he took them away to a large mountain, distant and far from reach without the knowledge or notice of anyone. He caused there a hillock, round and green, to be dug out of the middle, and the hole thus made to be covered carefully over so that a little company could dwell there together. This was done.

Deirdre and her foster-mother dwelt in the bothy mid the hills without the knowledge or the suspicion of any living person about them and without anything occurring, until Deirdre was sixteen years of age. Deirdre grew like the white sapling, straight and trim as the rash on the moss. She was the creature of fairest form, of loveliest aspect, and of gentlest nature that existed between earth and heaven in all Ireland – whatever colour of hue she had before, there was nobody that looked into her face but she would blush fiery red over it.

The woman that had charge of her, gave Deirdre every information and skill of which she herself had knowledge and skill. There was not a blade of grass growing from root, nor a bird singing in the wood, nor a star shining from heaven but Deirdre had a name for it. But one thing, she did not wish her to have either part or parley with any single living man of the rest of the world. But on a gloomy winter night, with black, scowling clouds, a hunter of game was wearily travelling the hills, and what happened but that he missed the trail of the hunt, and lost his course and companions. A drowsiness came upon the man as he wearily wandered over the hills, and he lay down by the side of the beautiful green knoll in which Deirdre lived, and he slept. The man was faint from hunger and wandering, and benumbed with cold, and a deep sleep fell upon him. When he lay down beside the green hill where Deirdre was, a troubled dream came to the man, and he thought that he enjoyed the warmth of a fairy broch, the fairies being inside playing music. The hunter shouted out in his dream, if there was anyone in the broch, to let him in for the Holy One's sake. Deirdre heard the voice and said to her foster mother, 'O foster-mother, what cry is that?' 'It is nothing at all, Deirdre – merely the birds of the air astray and seeking each other. But let them go past to the bosky glade. There is no shelter or house for them here.' 'Oh, foster-mother, the bird asked to get inside for the sake of the God of the Elements, and you yourself tell me that anything that is asked in His name we ought to do. If you will not allow the bird that is being benumbed with cold, and done to death with hunger, to be let in, I do not think much of your language or your faith. But since I give credence to your language and to your faith, which you taught me, I will myself let in the bird.' And Deirdre arose and drew the bolt from the leaf of the door, and she let in the hunter. She placed a seat in the place for sitting, food in the place for eating, and drink in the place for drinking for the man who came to the house. 'Oh, for this life and raiment, you man that came in, keep restraint on your tongue!' said the old woman. 'It is not a great thing for you to keep your mouth shut and your tongue quiet when you get a home and shelter of a hearth on a gloomy winter's night.' 'Well,' said the hunter, 'I may do that – keep my mouth shut and my tongue quiet, since I came to the house and received hospitality from you; but by the hand of thy father and grandfather, and by your own two hands, if some other of the people of the world saw this beauteous creature you have here hid away, they would not long leave her with you, I swear.'

'What men are these you refer to?' said Deirdre.

DEIRDRE.
O NURSE WHAT
CRY IS THAT?

ONLY THE BIRDS OF THE AIR
CALLING ONE TO THE OTHER —
THERE IS NO HOME FOR THEM HERE
LET THEM GO BY TO THE THICKET.

'Well, I will tell you, young woman,' said the hunter. 'They art Naois, son of Uisnech, and Allen and Arden his two brothers.'

'What like are these men when seen, if we were to see them?' said Deirdre.

'Why, the aspect and form of the men when seen are these,' said the hunter: 'they have the colour of the raven on their hair, their skin like swan on the wave in whiteness, and their cheeks as the blood of the brindled red calf, and their speed and their leap are those of the salmon of the torrent and the deer of the grey mountainside. And Naois is head and shoulders over the rest of the people of Erin.'

'However they are,' said the nurse, 'be you off from here and take another road. And, king ofLight and Sun! In good sooth and certainty, little are my thanks for yourself or for her that let you in!'

The hunter went away, and went straight to the palace of King Connachar. He sent word into the king that he wished to speak to him if he pleased. The king answered the message and came out to speak to the man. 'What is the reason of your journey?' said the king to the hunter.

'I have only to tell you, O king,' said the hunter, 'that I saw the fairest creature that ever was born in Erin, and I came to tell you of it.'

'Who is this beauty and where is she to be seen, when she was not seen before till you saw her, if you did see her?'

'Well, I did see her,' said the hunter. 'But, if I did, no man else can see her unless he get directions from me as to where she is dwelling.'

'And will you direct me to where she dwells? And the reward of your directing me will be as good as the reward of your message,' said the king.

'Well, I will direct you, O king, although it is likely that this will not be what they want,' said the hunter.

Connachar, king of Ulster, sent for his nearest kinsmen, and he told them of his intent. Though early rose the song of the birds mid the rocky caves and the music of the birds in the grove, earlier than that did Connachar, king of Ulster, arise, with his little troop of dear friends, in the delightful twilight of the fresh and gentle May; the dew was heavy on each bush and flower and stem, as they went to bring Deirdre forth from the green knoll where she stayed. Many a youth was there who had a lithe leaping and lissom step when they started whose step was faint, failing, and faltering when they reached the bothy on account of the length of the way and roughness of the road. 'Yonder, now, down in the bottom of the glen is the bothy where the woman dwells, but I will not go nearer than this to the old woman,' said the húnter.

Connachar with his band of kinsfolk went down to the green knoll where Deirdre dwelt and he knocked at the door of the bothy. The nurse replied, 'No less than a king's command and a king's army could put me out of my bothy tonight. And I should be obliged to you, were you to tell who it is that wants me to open my bothy door.' 'It is I, Connachar, king of Ulster.' When the poor woman heard who was at the door, she rose with haste and let in the king and all that could get in of his retinue.

When the king saw the woman that was before him that he had been in quest of, he thought he never saw in the course of the day nor in the dream of night a creature so fair as Deirdre and he gave his full heart's weight of love to her. Deirdre was raised on the topmost of the heroes' shoulders and she and her foster-mother were brought to the court of King Connachar of Ulster.

With the love that Connachar had for her, he wanted to marry Deirdre right off there and then, will she nill she marry him. But she said to him, 'I would be obliged to you if you will give me the respite of a year and a day.' He said, 'I will grant you that, hard though it is, if you will give me your unfailing promise that you will marry me at the year's end.' And she gave the promise. Connachar got for her a woman-teacher and merry modest maidens fair that would lie down and rise with her, that would play and speak with her. Deirdre was clever in maidenly duties and wifely understanding, and Connachar thought he never saw with bodily eye a creature that pleased him more.

Deirdre and her women companions were one day out on the hillock behind the house enjoying the scene, and drinking in the sun's heat. What did they see coming but three men a-journeying.

Deirdre was looking at the men that were coming, and wondering at them. When the men neared them, Deirdre remembered the language of the huntsman, and she said to herself that these were the three sons of Uisnech, and that this was Naois, he having what was above the bend of the two shoulders above the men of Erin all. The three brothers went past without taking any notice of them, without even glancing at the young girls on the hillock. What happened but that love for Naois struck the heart of Deirdre, so that she could not but follow after him. She girded up her raiment and went after the men that went past the base of the knoll, leaving her women attendants there. Allen and Arden had heard of the woman that Connachar, king of Ulster, had with him, and they thought that, if Naois, their brother, saw her, he would have her himself, more especially as she was not married to the king. They perceived the woman coming, and called on one another to hasten their step as they had a long distance to travel, and the dusk of night was coming on. They did so. She cried, 'Naois, son of Uisnech, will you leave me?' 'What piercing, shrill cry is that – the most melodious my ear ever heard, and the shrillest that ever struck my heart of all the cries I ever heard?' 'It is anything else but the wail of the wave-swans of Connachar,' said his brothers. 'No! Yonder is a woman's cry of distress,' said Naois, and he swore he would not go farther until he saw from whom the cry came, and Naois turned back. Naois and Deirdre met, and Deirdre kissed Naois three times, and a kiss each to his brothers. With the confusion that she was in, Deirdre went into a crimson blaze of fire, and her colour came and went as rapidly as the movement of the aspen by the stream side. Naois thought he never saw a fairer creature, and Naois gave Deirdre the love that he never gave to thing, to vision, or to creature but to herself.

Then Naois placed Deirdre on the topmost height of his shoulder, and told his brothers to keep up their pace, and they kept up their pace. Naois thought that it would not be well for him to remain in Erin on account of the way in which Connachar, king of Ulster, his uncle's son, had gone against him because of the woman, though he had not married her; and he turned back to Alba, that is, Scotland. He reached the side of Loch Ness and made his habitation there. He could kill the salmon of the torrent from out his own door, and the deer of the grey gorge from out his window. Naois and Deirdre and Allen and Arden dwelt in a tower, and they were happy so long a time as they were there.

By this time the end of the period came at which Deirdre had to marry Connachar, king of Ulster. Connachar made up his mind to take Deirdre away by the sword whether she was married to Naois or not. So he prepared a great and gleeful feast. He sent word far and wide through Erin all to his kinspeople to come to the feast. Connachar thought to himself that Naois would not come though he should bid him; and the scheme that arose in his mind was to send for his father's brother, Ferchar Mae Ro, and to send him on an embassy to Naois. He did so; and Connachar said to Ferchar, 'Tell Naois, son of Uisnech, that I am setting forth a great and gleeful feast to my friends and kinspeople throughout the wide extent of Erin all, and that I shall not have rest by day nor sleep by night if he and Allen and Arden be not partakers of the feast.'

Ferchar Mae Ro and his three sons went on their journey, and reached the tower where Naois was dwelling by the side of Loch Etive. The sons of Uisnech gave a cordial kindly welcome to Ferchar Mae Ro and his three sons, and asked of him the news of Erin. 'The best news that I have for you,' said the hardy hero, 'is that Connachar, king of Ulster, is setting forth a great sumptuous feast to his friends and kinspeople throughout the wide extent of Erin all, and he has vowed by the earth beneath him, by the high heaven above him, and by the sun that wends to the west, that he will have no rest by day nor sleep by night if the sons of Uisnech, the sons of his own father's brother, will not come back to the land of their home and the soil of their nativity, and to the feast likewise, and he has sent us on embassy to invite you.'

'We will go with you,' said Naois.

'We will,' said his brothers.

But Deirdre did not wish to go with Ferchar Mae Ro, and she tried every prayer to turn Naois from going with him – she said, 'I saw a vision, Naois, and do you interpret it to me,' said Deirdre – then she sang:

'O Naois, son of Uisnech, hear
    What was shown in a dream to me.

'There came three white doves out of the south
    Flying over the sea,
'And drops of honey were in their mouth
    From the hive of the honeybee.

'O Naois, son of Uisnech, hear,
    What was shown in a dream to me.

'I saw three grey hawks out of the south
    Come flying over the sea,
And the red red drops they bare in their mouth
    They were dearer than life to me.'

Said Naois:

'It is nought but the fear of woman's heart,
    And a dream of the night, Deirdre.

The day that Connachar sent the invitation to his feast will be unlucky for us if we don't go, O Deirdre.'

'You will go there,' said Ferchar Mac Ro; 'and if Connachar show kindness to you, show ye kindness to him; and if he will display wrath towards you, display ye wrath towards him, and I and my three sons will be with you.'

'We will,' said Daring Drop. 'We will,' said Hardy Holly. 'We will,' said Fiallan the Fair.

'I have three sons, and they are three heroes, and in any harm or danger that may befall you, they will be with you, and I myself will be along with them.' And Ferchar Mac Ro gave his vow and his word in presence of his arms that, in any harm or danger that came in the way of the sons of Uisnech, he and his three sons would not leave head on live body in Erin, despite sword or helmet, spear or shield, blade or mail, be they ever so good.

Deirdre was unwilling to leave Alba, but she went with Naois. Deirdre wept tears in showers and she sang:

> 'Dear is the land, the land over there,
>   Alba full of woods and lakes;
> Bitter to my heart is leaving thee,
>   But I go away with Naois.'

Ferchar Mae Ro did not stop till he got the sons of Uisnech away with him, despite the suspicion of Deirdre.

> The coracle was put to sea,
>   The sail was hoisted to it;
> And the second morrow they arrived
>   On the white shores of Erin.

As soon as the sons of Uisnech landed in Erin, Ferchar Mae Ro sent word to Connachar, king of Ulster, that the men whom he wanted were come, and let him now show kindness to them. 'Well,' said Connachar, 'I did not expect that the sons of Uisnech would come, though I sent for them, and I am not quite ready to receive them. But there is a house down yonder where I keep strangers, and let them go down to it today, and my house will be ready before them tomorrow.'

But he that was up in the palace felt it long that he was not getting word as to how matters were going on for those down in the house of the strangers. 'Go you, Gelban Grednach, son of Lochlin's king, go you down and bring me information as to whether her former hue and complexion are on Deirdre. If they be, I will take her out with edge of blade and point of sword, and if not, let Naois, son of Uisnech, have her for himself,' said Connachar.

Gelban, the cheering and charming son of Lochlin's king, went down to the place of the strangers, where the sons of Uisnech and Deirdre were staying. He looked in through the bicker-hole on the door-leaf. Now she that he gazed upon used to go into a crimson blaze of blushes when anyone looked at her. Naois looked at Deirdre and knew that someone was looking at her from the back of the door-leaf. He seized one of the dice on the table before him and fired it through the bicker-hole, and knocked the eye out of Gelban Grednach the cheerful and charming, right through the back of his head. Gelban returned back to the palace of King Connachar.

'You were cheerful, charming, going away, but you are cheerless, charmless, returning. What has happened to you, Gelban? But have you seen her, and are Deirdre's hue and complexion as before?' said Connachar.

'Well, I have seen Deirdre, and I saw her also truly, and while I was looking at her through the bicker-hole on the door, Naois, son of Uisnech, knocked out my eye with one of the dice in his hand. But of a truth and verity, although he put out even my eye, it were my desire still to remain looking at her with the other eye, were it not for the hurry you told me to be in,' said Gelban.

'That is true,' said Connachar. 'Let three hundred brave heroes go down to the abode of the strangers, and let them bring hither to me Deirdre, and kill the rest.'

Connachar ordered three hundred active heroes to go down to the abode of the strangers and to take Deirdre up with them and kill the rest. 'The pursuit is coming,' said Deirdre.

'Yes, but I will myself go out and stop the pursuit,' said Naois.

'It is not you, but we that will go,' said Daring Drop, and Hardy Holly and Fiallan the Fair; 'it is to us that our father entrusted your defence from harm and danger when he himself left for home.' And the gallant youths, full noble, full manly, full handsome, with beauteous brown locks, went forth girt with battle arms fit for fierce fight and clothed with combat dress for fierce contest fit, which was burnished, bright, brilliant, bladed, blazing, on which were many pictures of beasts and birds and creeping things, lions and lithe-limbed tigers, brown eagle and harrying hawk and adder fierce; and the young heroes laid low three-thirds of the company.

Connachar came out in haste and cried with wrath, 'Who is there on the floor of fight, slaughtering my men?'

'We, the three sons of Ferchar Mac Ro.'

'Well,' said the king, 'I will give a free bridge to your grandfather, a free bridge to your father, and a free bridge each to you three brothers, if you come over to my side tonight.'

'Well, Connachar, we will not accept that offer from you nor thank you for it. Greater by far do we prefer to go home to our father and tell the deeds of heroism we have done, than accept anything on these terms from you. Naois, son of Uisnech, and Allen and Arden are as nearly related to yourself as they are to us, though you are so keen to shed their blood, and you would shed our blood also, Connachar.' And the noble, manly, handsome youths with beauteous, brown locks returned inside. 'We are now,' said they, 'going home to tell our father that you are now safe from the hands of the king.' And the youths all fresh and tall and lithe and beautiful, went home to their father to tell that the sons of Uisnech were safe. This happened at the parting of the day and night in the morning twilight time, and Naois said they must go away, leave that house, and return to Alba.

Naois and Deirdre, Allan and Arden started to return to Alba. Word came to the king that the company he was in pursuit of were gone. The king then sent for Duanan Gacha Druid, the best magician he had, and he spoke to him as follows. 'Much wealth have I expended on you, Duanan Gacha Druid, to give schooling and learning and magic mystery to you, if these people get away from me today without care, without consideration or regard for me, without chance of overtaking them, and without power to stop them.'

'Well, I will stop them,' said the magician, 'until the company you send in pursuit return.' And the magician placed a wood before them through which no man could go, but the sons of Uisnech marched through the wood without halt or hesitation, and Deirdre held on to Naois's hand.

'What is the good of that? That will not do yet,' said Connachar. 'They are off without bending of their feet or stopping of their step, without heed or respect to me, and I am without power to keep up to them or opportunity to turn them back this night.'

'I will try another plan on them,' said the druid; and he placed before them a grey sea instead of a green plain. The three heroes stripped and tied their clothes behind their heads, and Naois placed Deirdre on the top of his shoulder.

> They stretched their sides to the stream,
> And sea and land were to them the same,
> The rough grey ocean was the same
> As meadow-land green and plain.

'Though that be good, O Duanan, it will not make the heroes return,' said Connachar; 'they are gone without regard for me, and without honour to me, and without power on my part to pursue them or to force them to return this night.'

'We shall try another method on them, since yon one did not stop them,' said the druid. And the druid froze the grey ridged sea into hard rocky knobs, the sharpness of sword being on the one edge and the poison power of adders on the other. Then Arden cried that he was getting tired, and nearly giving over. 'Come you, Arden, and sit on my right shoulder,' said Naois. Arden came and sat on Naois's shoulder. Arden was long in this posture when he died; but though he was dead Naois would not let him go. Allen then cried out that he was getting faint and nigh-well giving up. When Naois heard his prayer, he gave forth the piercing sigh of death, and asked Allen to lay hold of him and he would bring him to land. Allen was not long when the weakness of death came on him and his hold failed. Naois looked around, and when he saw his two well-beloved brothers dead, he cared not whether he lived or died, and he gave forth the bitter sigh of death, and his heart burst.

'They are gone,' said Duanan Gacha Druid to the king, 'and I have done what you desired me. The sons of Uisnech are dead and they will trouble you no more; and you have your wife hale and whole to yourself.'

'Blessings for that upon you and may the good results accrue to me, Duanan. I count it no loss what I spent in the schooling and teaching of you. Now dry up the flood, and let me see if I can behold Deirdre,' said Connachar. And Duanan Gacha Druid dried up the flood from the plain and the three sons of Uisnech were lying together dead, without breath of life, side by side on the green meadow plain and Deirdre bending above showering down her tears.

Then Deirdre said this lament. 'Fair one, loved one, flower of beauty; beloved upright and strong; beloved noble and modest warrior. Fair one, blue-eyed, beloved of thy wife; lovely to me at the trysting-place came thy clear voice through the woods of Ireland. I cannot eat or smile henceforth. Break not today, my heart: soon enough shall I lie within my grave. Strong are the waves of sorrow, but stronger is sorrow's self, Connachar.'

The people then gathered round the heroes' bodies and asked Connachar what was to be done with the bodies. The order that he gave was that they should dig a pit and put the three brothers in it side by side.

Deirdre kept sitting on the brink of the grave, constantly asking the grave diggers to dig the pit wide and free. When the bodies of the brothers were put in the grave, Deirdre said:

'Come over hither, Naois, my love,
Let Arden close to Allen lie;
If the dead had any sense to feel,
Ye would have made a place for Deirdre.'

The men did as she told them. She jumped into the grave and lay down by Naois, and she was dead by his side.

The king ordered the body to be raised from out the grave and to be buried on the other side of the loch. It was done as the king bade, and the pit closed. Thereupon a fir shoot grew out of the grave of Deirdre and a fir shoot from the grave of Naois, and the two shoots united in a knot above the loch. The king ordered the shoots to be cut down, and this was done twice, until, at the third time, the wife whom the king had married caused him to stop this work of evil and his vengeance on the remains of the dead.

Munachar and Manachar

There once lived a Munachar and a Manachar, a long time ago, and it is a long time since it was, and if they were alive now they would not be alive then. They went out together to pick raspberries, and as many as Munachar used to pick Manachar used to eat. Munachar said he must go look for a rod to make a gad to hang Manachar, who ate his raspberries everyone; and he came to the rod. 'What news the day?' said the rod. 'It is my own news that I'm seeking. Going looking for a rod, a rod to make a gad, a gad to hang Manachar, who ate my raspberries every one.'

'You will not get me,' said the rod, 'until you get an axe to cut me.' He came to the axe. 'What news today?' said the axe. 'It's my own news I'm seeking. Going looking for an axe, an axe to cut a rod, a rod to make a gad, a gad to hang Manachar who ate my raspberries every one.'

'You will not get me,' said the axe, 'until you get a flag to edge me.' He came to the flag. 'What news today?' says the flag. 'It's my own news I'm seeking. Going looking for a flag, flag to edge axe, axe to cut a rod, a rod to make a gad, a gad to hang Manachar, who ate my raspberries every one.'

'You will not get me,' says the flag, 'till you get water to wet me.'
He came to the water. 'What news today?' says the water. 'It's my
own news that I'm seeking. Going looking for water, water to wet
flag to edge axe, axe to cut a rod, a rod to make a gad, a gad to hang
Manachar, who ate my raspberries everyone.'

'You will not get me,' said the water, 'until you get a deer who
will swim me.' He came to the deer. 'What news today?' says the
deer. 'It's my own news I'm seeking. Going looking for a deer,
deer to swim water, water to wet flag, flag to edge axe, axe to cut a
rod, a rod to make a gad, a gad to hang Manachar, who ate my
raspberries every one.'

'You will not get me,' said the deer, 'until you get a hound who
will hunt me.' He came to the hound. 'What news today?' says the
hound. 'It's my own news I'm seeking. Going looking for a hound,
hound to hunt deer, deer to swim water, water to wet flag, flag to
edge axe, axe to cut a rod, a rod to make a gad, a gad to hang
Manachar, who ate my raspberries every one.'

'You will not get me,' said the hound, 'until you get a bit of
butter to put in my claw.' He came to the butter. 'What news
today?' says the butter. 'It's my own news I'm seeking. Going
looking for butter, butter to go in claw of hound, hound to hunt
deer, deer to swim water, water to wet flag, flag to edge axe, axe to
cut a rod, a rod to make a gad, a gad to hang Manachar, who ate
my raspberries every one.'

'You will not get me,' said the butter, 'until you get a cat who
shall scrape me.' He came to the cat. 'What news today?' said the
cat. 'It's my own news I'm seeking. Going looking for a cat, cat to
scrape butter, butter to go in claw of hound, hound to hunt deer,
deer to swim water, water to wet flag, flag to edge axe, axe to cut
a rod, a rod to make a gad, gad to hang Manachar, who ate my
raspberries every one.'

'You will not get me,' said the cat, 'until you will get milk which
you will give me.' He came to the cow. 'What news today?' said
the cow. It's my own news I'm seeking. Going looking for a cow,
cow to give me milk, milk I will give to the cat, cat to scrape
butter, butter to go in claw of hound, hound to hunt deer, deer to
swim water, water to wet flag, flag to edge axe, axe to cut a rod, a

rod to make a gad, a gad to hang Manachar, who ate my raspberries every one.'

'You will not get any milk from me,' said the cow, 'until you bring me a whisp of straw from those threshers yonder.' He came to the threshers. 'What news today?' said the threshers. 'It's my own news I'm seeking. Going looking for a whisp of straw from ye to give to the cow, the cow to give me milk, milk I will give to the cat, cat to scrape butter, butter to go in claw of hound, hound to hunt deer, deer to swim water, water to wet flag, flag to edge axe, axe to cut a rod, a rod to make a gad, a gad to hang Manachar, who ate my raspberries every one.'

You will not get any whisp of straw from us,' said the threshers, 'until you bring us the makings of a cake from the miller over yonder.' He came to the miller. 'What news today?' said the miller. 'It's my own news I'm seeking. Going looking for the makings of a cake which I will give to the threshers, the threshers to give me a whisp of straw, the whisp of straw I will give to the cow, the cow to give me milk, milk I will give to the cat, cat to scrape butter, butter to go in claw of hound, hound to hunt deer, deer to swim water, water to wet flag, flag to edge axe, axe to cut a rod, a rod to make a gad, a gad to hang Manachar, who ate my raspberries every one.'

'You will not get any makings of a cake from me,' said the miller, 'till you bring me the full of that sieve of water from the river over there.'

He took the sieve in his hand and went over to the river, but as often as ever he would stoop and fill it with water, the moment he raised it the water would run out of it again, and sure, if he had been there from that day till this, he never could have filled it. A crow went flying by him, over his head. 'Daub! Daub!' said the crow. 'My blessings on ye, then,' said Munachar, 'but it's the good advice you have,' and he took the red clay and the daub that was by the brink, and he rubbed it to the bottom of the sieve, until all the holes were filled, and then the sieve held the water, and he brought the water to the miller, and the miller gave him the makings of a cake, and he gave the makings of the cake to the threshers, and the threshers gave him a whisp of straw, and he gave the whisp of straw to the cow, and the cow gave him milk, the milk he gave to the cat, the cat scraped the butter, the butter went into the claw of the hound, the hound hunted the deer, the deer swam the water, the water wet the flag, the flag sharpened the axe, the axe cut the rod, and the rod made a gad, and when he had it ready to hang Manachar he found that Manachar had BURST.

King O'Toole and his Goose

Och, I thought all the world, far and near, had heerd o' King O'Toole – well, well, but the darkness of mankind is untellible! Well, sir, you must know, as you didn't hear it afore, that there was a king, called King O'Toole, who was a fine old king in the old ancient times, long ago; and it was he that owned the churches in the early days. The king, you see, was the right sort; he was the real boy, and loved sport as he loved his life, and hunting in particular; and from the rising o' the sun, up he got, and away he went over the mountains after the deer; and fine times they were.

Well, it was all mighty good, as long as the king had his health; but, you see, in course of time the king grew old, by raison he was stiff in his limbs, and when he got stricken in years, his heart failed him, and he was lost entirely for want o' diversion, because he couldn't go a-hunting no longer; and, by dad, the poor king was obliged at last to get a goose to divert him. Oh, you may laugh, if you like, but it's truth I'm telling you; and the way the goose diverted him was this-a-way: You see, the goose used to swim across the lake, and go diving for trout, and catch fish on a Friday for the king, and flew every other day round about the lake, diverting the poor king. All went on mighty well until, by dad, the goose got stricken in years like her master, and couldn't divert him no longer, and then it was that the poor king was lost entirely. The king was walkin' one mornin' by the edge of the lake, lamentin' his cruel fate, and thinking of drowning himself, that could get no diversion in life, when all of a sudden, turning round the corner, who should he meet but a mighty decent young man coming up to him.

'God save you,' says the king to the young man.

'God save you kindly, King O'Toole,' says the young man.

'True for you,' says the king. 'I am King O'Toole,' says he, 'prince and plennypennytinchery of these parts,' says he; 'but how came ye to know that?' says he.

'Oh, never mind,' says St Kavin.

You see it was St Kavin, sure enough – the saint himself in disguise, and nobody else. 'Oh, never mind,' says he, 'I know more than that. May I make bold to ask how is your goose, King O'Toole?' says he.

'Blur-an-agers, how came ye to know about my goose?' says the king.

'Oh, no matter; I was given to understand it,' says St Kavin.

After some more talk the king says, 'What are you?'

'I'm an honest man,' says St Kavin.

'Well, honest man,' says the king, 'and how is it you make your money so aisy?'

'By makin' old things as good as new,' says St Kavin.

'Is it a tinker you are?' says the king.

'No,' says the saint; 'I'm no tinker by trade, King O'Toole; I've a better trade than a tinker,' says he – 'what would you say,' says he, 'if I made your old goose as good as new?'

My dear, at the word of making his goose as good as new, you'd think the poor old king's eyes were ready to jump out of his head. With that the king whistled, and down came the poor goose, just like a hound, waddling up to the poor cripple, her master, and as like him as two peas. The minute the saint clapped his eyes on the goose, 'I'll do the job for you,' says he, 'King O'Toole.'

'By *Jaminee*!' says King O'Toole. 'If you do, I'll say you're the cleverest fellow in the seven parishes.'

'Oh, by dad,' says St Kavin, 'you must say more nor that – my horn's not so soft all out,' says he, 'as to repair your old goose for nothing; what'll you gi' me if I do the job for you? – that's the chat,' says St Kavin.

'I'll give you whatever you ask,' says the king; 'isn't that fair?'

'Divil a fairer,' says the saint; 'that's the way to do business. Now,' says he, 'this is the bargain I'll make with you, King O'Toole: will you gi' me all the ground the goose flies over, the first offer, after I make her as good as new?'

'I will,' says the king.

'You won't go back o' your word?' says St Kavin.

'Honour bright!' says King O'Toole, holding out his fist.

'Honour bright!' says St Kavin, back agin, 'it's a bargain. Come here!' says he to the poor old goose – 'come here, you unfortunate ould cripple, and it's I that'll make you the sporting bird.' With that, my dear, he took up the goose by the two wings – 'Criss o' my cross an you,' says he, markin' her to grace with the blessed sign at the same minute – and throwing her up in the air. 'Whew,' says he, jist givin' her a blast to help her; and with that, my jewel, she took to her heels, flyin' like one o' the eagles themselves, and cutting as many capers as a swallow before a shower of rain.

Well, my dear, it was a beautiful sight to see the king standing with his mouth open, looking at his poor old goose flying as light as a lark, and better than ever she was: and when she lit at his feet, patted her on the head, and '*Ma vourneen*,' says he, 'but you are the *darlint* o' the world.'

'And what do you say to me,' says St Kavin, 'for making her the like?'

'By Jabers,' says the king, 'I say nothing beats the art o' man, barring the bees.'

'And do you say no more nor that?' says St Kavin.

'And that I'm beholden to you,' says the king.

'But will you gi'e all the ground the goose flew over?' says St Kavin.

'I will,' says King O'Toole, 'and you're welcome to it,' says he, 'though it's the last acre I have to give.'

'But you'll keep your word true?' says the saint.

'As true as the sun,' says the king.

'It's well for you, King O'Toole, that you said that word,' says he; 'for if you didn't say that word, the devil the bit o' your goose would ever fly agin.'

When the king was as good as his word, St Kavin was pleased with him, and then it was that he made himself known to the king. 'And,' says he, 'King O'Toole, you're a decent man, for I only came here to try you. You don't know me,' says he, 'because I'm disguised.'

'Musha! Then,' says the king, 'who are you?'

'I'm St Kavin,' said the saint, blessing himself.

'Oh, queen of heaven!' says the king, making the sign of the cross between his eyes, and falling down on his knees before the saint. 'Is it the great St Kavin,' says he, 'that I've been discoursing all this time without knowing it,' says he, 'all as one as if he was a lump of a *gossoon*? – and so you're a saint?' says the king.

'I am,' says St Kavin.

'By Jabers, I thought I was only talking to a dacent boy,' says the king.

'Well, you know the difference now,' says the saint. 'I'm St Kavin,' says he, 'the greatest of all the saints.'

And so the king had his goose as good as new, to divert him as long as he lived and the saint supported him after he came into his property, as I told you, until the day of his death – and that was soon after; for the poor goose thought he was catching a trout one Friday; but, my jewel, it was a mistake he made – and instead of a trout, it was a thieving horse-eel; and instead of the goose killing a trout for the king's supper – by dad, the eel killed the king's goose – and small blame to him; but he didn't ate her, because he darn't ate what St Kavin had laid his blessed hands on.

Jack and his Comrades

Once there was a poor widow, as often there has been, and she had one son. A very scarce summer came, and they didn't know how they'd live till the new potatoes would be fit for eating. So Jack said to his mother one evening, 'Mother, bake my cake, and kill my hen, till I go seek my fortune; and if I meet it, never fear but I'll soon be back to share it with you.'

So she did as he asked her, and he set out at break of day on his journey. His mother came along with him to the yard gate, and says she, 'Jack, which would you rather have, half the cake and half the hen with my blessing, or the whole of 'em with my curse?'

'O musha, mother,' says Jack, 'why do you ax me that question? Sure you know I wouldn't have your curse and Damer's estate along with it.'

'Well, then, Jack,' says she, 'here's the whole lot of 'em, with my thousand blessings along with them.' So she stood on the yard fence and blessed him as far as her eyes could see him.

Well, he went along and along till he was tired, and ne'er a farmer's house he went into wanted a boy. At last his road led by the side of a bog, and there was a poor ass up to his shoulders near a big bunch of grass he was striving to come at.

'Ah, then, Jack asthore,' says he, 'help me out or I'll be drowned.'

'Never say't twice,' says Jack, and he pitched in big stones and sods into the slob, till the ass got good ground under him.

'Thank you, Jack,' says he, when he was out on the hard road; 'I'll do as much for you another time. Where are you going?'

'Faith, I'm going to seek my fortune till harvest comes in, God bless it!'

'And if you like,' says the ass, 'I'll go along with you; who knows what luck we may have!'

'With all my heart, it's getting late, let us be jogging.'

'Well, they were going through a village, and a whole army of gossoons were hunting a poor dog with a kettle tied to his tail. He ran up to Jack for protection, and the ass let such a roar out of him, that the little thieves took to their heels as if the ould boy was after them.

'More power to you, Jack,' says the dog.

'I'm much obleeged to you; where is the baste and yourself going?'

'We're going to seek our fortune till harvest comes in.'

'And wouldn't I be proud to go with you!' says the dog. 'And get rid of them ill-conducted boys; purshuin' to 'em.'

'Well, well, throw your tail over your arm, and come along.'

They got outside the town, and sat down under an old wall, and Jack pulled out his bread and meat, and shared with the dog; and the ass made his dinner on a bunch of thistles. While they were eating and chatting, what should come by but a poor half-starved cat, and the moll-row he gave out of him would make your heart ache.

'You look as if you saw the tops of nine houses since breakfast,' says Jack; 'here's a bone and something on it.'

'May your child never know a hungry belly!' says Tom. 'It's myself that's in need of your kindness. May I be so bold as to ask where yez are all going?'

'We're going to seek out fortune till the harvest comes in, and you may join us if you like.'

'And that I'll do with a heart and a half,' says the cat, 'and thank'ee for asking me.'

Off they set again, and just as the shadows of the trees were three times as long as themselves, they heard a great cackling in a field inside the road, and out over the ditch jumped a fox with a fine black cock in his mouth.

'Oh, you anointed villain!' says the ass, roaring like thunder.

'At him, good dog!' says Jack, and the word wasn't out of his mouth when Coley was in full sweep after the Red Dog. Reynard dropped his prize like a hot potato, and was off like shot, and the poor cock came back fluttering and trembling to Jack and his comrades.

'O musha, naybours!' says he. 'Wasn't it the heigth o' luck that threw you in my way! Maybe I won't remember your kindness if ever I find you in hardship; and where in the world are you all going?'

'We're going to seek our fortune till the harvest comes in; you may join our party if you like, and sit on Neddy's crupper when your legs and wings are tired.'

Well, the march began again, and just as the sun was gone down they looked around, and there was neither cabin nor farm house in sight.

'Well, well,' says Jack, 'the worse luck now the better another time, and it's only a summer night after all. We'll go into the wood, and make our bed on the long grass.'

No sooner said than done. Jack stretched himself on a bunch of dry grass, the ass lay near him, the dog and cat lay in the ass's warm lap, and the cock went to roost in the next tree.

Well, the soundness of deep sleep was over them all, when the cock took a notion of crowing.

'Bother you, Black Cock!' says the ass. 'You disturbed me from as nice a wisp of hay as ever I tasted. What's the matter?'

'It's daybreak that's the matter: don't you see light yonder?'

'I see a light indeed,' says Jack, 'but it's from a candle it's coming, and not from the sun. As you've roused us we may as well go over, and ask for lodging.'

So they all shook themselves, and went on through grass, and rocks, and briars, till they got down into a hollow, and there was the light coming through the shadow, and along with it came singing, and laughing, and cursing.

'Easy, boys!' says Jack. 'Walk on your tippy toes till we see what sort of people we have to deal with.'

So they crept near the window, and there they saw six robbers inside, with pistols, and blunderbushes, and cutlashes, sitting at a table, eating roast beef and pork, and drinking mulled beer, and wine, and whiskey punch.

'Wasn't that a fine haul we made at the Lord of Dunlavin's!' says one ugly-looking thief with his mouth full. 'And it's little we'd get only for the honest porter! Here's his purty health!'

'The porter's purty health!' cried out every one of them, and Jack bent his finger at his comrades.

'Close your ranks, my men,' says he in a whisper, 'and let everyone mind the word of command.'

So the ass put his fore-hoofs on the sill of the window, the dog got on the ass's head, the cat on the dog's head, and the cock on the cat's head. Then Jack made a sign, and they all sung out like mad.

'Hee-haw, hee-haw!' roared the ass; 'Bow-wow!' barked the dog; 'Meaw-meaw!' cried the cat; 'Cocka-doodle-doo!' crowed the cock.

'Level your pistols!' cried Jack, 'and make smithereens of 'em. Don't leave a mother's son of 'em alive; present, fire!'

With that they gave another halloo, and smashed every pane in the window. The robbers were frightened out of their lives. They blew out the candles, threw down the table, and skelped out at the back door as if they were in earnest, and never drew rein till they were in the very heart of the wood.

Jack and his party got into the room, closed the shutters, lighted the candles, and ate and drank till hunger and thirst were gone. Then they lay down to rest – Jack in the bed, the ass in the stable, the dog on the doormat, the cat by the fire, and the cock on the perch.

At first the robbers were very glad to find themselves safe in the thick wood, but they soon began to get vexed.

'This damp grass is very different from our warm room,' says one.

'I was obliged to drop a fine pig's foot,' says another.

'I didn't get a tayspoonful of my last tumbler,' says another.

'And all the Lord of Dunlavin's gold and silver that we left behind!' says the last.

'I think I'll venture back,' says the captain, 'and see if we can recover anything.'

'That's a good boy!' said they all, and away he went.

The lights were all out, and so he groped his way to the fire, and there the cat flew in his face, and tore him with teeth and claws. He let a roar out of him, and made for the room door, to look for a candle inside. He trod on the dog's tail, and if he did, he got the marks of his teeth in his arms, and legs, and thighs.

'Thousand murders!' cried he; 'I wish I was out of this unlucky house.'

When he got to the street door, the cock dropped down upon him with his claws and bill, and what the cat and dog done to him was only a flay-bite to what he got from the cock.

'Oh, tattheration to you all, you unfeeling vagabones!' says he, when he recovered his breath; and he staggered and spun round and round till he reeled into the stable, back foremost, but the ass received him with a kick on the broadest part of his small clothes, and laid him comfortably on the dunghill.

When he came to himself, he scratched his head, and began to think what happened him; and as soon as he found that his legs were able to carry him, he crawled away, dragging one foot after another, till he reached the wood.

'Well, well,' cried them all, when he came within hearing, 'any chance of our property?'

'You may say chance,' says he, 'and it's itself is the poor chance all out. Ah, will any of you pull a bed of dry grass for me? All the sticking-plaster in Enniscorthy will be too little for the cuts and bruises I have on me. Ah, if you only knew what I have gone through for you! When I got to the kitchen fire, looking for a sod of lighted turf, what should be there but an old woman carding flax, and you may see the marks she left on my face with the cards. I made to the room door as fast as I could, and who should I stumble over but a cobbler and his seat, and if he did not work at me with his awls and his pinchers you may call me a rogue. Well, I got away from him somehow, but when I was passing through the door, it must be the divel himself that pounced down on me with his claws, and his teeth, that were equal to sixpenny nails, and his wings – ill luck he in his road! Well, at last I reached the stable, and there, by way of salute, I got a pelt from a sledgehammer that sent me half a mile off. If you don't believe me, I'll give you leave to go and judge for yourselves.'

'Oh, my poor captain,' says they, 'we believe you to the nines. Catch us, indeed, going within a hen's race of that unlucky cabin!'

Well, before the sun shook his doublet next morning, Jack and his comrades were up and about. They made a hearty breakfast on what was left the night before, and then they all agreed to set off to the castle of the Lord of Dunlavin, and give him back all his gold and silver. Jack put it all in the two ends of a sack and laid it across Neddy's back, and all took the road in their hands. Away they went, through bogs, up hills, down dales, and sometimes along the yellow high road, till they came to the hall door of the Lord of Dunlavin, and who should be there, airing his powdered head, his white stockings, and his red breeches, but the thief of a porter.

He gave a cross look to the visitors, and says he to Jack, 'What do you want here, my fine fellow? There isn't room for you all.'

'We want,' says Jack, 'what I'm sure you haven't to give us – and that is, common civility.'

'Come, be off, you lazy strollers!' says he. 'While a cat 'ud be licking her ear, or I'll let the dogs at you.'

'Would you tell a body,' says the cock that was perched on the ass's head, 'who was it that opened the door for the robbers the other night?'

Ah! Maybe the porter's red face didn't turn the colour of his frill, and the Lord of Dunlavin and his pretty daughter, that were standing at the parlour window unknownst to the porter, put out their heads.

'I'd be glad, Barney,' says the master, 'to hear your answer to the gentleman with the red comb on him.'

'Ah, my lord, don't believe the rascal; sure I didn't open the door to the six robbers.'

'And how did you know there were six, you poor innocent?' said the lord.

'Never mind, sir,' says Jack, 'all your gold and silver is there in that sack, and I don't think you will begrudge us our supper and bed after our long march from the wood of Athsalach.'

'Begrudge, indeed! Not one of you will ever see a poor day if I can help it.'

So all were welcomed to their heart's content, and the ass and the dog and the cock got the best posts in the farmyard, and the cat took possession of the kitchen. The lord took Jack in hand, dressed him from top to toe in broadcloth, and frills as white as snow, and turnpumps, and put a watch in his fob. When they sat down to dinner, the lady of the house said Jack had the air of a born gentleman about him, and the lord said he'd make him his steward. Jack brought his mother, and settled her comfortably near the castle, and all were as happy as you please.

The Shee an Gannon and the Gruagach Gaire

The Shee an Gannon was born in the morning, named at noon, and went in the evening to ask his daughter of the king of Erin.

'I will give you my daughter in marriage,' said the king of Erin; 'you won't get her, though, unless you go and bring me back the tidings that I want, and tell me what it is that put a stop to the laughing of the Gruagach Gaire, who before this laughed always, and laughed so loud that the whole world heard him. There are twelve iron spikes out here in the garden behind my castle. On eleven of the spikes are the heads of kings' sons who came seeking my daughter in marriage, and all of them went away to get the knowledge I wanted. Not one was able to get it and tell me what stopped the Gruagach Gaire from laughing. I took the heads off them all when they came back without the tidings for which they went, and I'm greatly in dread that your head'll be on the twelfth spike, for I'll do the same to you that I did to the eleven kings' sons unless you tell what put a stop to the laughing of the Gruagach.'

The Shee an Gannon made no answer, but left the king and pushed away to know could he find why the Gruagach was silent.

He took a glen at a step, a hill at a leap, and travelled all day till evening. Then he came to a house. The master of the house asked him what sort was he, and he said, 'A young man looking for hire.'

'Well,' said the master of the house, 'I was going tomorrow to look for a man to mind my cows. If you'll work for me, you'll have a good place, the best food a man could have to eat in this world, and a soft bed to lie on.'

The Shee an Gannon took service, and ate his supper. Then the master of the house said, 'I am the Gruagach Gaire; now that you are my man and have eaten your supper, you'll have a bed of silk to sleep on.'

Next morning after breakfast the Gruagach said to the Shee an Gannon, 'Go out now and loosen my five golden cows and my bull without horns, and drive them to pasture; but when you have them out on the grass, be careful you don't let them go near the land of the giant.'

The new cowboy drove the cattle to pasture, and when near the land of the giant, he saw it was covered with woods and surrounded by a high wall. He went up, put his back against the wall, and threw in a great stretch of it; then he went inside and threw out another great stretch of the wall, and put the five golden cows and the bull without horns on the land of the giant.

Then he climbed a tree, ate the sweet apples himself, and threw the sour ones down to the cattle of the Gruagach Gaire.

Soon a great crashing was heard in the woods – the noise of young trees bending, and old trees breaking. The cowboy looked around, and saw a five-headed giant pushing through the trees; and soon he was before him.

'Poor miserable creature!' said the giant. 'But weren't you impudent to come to my land and trouble me in this way? You're too big for one bite, and too small for two. I don't know what to do, but tear you to pieces.'

'You nasty brute,' said the cowboy, coming down to him from the tree, ' 'tis little I care for you;' and then they went at each other. So great was the noise between them that there was nothing in the world but what was looking on and listening to the combat.

They fought till late in the afternoon, when the giant was getting the upper hand; and then the cowboy thought that if the giant should kill him, his father and mother would never find him or set eyes on him again, and he would never get the daughter of the king of Erin. The heart in his body grew strong at this thought. He sprang on the giant, and with the first squeeze and thrust he put him to his knees in the hard ground, with the second thrust to his waist, and with the third to his shoulders.

'I have you at last; you're done for now!' said the cowboy.

Then he took out his knife, cut the five heads off the giant, and when he had them off he cut out the tongues and threw the heads over the wall.

Then he put the tongues in his pocket and drove home the cattle. That evening the Gruagach couldn't find vessels enough in all his place to hold the milk of the five golden cows.

But when the cowboy was on the way home with the cattle, the son of the king of Tisean came and took the giant's heads and claimed the princess in marriage when the Gruagach Gaire should laugh.

After supper the cowboy would give no talk to his master, but kept his mind to himself, and went to the bed of silk to sleep.

On the morning the cowboy rose before his master, and the first words he said to the Gruagach were, 'What keeps you from laughing, you who used to laugh so loud that the whole world heard you?'

'I'm sorry,' said the Gruagach, 'that the daughter of the king of Erin sent you here.'

'If you don't tell me of your own will, I'll make you tell me,' said the cowboy; and he put a face on himself that was terrible to look at, and running through the house like a madman, could find nothing that would give pain enough to the Gruagach but some ropes made of untanned sheepskin hanging on the wall.

He took these down, caught the Gruagach, fastened him by the three smalls, and tied him so that his little toes were whispering to his ears. When he was in this state the Gruagach said, 'I'll tell you what stopped my laughing if you set me free,'

So the cowboy unbound him, the two sat down together, and the Gruagach said, 'I lived in this castle here with my twelve sons. We ate, drank, played cards, and enjoyed ourselves, till one day when my sons and I were playing, a slender brown hare came rushing in, jumped on to the hearth, tossed up the ashes to the rafters and ran away.

'On another day he came again; but if he did, we were ready for him, my twelve sons and myself. As soon as he tossed up the ashes and ran off; we made after him, and followed him till nightfall, when he went into a glen. We saw a light before us. I ran on, and came to a house with a great apartment, where there was a man named Yellow Face with twelve daughters, and the hare was tied to the side of the room near the women.

'There was a large pot over the fire in the room, and a great stork boiling in the pot. The man of the house said to me, "There are bundles of rushes at the end of the room, go there and sit down with your men!"

'He went into the next room and brought out two pikes, one of wood, the other of iron, and asked me which of the pikes would I take. I said, "I'll take the iron one;" for I thought in my heart that if an attack should come on me, I could defend myself better with the iron than the wooden pike.

'Yellow Face gave me the iron pike, and the first chance of taking what I could out of the pot on the point of the pike. I got but a small piece of the stork, and the man of the house took all the rest on his wooden pike. We had to fast that night; and when the man and his twelve daughters ate the flesh of the stork, they hurled the bare bones in the faces of my sons and myself.

'We had to stop all night that way, beaten on the faces by the bones of the stork.

'Next morning, when we were going away, the man of the house asked me to stay a while; and going into the next room, he brought out twelve loops of iron and one of wood, and said to me: "Put the heads of your twelve sons into the iron loops, and keep my own head into the wooden one;" and I said, "I'll put the twelve heads of my sons in the iron loops, and keep my own out of the wooden one."

'He put the iron loops on the necks of my twelve sons, and put the wooden one on his own neck. Then he snapped the loops one after another, till he took the heads off my twelve sons and threw the heads and bodies out of the house; but he did nothing to hurt his own neck.

'When he had killed my sons he took hold of me and stripped the skin and flesh from the small of my back down, and when he had done that he took the skin of a black sheep that had been hanging on the wall for seven years and clapped it on my body in place of my own flesh and skin; and the sheepskin grew on me, and every year since then I shear myself, and every bit of wool I use for the stockings that I wear I clip off my own back.'

When he had said this, the Gruagach showed the cowboy his back covered with thick black wool.

After what he had seen and heard, the cowboy said, 'I know now why you don't laugh, and small blame to you. But does that hare come here still?'

'He does indeed,' said the Gruagach.

Both went to the table to play, and they were not long playing cards when the hare ran in; and before they could stop him he was out again.

But the cowboy made after the hare, and the Gruagach after the cowboy, and they ran as fast as ever their legs could carry them till nightfall; and when the hare was entering the castle where the twelve sons of the Gruagach were killed, the cowboy caught him by the two hind legs and dashed out his brains against the wall; and the skull of the hare was knocked into the chief room of the castle, and fell at the feet of the master of the place.

'Who has dared to interfere with my fighting pet?' screamed Yellow Face.

'I,' said the cowboy; 'and if your pet had had manners, he might be alive now.'

The cowboy and the Gruagach stood by the fire. A stork was boiling in the pot, as when the Gruagach came the first time. The master of the house went into the next room and brought out an iron and a wooden pike, and asked the cowboy which would he choose.

'I'll take the wooden one,' said the cowboy; 'and you may keep the iron one for yourself.'

So he took the wooden one; and going to the pot, brought out on the pike all the stork except a small bite, and he and the Gruagach fell to eating, and they were eating the flesh of the stork all night. The cowboy and the Gruagach were at home in the place that time.

In the morning the master of the house went into the next room, took down the twelve iron loops with a wooden one, brought them out, and asked the cowboy which would he take, the twelve iron or the one wooden loop.

'What could I do with the twelve iron ones for myself or my master? I'll take the wooden one.'

He put it on, and taking the twelve iron loops, put them on the necks of the twelve daughters of the house, then snapped the twelve heads off them, and turning to their father, said, 'I'll do the same thing to you unless you bring the twelve sons of my master to life, and make them as well and strong as when you took their heads.'

The master of the house went out and brought the twelve to life again; and when the Gruagach saw all his sons alive and as well as ever, he let a laugh out of himself, and all the Eastern world heard the laugh.

Then the cowboy said to the Gruagach, 'It's a bad thing you have done to me, for the daughter of the king of Erin will be married the day after your laugh is heard.'

'Oh! Then we must be there in time,' said the Gruagach; and they all made away from the place as fast as ever they could, the cowboy, the Gruagach, and his twelve sons.

They hurried on; and when within three miles of the king's castle there was such a throng of people that no one could go a step ahead. 'We must clear a road through this,' said the cowboy.

'We must indeed,' said the Gruagach; and at it they went, threw the people some on one side and some on the other, and soon they had an opening for themselves to the king's castle.

As they went in, the daughter of the king of Erin and the son of the king of Tisean were on their knees just going to be married. The cowboy drew his hand on the bridegroom, and gave a blow that sent him spinning till he stopped under a table at the other side of the room.

'What scoundrel struck that blow?' asked the king of Erin.

'It was I,' said the cowboy.

'What reason had you to stroke the man who won my daughter?'

'It was I who won your daughter, not he; and if you don't believe me, the Gruagach Gaire is here himself. He'll tell you the whole story from beginning to end, and show you the tongues of the giant.'

So the Gruagach came up and told the king the whole story, how the Shee an Gannon had become his cowboy, had guarded the five golden cows and the bull without horns, cut off the heads of the five-headed giant, killed the wizard hare, and brought his own twelve sons to life. 'And then,' said the Gruagach, 'he is the one man in the whole world I have ever told why I stopped laughing, and the only one who had ever seen my fleece of wool.'

When the king of Erin heard what the Gruagach said, and saw the tongues of the giant fitted in the head, he made the Shee an Gannon kneel down by his daughter, and they were married on the spot.

Then the son of the king of Tisean was thrown into prison, and the next day they put down a great fire, and the deceiver was burned to ashes.

The wedding lasted nine days, and the last day was better than the first.

The Storyteller at Fault

At the time when the Tuatha De Dannan held the sovereignty of Ireland, there reigned in Leinster a king, who was remarkably fond of hearing stories. Like the other princes and chieftains of the island, he had a favourite storyteller, who held a large estate from his majesty, on condition of telling him a new story every night of his life, before he went to sleep. Many indeed were the stories he knew, so that he had already reached a good old age without failing even for a single night in his task; and such was the skill he displayed that whatever cares of state or other annoyances might prey upon the monarch's mind, his storyteller was sure to send him to sleep.

One morning the storyteller arose early, and as his custom was, strolled out into his garden turning over in his mind incidents which he might weave into a story for the king at night. But this morning he found himself quite at fault; after pacing his whole demesne, he returned to his house without being able to think of anything new or strange, He found no difficulty in 'there was once a king who had three sons' or 'one day the king of all Ireland', but further than that he could not get. At length he went into breakfast, and found his wife much perplexed at his delay.

'Why don't you come to breakfast, my dear?' said she.

'I have no mind to eat anything,' replied the storyteller; 'long as I have been in the service of the king of Leinster, I never sat down to breakfast without having a new story ready for the evening, but this morning my mind is quite shut up, and I don't know what to do. I might as well lie down and die at once. I'll be disgraced for ever this evening, when the king calls for his storyteller.'

Just at this moment the lady looked out of the window.

'Do you see that black thing at the end of the field?' said she.

'I do,' replied her husband.

They drew nigh, and saw a miserable looking old man lying on the ground with a wooden leg placed beside him.

'Who are you, my good man?' asked the storyteller.

'Oh, then 'tis little matter who I am. I'm a poor, old, lame, decrepit, miserable creature, sitting down here to rest awhile.'

'An' what are you doing with that box and dice I see in your hand?'

'I am waiting here to see if anyone will play a game with me,' replied the beggar-man.

'Play with you! Why what has a poor old man like you to play for?'

'I have one hundred pieces of gold in this leathern purse,' replied the old man.

'You may as well play with him,' said the storyteller's wife; 'and perhaps you'll have something to tell the king in the evening.'

A smooth stone was placed between them, and upon it they cast their throws.

It was but a little while and the storyteller lost every penny of his money.

'Much good may it do you, friend,' said he. 'What better hap could I look for, fool that I am!'

'Will you play again?' asked the old man.

'Don't be talking, man: you have all my money.'

'Haven't you chariot and horses and hounds?'

'Well, what of them!'

'I'll stake all the money I have against thine.'

'Nonsense, man! Do you think for all the money in Ireland, I'd run the risk of seeing my lady tramp home on foot?'

'Maybe you'd win,' said the bocough.

'Maybe I wouldn't,' said the storyteller.

'Play with him, husband,' said his wife. 'I don't mind walking, if you do, love.'

'I never refused you before,' said the storyteller, 'and I won't do so now.'

Down he sat again, and in one throw lost houses, hounds, and chariot.

'Will you play again?' asked the beggar.

'Are you making game of me, man; what else have I to stake?'

'I'll stake all my winnings against your wife,' said the old man.

The storyteller turned away in silence, but his wife stopped him.

'Accept his offer,' said she. 'This is the third time, and who knows what luck you may have? You'll surely win now.'

They played again, and the storyteller lost. No sooner had he done so, than to his sorrow and surprise, his wife went and sat down near the ugly old beggar.

'Is that the way you're leaving me?' said the storyteller.

'Sure I was won,' said she. 'You would not cheat the poor man, would you?'

'Have you any more to stake?' asked the old man.

'You know very well I have not,' replied the storyteller.

'I'll stake the whole now, wife and all, against your own self,' said the old man.

Again they played, and again the storyteller lost.

'Well! Here I am, and what do you want with me?'

'I'll soon let you know,' said the old man, and he took from his pocket a long cord and a wand.

'Now,' said he to the storyteller, 'what kind of animal would you rather be, a deer, a fox or a hare? You have your choice now, but you may not have it later.'

To make a long story short, the storyteller made his choice of a hare; the old man threw the cord round him, struck him with the wand, and lo! A long-eared, frisking hare was skipping and jumping on the green.

But it wasn't for long; who but his wife called the hounds, and set them on him. The hare fled, the dogs followed. Round the field ran a high wall, so that run as he might, he couldn't get out, and mightily diverted were beggar and lady to see him twist and double.

In vain did he take refuge with his wife, she kicked him back again to the hounds, until at length the beggar stopped the hounds, and with a stroke of the wand, panting and breathless, the storyteller stood before them again.

'And how did you like the sport?' said the beggar.

'It might be sport to others,' replied the storyteller looking at his wife, 'for my part I could well put up with the loss of it.

'Would it be asking too much,' he went on to the beggar, 'to know who you are at all, or where you come from or why you take a pleasure in plaguing a poor old man like me?'

'Oh!' replied the stranger, 'I'm an odd kind of good-for-little fellow, one day poor, another day rich, but if you wish to know more about me or my habits, come with me and perhaps I may show you more than you would make out if you went alone.'

'I'm not my own master to go or stay,' said the storyteller, with a sigh.

The stranger put one hand into his wallet and drew out of it before their eyes a well-looking middle-aged man, to whom he spoke as follows, 'By all you heard and saw since I put you into my wallet, take charge of this lady and of the carriage and horses, and have them ready for me whenever I want them.'

Scarcely had he said these words when all vanished, and the storyteller found himself at the Foxes' Ford, near the castle of Red Hugh O'Donnell. He could see all but none could see him.

O'Donnell was in his hall, and heaviness of flesh and weariness of spirit were upon him.

'Go out,' said he to his doorkeeper, 'and see who or what may be coming.'

The doorkeeper went, and what he saw was a lank, grey beggar-man; half his sword bared behind his haunch, his two shoes full of cold road-a-wayish wa-ter sousing about him, the tips of his two ears out through his old hat, his two shoulders out through his scant tattered cloak, and in his hand a green wand of holly.

'Save you, O'Donnell,' said the lank grey beggar-man.

'And you likewise,' said O'Donnell. 'Whence come you, and what is your craft?'

> 'I come from the outmost stream of earth,
> From the glens where the white swans glide,
> A night in Islay, a night in Man,
> A night on the cold hillside.'

'It's the great traveller you are,' said O'Donnell. 'Maybe you've learnt something on the road.'

'I am a juggler,' said the lank grey beggar-man, 'and for five pieces of silver you shall see a trick of mine.'

'You shall have them,' said O'Donnell; and the lank grey beggar-man took three small straws and placed them in his hand.

'The middle one,' said he, 'I'll blow away; the other two I'll leave.'

'Thou canst not do it,' said one and all.

But the lank grey beggar-man put a finger on either outside straw and, whiff, away he blew the middle one.

''Tis a good trick,' said O'Donnell; and he paid him his five pieces of silver.

'For half the money,' said one of the chief's lads, 'I'll do the same trick.'

'Take him at his word, O'Donnell.'

The lad put the three straws on his hand, and a finger on either outside straw and he blew; and what happened but that the fist was blown away with the straw.

'Thou art sore, and thou wilt be sorer,' said O'Donnell.

'Six more pieces, O'Donnell, and I'll do another trick for thee,' said the lank grey beggar-man.

'Six shalt thou have.'

'Seest thou my two ears! One I'll move but not t'other.'

' 'Tis easy to see them, they're big enough, but thou canst never move one ear and not the two together.'

The lank grey beggar-man put his hand to his ear, and he gave it a pull.

O'Donnell laughed and paid him the six pieces.

'Call that a trick,' said the fistless lad, 'anyone can do that,' and so saying, he put up his hand, pulled his ear, and what happened was that he pulled away ear and head.

'Sore thou art, and sorer thou'lt be,' said O'Donnell.

'Well, O'Donnell,' said the lank grey beggar-man, 'stranger are the tricks I've shown thee, but I'll show thee a stranger one yet for the same money.'

'Thou hast my word for it,' said O'Donnell.

With that the lank grey beggar-man took a bag from under his armpit, and from out the bag a ball of silk, and he unwound the ball and he flung it slantwise up into the clear blue heavens, and it became a ladder; then he took a hare and placed it upon the thread, and up it ran; again he took out a red-eared hound, and it swiftly ran up after the hare.

'Now,' said the lank grey beggar-man. 'Has anyone a mind to run after the dog and on the course?'

'I will,' said a lad of O'Donnell's.

'Up with you then,' said the juggler; 'but I warn you if you let my hare be killed I'll cut off your head when you come down.'

The lad ran up the thread and all three soon disappeared. After looking up for a long time, the lank grey beggar-man said, 'I'm afraid the hound is eating the hare, and that our friend has fallen asleep.'

Saying this he began to wind the thread, and down came the lad fast asleep; and down came the red-eared hound and in his mouth the last morsel of the hare.

He struck the lad a stroke with the edge of his sword, and so cast his head off. As for the hound, if he used it no worse, he used it no better.

'It's little I'm pleased, and sore I'm angered,' said O'Donnell, 'that a hound and a lad should be killed at my court.'

'Five pieces of silver twice over for each of them,' said the juggler, 'and their heads shall be on them as before.'

'Thou shalt get that,' said O'Donnell.

Five pieces, and again five were paid him, and lo! The lad had his head and the hound his. And though they lived to the uttermost end of time, the hound would never touch a hare again, and the lad took good care to keep his eyes open.

Scarcely had the lank grey beggar-man done this when he vanished from out their sight, and no one present could say if he had flown through the air or if the earth had swallowed him up.

> He moved as wave tumbling o'er wave
> As whirlwind following whirlwind,
> As a furious wintry blast,
> So swiftly, sprucely, cheerily,
> Right proudly,
> And no stop made
> Until he came
> To the court of Leinster's King,
> He gave a cheery light leap
> O'er top of turret,
> Of court and city
> Of Leinster's King.

Heavy was the flesh and weary the spirit of Leinster's king. 'Twas the hour he was wont to hear a story, but send he might right and left, not a jot of tidings about the storyteller could he get.

'Go to the door,' said he to his doorkeeper, 'and see if a soul is in sight who may tell me something about my storyteller.'

The doorkeeper went, and what he saw was a lank grey beggar-man, half his sword bared behind his haunch, his two old shoes full of cold road-a-wayish water sousing about him, the tips of his two ears out through his old hat, his two shoulders out through his scant tattered cloak, and in his hand a three-stringed harp.

'What canst thou do?' said the doorkeeper.

'I can play,' said the lank grey beggar-man. 'Never fear,' added he to the storyteller, 'thou shalt see all, and not a man shall see thee.'

When the king heard a harper was outside, he bade him in.

'It is I that have the best harpers in the five-fifths of Ireland,' said he, and he signed them to play. They did so, and if they played, the lank grey beggar-man listened.

'Heardst thou ever the like?' said the king.

'Did you ever, O king, hear a cat purring over a bowl of broth, or the buzzing of beetles in the twilight, or a shrill-tongued old woman scolding your head off?'

'That I have often,' said the king.

'More melodious to me,' said the lank grey beggar-man, 'were the worst of these sounds than the sweetest harping of thy harpers.'

When the harpers heard this, they drew their swords and rushed at him, but instead of striking him, their blows fell on each other, and soon not a man but was cracking his neighbour's skull and getting his own cracked in turn.

When the king saw this, he thought it hard the harpers weren't content with murdering their music, but must needs murder each other.

'Hang the fellow who began it all,' said he; 'and if I can't have a story, let me have peace.'

Up came the guards, seized the lank grey beggar-man, marched him to the gallows and hanged him high and dry. Back they marched to the hall, and who should they see but the lank grey beggar-man seated on a bench with his mouth to a flagon of ale.

'Never welcome you in,' cried the captain of the guard, 'didn't we hang you this minute, and what brings you here?'

'Is it me myself, you mean?'

'Who else?' said the captain.

'May your hand turn into a pig's foot with you when you think of tying the rope; why should you speak of hanging me?'

Back they scurried to the gallows, and there hung the king's favourite brother.

Back they hurried to the king who had fallen fast asleep.

'Please, your majesty,' said the captain, 'we hanged that strolling vagabond, but here he is back again as well as ever.'

'Hang him again,' said the king, and off he went to sleep once more.

They did as they were told, but what happened was that they found the king's chief harper hanging where the lank grey beggar-man should have been.

The captain of the guard was sorely puzzled.

'Are you wishful to hang me a third time?' said the lank grey beggar-man.

'Go where you will,' said the captain, 'and as fast as you please if you'll only go far enough. It's trouble enough you've given us already.'

'Now you're reasonable,' said the beggar-man; 'and since you've given up trying to hang a stranger because he finds fault with your music, I don't mind telling you that if you go back to the gallows you'll find your friends sitting on the sward none the worse for what has happened.'

As he said these words he vanished; and the storyteller found himself on the spot where they first met, and where his wife still was with the carriage and horses.

'Now,' said the lank grey beggar-man, 'I'll torment you no longer. There's your carriage and your horses, and your money and your wife; do what you please with them.'

'For my carriage and my horses and my hounds,' said the story-teller, 'I thank you; but my wife and my money you may keep.'

'No,' said the other. 'I want neither, and as for your wife, don't think ill of her for what she did, she couldn't help it.'

'Not help it! Not help kicking me into the mouth of my own hounds! Not help casting me off for the sake of a beggarly old – '

'I'm not as beggarly or as old as ye think. I am Angus of the Bruff; many a good turn you've done me with the king of Leinster. This morning my magic told me the difficulty you were in, and I made up my mind to get you out of it. As for your wife there, the power that changed your body changed her mind. Forget and forgive as man and wife should do, and now you have a story for the king of Leinster when he calls for one;' and with that he disappeared.

It's true enough he now had a story fit for a king. From first to last he told all that had befallen him; so long and loud laughed the king that he couldn't go to sleep at all. And he told the storyteller never to trouble for fresh stories, but every night as long as he lived he listened again and he laughed afresh at the tale of the lank grey beggar-man.

A Legend of Knockmany

What Irish man, woman, or child has not heard of our renowned Hibernian Hercules, the great and glorious Fin M'Coul? Not one, from Cape Clear to the Giant's Causeway, nor from that back again to Cape Clear. And, by the way, speaking of the Giant's Causeway brings me at once to the beginning of my story. Well, it so happened that Fin and his men were all working at the Causeway, in order to make a bridge across to Scotland; when Fin, who was very fond of his wife Oonagh, took it into his head that he would go home and see how the poor woman got on in his absence. So, accordingly, he pulled up a fir-tree, and, after lopping off the roots and branches, made a walking-stick of it, and set out on his way to Oonagh.

Oonagh, or rather Fin, lived at this time on the very tip-top of Knockmany Hill, which faces a cousin of its own called Cullamore, that rises up, half-hill, half-mountain, on the opposite side.

There was at that time another giant, named Cucullin – some say he was Irish, and some say he was Scots – but whether Scots or Irish, sorrow doubt of it but he was a targer. No other giant of the day could stand before him; and such was his strength, that, when well vexed, he could give a stamp that shook the country about him. The fame and name of him went far and near; and nothing in the shape of a man, it was said, had any chance with him in a fight. By one blow of his fists he flattened a thunderbolt and kept it in his pocket, in the shape of a pancake, to show to all his enemies, when they were about to fight him. Undoubtedly he had given every giant in Ireland a considerable beating, barring Fin M'Coul himself; and he swore that he would never rest, night or day, winter or summer, till he would serve Fin with the same sauce, if he could catch him. However, the short and long of it was, with reverence be it spoken, that Fin heard Cucullin was coming to the Causeway to have a trial of strength with him; and he was seized with a very warm and sudden fit of affection for his wife, poor woman, leading a very lonely, uncomfortable life of it in his absence. He accordingly pulled up the fir-tree, as I said before, and having snedded it into a walking-stick, set out on his travels to see his darling Oonagh on the top of Knockmany, by the way.

In truth, the people wondered very much why it was that Fin selected such a windy spot for his dwelling-house, and they even went so far as to tell him as much.

'What can you mane, Mr M'Coul,' said they, 'by pitching your tent upon the top of Knockmany, where you never are without a breeze, day or night, winter or summer, and where you're often forced to take your nightcap without either going to bed or turning up your little finger; ay, an' where, besides this, there's the sorrow's own want of water?'

'Why,' said Fin, 'ever since I was the height of a round tower, I was known to be fond of having a good prospect of my own; and where the dickens, neighbours, could I find a better spot for a good prospect than the top of Knockmany? As for water, I am sinking a pump, and, plase goodness, as soon as the Causeway's made, I intend to finish it.'

Now, this was more of Fin's philosophy; for the real state of the case was, that he pitched upon the top of Knockmany in order that he might be able to see Cucullin coming towards the house. All we have to say is, that if he wanted a spot from which to keep a sharp lookout – and, between ourselves, he did want it grievously – barring Slieve Croob, or Slieve Donard, or its own cousin, Cullamore, he could not find a neater or more convenient situation for it in the sweet and sagacious province of Ulster.

'God save all here!' said Fin, good-humouredly, on putting his honest face into his own door.

'Musha, Fin, avick, an' you're welcome home to your own Oonagh, you darlin' bully.' Here followed a smack that is said to have made the waters of the lake at the bottom of the hill curl, as it were, with kindness and sympathy.

Fin spent two or three happy days with Oonagh, and felt

himself very comfortable, considering the dread he had of Cucullin. This, however, grew upon him so much that his wife could not but perceive something lay on his mind which he kept altogether to himself. Let a woman alone, in the meantime, for ferreting or wheedling a secret out of her good man, when she wishes. Fin was a proof of this.

'It's this Cucullin,' said he, 'that's troubling me. When the fellow gets angry, and begins to stamp, he'll shake you a whole townland; and it's well known that he can stop a thunderbolt, for he always carries one about him in the shape of a pancake, to show to anyone that might misdoubt it.'

As he spoke, he clapped his thumb in his mouth, which he always did when he wanted to prophesy, or to know anything that happened in his absence; and the wife asked him what he did it for.

'He's coming,' said Fin; 'I see him below Dungannon.'

'Thank goodness, dear! An' who is it, avick? Glory be to God!'

'That baste, Cucullin,' replied Fin; 'and how to manage I don't know. If I run away, I am disgraced; and I know that sooner or later I must meet him, for my thumb tells me so.'

'When will he be here?' said she.

'Tomorrow, about two o'clock,' replied Fin, with a groan.

'Well, my bully, don't be cast down,' said Oonagh. 'Depend on me, and maybe I'll bring you better out of this scrape than ever you could bring yourself, by your rule o'thumb.'

She then made a high smoke on the top of the hill, after which she put her finger in her mouth, and gave three whistles, and by that Cucullin knew he was invited to Cullamore – for this was the way that the Irish long ago gave a sign to all strangers and travellers, to let them know they were welcome to come and take share of whatever was going.

In the meantime, Fin was very melancholy, and did not know what to do, or how to act at all. Cucullin was an ugly customer to meet with; and, the idea of the 'cake' aforesaid flattened the very heart within him. What chance could he have, strong and brave though he was, with a man who could, when put in a passion, walk the country into earthquakes and knock thunderbolts into pancakes? Fin knew not on what hand to turn him. Right or left –

backward or forward – where to go he could form no guess whatsoever.

'Oonagh,' said he, 'can you do nothing for me? Where's all your invention? Am I to be skivered like a rabbit before your eyes, and to have my name disgraced for ever in the sight of all my tribe, and me the best man among them? How am I to fight this man-mountain – this huge cross between an earthquake and a thunderbolt? – with a pancake in his pocket that was once – '

'Be easy, Fin,' replied Oonagh. 'Troth, I'm ashamed of you. Keep your toe in your pump, will you? Talking of pancakes, maybe, we'll give him as good as any he brings with him – thunderbolt or otherwise. If I don't treat him to as smart feeding as he's got this many a day, never trust Oonagh again. Leave him to me, and do just as I bid you.'

This relieved Fin very much; for, after all, he had great confidence in his wife, knowing, as he did, that she had got him out of many a quandary before. Oonagh then drew the nine woollen threads of different colours, which she always did to find out the best way of succeeding in anything of importance she went about. She then platted them into three plats with three colours in each, putting one on her right arm, one round her heart, and the third round her right ankle, for then she knew that nothing could fail with her that she undertook.

Having everything now prepared, she sent round to the neighbours and borrowed one-and-twenty iron griddles, which she took and kneaded into the hearts of one-and-twenty cakes of bread, and these she baked on the fire in the usual way, setting them aside in the cupboard according as they were done. She then put down a large pot of new milk, which she made into curds and whey. Having done all this, she sat down quite contented, waiting for his arrival on the next day about two o'clock, that being the hour at which he was expected – for Fin knew as much by the sucking of his thumb. Now this was a curious property that Fin's thumb had. In this very thing, moreover, he was very much resembled by his great foe, Cucullin; for it was well known that the huge strength he possessed all lay in the middle finger of his right hand, and that, if he happened by any mischance to lose it, he was no more, for all his bulk, than a common man.

At length, the next day, Cucullin was seen coming across the valley, and Oonagh knew that it was time to commence operations. She immediately brought the cradle, and made Fin to lie down in it, and cover himself up with the clothes.

'You must pass for your own child,' said she; 'so just lie there snug, and say nothing, but be guided by me.'

About two o'clock, as he had been expected, Cucullin came in. 'God save all here!' said he. 'Is this where the great Fin M'Coul lives?'

'Indeed it is, honest man,' replied Oonagh; 'God save you kindly – won't you be sitting?'

'Thank you, ma'am,' says he, sitting down. 'You're Mrs M'Coul, I suppose?'

'I am,' said she, 'and I have no reason, I hope, to be ashamed of my husband.'

'No,' said the other, 'he has the name of being the strongest and bravest man in Ireland; but for all that, there's a man not far from you that's very desirous of taking a shake with him. Is he at home?'

'Why, then, no,' she replied, 'and if ever a man left his house in a fury, he did. It appears that someone told him of a big basthoon of a giant called Cucullin being down at the Causeway to look for him, and so he set out there to try if he could catch him. Troth, I hope, for the poor giant's sake, he won't meet with him, for if he does, Fin will make paste of him at once.'

'Well,' said the other, 'I am Cucullin, and I have been seeking him these twelve months, but he always kept clear of me; and I will never rest night or day till I lay my hands on him.'

At this Oonagh set up a loud laugh, of great contempt, by the way, and looked at him as if he was only a mere handful of a man.

'Did you ever see Fin?' said she, changing her manner all at once.

'How could I?' said he. 'He always took care to keep his distance.'

'I thought so,' she replied. 'I judged as much; and if you take my advice, you poor-looking creature, you'll pray night and day that you may never see him, for I tell you it will be a black day for you when you do. But, in the meantime, you perceive that the wind's on the door, and as Fin himself is from home, maybe you'd be civil enough to turn the house, for it's always what Fin does when he's here.'

This was a startler even to Cucullin; but he got up, however, and after pulling the middle finger of his right hand until it cracked three times, he went outside, and getting his arms about the house, turned it as she had wished. When Fin saw this, he felt the sweat of fear oozing out through every pore of his skin; but Oonagh, depending upon her woman's wit, felt not a whit daunted.

'Arrah, then,' said she, 'as you are so civil, maybe you'd do another obliging turn for us, as Fin's not here to do it himself. You see, after this long stretch of dry weather we've had, we feel very badly off for want of water. Now, Fin says there's a fine spring-well somewhere under the rocks behind the hill here below, and it was his intention to pull them asunder; but having heard of you, he left the place in such a fury, that he never thought of it. Now, if you try to find it, troth I'd feel it a kindness.'

She then brought Cucullin down to see the place, which was then all one solid rock; and, after looking at it for some time, he cracked his right middle finger nine times, and, stooping down, tore a cleft about four hundred feet deep, and a quarter of a mile in length, which has since been christened by the name of Lumford's Glen.

'You'll now come in,' said she, 'and eat a bit of such humble fare as we can give you. Fin, even although he and you are enemies, would scorn not to treat you kindly in his own house; and, indeed, if I didn't do it even in his absence, he would not be pleased with me.'

She accordingly brought him in, and placing half-a-dozen of the cakes we spoke of before him, together with a can or two of butter, a side of boiled bacon, and a stack of cabbage, she desired him to help himself – for this, be it known, was long before the invention of potatoes. Cucullin put one of the cakes in his mouth to take a huge whack out of it, when he made a thundering noise, something between a growl and a yell. 'Blood and fury!' he shouted. 'How is this? Here are two of my teeth out! What kind of bread is this you gave me?'

'What's the matter?' said Oonagh coolly.

'Matter!' shouted the other again. 'Why, here are the two best teeth in my head gone.'

'Why,' said she, 'that's Fin's bread – the only bread he ever eats when at home; but, indeed, I forgot to tell you that nobody can eat it but himself, and that child in the cradle there. I thought, however, that, as you were reported to be rather a stout little fellow of your size, you might be able to manage it, and I did not wish to affront a man that thinks himself able to fight Fin. Here's another cake – maybe it's not so hard as that.'

Cucullin at the moment was not only hungry, but ravenous, so he accordingly made a fresh set at the second cake, and immediately another yell was heard twice as loud as the first. 'Thunder and gibbets!' he roared. 'Take your bread out of this, or I will not have a tooth in my head; there's another pair of them gone!'

'Well, honest man,' replied Oonagh, 'if you're not able to eat

the bread, say so quietly, and don't be wakening the child in the
cradle there. There, now, he's awake upon me.'

Fin now gave a skirl that startled the giant, as coming from such
a youngster as he was supposed to be.

'Mother,' said he, 'I'm hungry – get me something to eat.'
Oonagh went over, and putting into his hand a cake that had no
griddle in it, Fin, whose appetite in the meantime had been
sharpened by seeing eating going forward, soon swallowed it.
Cucullin was thunderstruck, and secretly thanked his stars that he
had the good fortune to miss meeting Fin, for, as he said to
himself, 'I'd have no chance with a man who could eat such bread
as that, which even his son that's but in his cradle can munch
before my eyes.'

'I'd like to take a glimpse at the lad in the cradle,' said he to
Oonagh, 'for I can tell you that the infant who can manage that
nutriment is no joke to look at, or to feed of a scarce summer.'

'With all the veins of my heart,' replied Oonagh. 'Get up,
acushla, and show this decent little man something that won't be
unworthy of your father, Fin M'Coul.'

Fin, who was dressed for the occasion as much like a boy as
possible, got up, and bringing Cucullin out, 'Are you strong?'
said he.

'Thunder an' ounds!' exclaimed the other. 'What a voice in so
small a chap!'

'Are you strong?' said Fin again. 'Are you able to squeeze water
out of that white stone?' he asked, putting one into Cucullin's
hand. The latter squeezed and squeezed the stone, but in vain.

'Ah, you're a poor creature!' said Fin. 'You a giant! Give me the
stone here, and when I'll show what Fin's little son can do, you
may then judge of what my daddy himself is.'

Fin then took the stone, and exchanging it for the curds, he
squeezed the latter until the whey, as clear as water, oozed out in
a little shower from his hand.

'I'll now go in,' said he, 'to my cradle; for I scorn to lose my time
with anyone that's not able to eat my daddy's bread, or squeeze
water out of a stone. Bedad, you had better be off out of this
before he comes back; for if he catches you, it's in flummery he'd

have you in two minutes.'

Cucullin, seeing what he had seen, was of the same opinion himself; his knees knocked together with the terror of Fin's return, and he accordingly hastened to bid Oonagh farewell, and to assure her, that from that day out, he never wished to hear of, much less to see, her husband. 'I admit fairly that I'm not a match for him,' said he, 'strong as I am; tell him I will avoid him as I would the plague, and that I will make myself scarce in this part of the country while I live.'

Fin, in the meantime, had gone into the cradle, where he lay very quietly, his heart at his mouth with delight that Cucullin was about to take his departure, without discovering the tricks that had been played off on him.

'It's well for you,' said Oonagh, 'that he doesn't happen to be here, for it's nothing but hawk's meat he'd make of you.'

'I know that,' says Cucullin. 'Divil a thing else he'd make of me; but before I go, will you let me feel what kind of teeth Fin's lad has got that can eat griddle-bread like that?'

'With all pleasure in life,' said she. 'Only, as they're far back in his head, you must put your finger a good way in.'

Cucullin was surprised to find such a powerful set of grinders in one so young; but he was still much more so on finding, when he took his hand from Fin's mouth, that he had left the very finger upon which his whole strength depended, behind him. He gave one loud groan, and fell down at once with terror and weakness. This was all Fin wanted, who now knew that his most powerful and bitterest enemy was at his mercy. He started out of the cradle, and in a few minutes the great Cucullin, that was for such a length of time the terror of him and all his followers, lay a corpse before him. Thus did Fin, through the wit and invention of Oonagh, his wife, succeed in overcoming his enemy by cunning, which he never could have done by force.

Fair, Brown and Trembling

King Hugh Curucha lived in Tir Conal, and he had three daughters, whose names were Fair, Brown and Trembling.

Fair and Brown had new dresses, and went to church every Sunday. Trembling was kept at home to do the cooking and work. They would not let her go out of the house at all; for she was more beautiful than the other two, and they were in dread she might marry before themselves.

They carried on in this way for seven years. At the end of seven years the son of the king of Emania fell in love with the eldest sister.

One Sunday morning, after the other two had gone to church, the old henwife came into the kitchen to Trembling, and said, 'It's at church you ought to be this day, instead of working here at home.'

'How could I go?' said Trembling. 'I have no clothes good enough to wear at church; and if my sisters were to see me there, they'd kill me for going out of the house.'

'I'll give you,' said the henwife, 'a finer dress than either of them has ever seen. And now tell me what dress will you have?'

'I'll have,' said Trembling, 'a dress as white as snow, and green shoes for my feet.'

Then the henwife put on the cloak of darkness, clipped a piece from the old clothes the young woman had on, and asked for the whitest robes in the world and the most beautiful that could be found, and a pair of green shoes.

That moment she had the robe and the shoes, and she brought them to Trembling, who put them on. When Trembling was dressed and ready, the henwife said, 'I have a honey-bird here to sit on your right shoulder, and a honey-finger to put on your left. At the door stands a milk-white mare, with a golden saddle for you to sit on, and a golden bridle to hold in your hand.'

Trembling sat on the golden saddle; and when she was ready to start, the henwife said, 'You must not go inside the door of the church, and the minute the people rise up at the end of Mass, do you make off, and ride home as fast as the mare will carry you.'

When Trembling came to the door of the church there was no one inside who could get a glimpse of her but was striving to know who she was; and when they saw her hurrying away at the end of Mass, they ran out to overtake her. But no use in their running; she was away before any man could come near her. From the minute she left the church till she got home, she overtook the wind before her, and outstripped the wind behind.

She came down at the door, went in, and found the henwife had dinner ready. She put off the white robes, and had on her old dress in a twinkling.

When the two sisters came home the henwife asked, 'Have you any news today from the church?'

'We have great news,' said they. 'We saw a wonderful grand lady at the church-door. The like of the robes she had we have never seen on woman before. It's little that was thought of our dresses beside what she had on; and there wasn't a man at the church, from the king to the beggar, but was trying to look at her and know who she was.'

The sisters would give no peace till they had two dresses like the robes of the strange lady; but honey-birds and honey-fingers were not to be found.

Next Sunday the two sisters went to church again, and left the youngest at home to cook the dinner.

After they had gone, the henwife came in and asked, 'Will you go to church today?'

'I would go,' said Trembling, 'if I could get the going.'

'What robe will you wear?' asked the henwife.

'The finest black satin that can be found, and red shoes for my feet.'

'What colour do you want the mare to be?'

'I want her to be so black and so glossy that I can see myself in her body.'

The henwife put on the cloak of darkness, and asked for the

robes and the mare. That moment she had them. When Trembling was dressed, the henwife put the honey-bird on her right shoulder and the honey-finger on her left. The saddle on the mare was silver, and so was the bridle.

When Trembling sat in the saddle and was going away, the henwife ordered her strictly not to go inside the door of the church, but to rush away as soon as the people rose at the end of Mass, and hurry home on the mare before any man could stop her.

That Sunday the people were more astonished than ever, and gazed at her more than the first time; and all they were thinking of was to know who she was. But they had no chance; for the moment the people rose at the end of Mass she slipped from the church, was in the silver saddle, and home before a man could stop her or talk to her.

The henwife had the dinner ready. Trembling took off her satin robe, and had on her old clothes before her sisters got home.

'What news have you today?' asked the henwife of the sisters when they came from the church.

'Oh, we saw the grand strange lady again! And it's little that any man could think of our dresses after looking at the robes of satin that she had on! And all at church, from high to low, had their mouths open, gazing at her, and no man was looking at us.'

The two sisters gave neither rest nor peace till they got dresses as nearly like the strange lady's robes as they could find. Of course they were not so good; for the like of those robes could not be found in Erin.

When the third Sunday came, Fair and Brown went to church dressed in black satin. They left Trembling at home to work in the kitchen, and told her to be sure and have dinner ready when they came back.

After they had gone and were out of sight, the henwife came to the kitchen and said, 'Well, my dear, are you for church today?'

'I would go if I had a new dress to wear.'

'I'll get you any dress you ask for. What dress would you like?' asked the henwife.

'A dress red as a rose from the waist down, and white as snow

Trembling at the church door

from the waist up; a cape of green on my shoulders; and a hat on my head with a red, a white, and a green feather in it; and shoes for my feet with the toes red, the middle white, and the backs and heels green.'

The henwife put on the cloak of darkness, wished for all these things, and had them. When Trembling was dressed, the henwife put the honey-bird on her right shoulder and the honey-finger on her left, and, placing the hat on her head, clipped a few hairs from one lock and a few from another with her scissors, and that moment the most beautiful golden hair was flowing down over the girl's shoulders. Then the henwife asked what kind of a mare she would ride. She said white, with blue and gold-coloured diamond-shaped spots all over her body, on her back a saddle of gold, and on her head a golden bridle.

The mare stood there before the door, and a bird sitting between her ears, which began to sing as soon as Trembling was in the saddle, and never stopped till she came home from the church.

The fame of the beautiful strange lady had gone out through the world, and all the princes and great men that were in it came to church that Sunday, each one hoping that it was himself would have her home with him after Mass.

The son of the king of Emania forgot all about the eldest sister, and remained outside the church, so as to catch the strange lady before she could hurry away.

The church was more crowded than ever before, and there were three times as many outside. There was such a throng before the church that Trembling could only come inside the gate.

As soon as the people were rising at the end of Mass, the lady slipped out through the gate, was in the golden saddle in an instant, and sweeping away ahead of the wind. But if she was, the prince of Emania was at her side, and, seizing her by the foot, he ran with the mare for thirty perches, and never let go of the beautiful lady till the shoe was pulled from her foot, and he was left behind with it in his hand. She came home as fast as the mare could carry her, and was thinking all the time that the henwife would kill her for losing the shoe.

Seeing her so vexed and so changed in the face, the old woman asked, 'What's the trouble that's on you now?'

'Oh! I've lost one of the shoes off my feet,' said Trembling.

'Don't mind that; don't be vexed,' said the henwife. 'Maybe it's the best thing that ever happened to you.'

Then Trembling gave up all the things she had to the henwife, put on her old clothes, and went to work in the kitchen. When the sisters came home, the henwife asked, 'Have you any news from the church?'

'We have indeed,' said they, 'for we saw the grandest sight today. The strange lady came again, in grander array than before. On herself and the horse she rode were the finest colours of the world, and between the ears of the horse was a bird which never stopped singing from the time she came till she went away. The lady herself is the most beautiful woman ever seen by man in Erin.'

After Trembling had disappeared from the church, the son of the king of Emania said to the other kings' sons, 'I will have that lady for my own.'

They all said, 'You didn't win her just by taking the shoe off her foot; you'll have to win her by the point of the sword; you'll have to fight for her with us before you can call her your own.'

'Well,' said the son of the king of Emania, 'when I find the lady that shoe will fit, I'll fight for her, never fear, before I leave her to any of you.'

Then all the kings' sons were uneasy, and anxious to know who was she that lost the shoe; and they began to travel all over Erin to know could they find her. The prince of Emania and all the others went in a great company together, and made the round of Erin; they went everywhere – north, south, east, and west. They visited every place where a woman was to be found, and left not a house in the kingdom they did not search, to know could they find the woman the shoe would fit, not caring whether she was rich or poor, of high or low degree.

The prince of Emania always kept the shoe; and when the young women saw it, they had great hopes, for it was of proper size, neither large nor small, and it would beat any man to know of what material it was made. One thought it would fit her if she cut a little from her great toe; and another, with too short a foot, put something in the tip of her stocking. But no use; they only spoiled their feet, and were curing them for months afterwards.

The two sisters, Fair and Brown, heard that the princes of the world were looking all over Erin for the woman that could wear the shoe, and every day they were talking of trying it on; and one day Trembling spoke up and said, 'Maybe it's my foot that the shoe will fit.'

'Oh, the breaking of the dog's foot on you! Why say so when you were at home every Sunday?'

They were that way waiting, and scolding the younger sister, till the princes were near the place. The day they were to come, the sisters put Trembling in a closet, and locked the door on her. When the company came to the house, the prince of Emania gave the shoe to the sisters. But though they tried and tried, it would fit neither of them.

'Is there any other young woman in the house?' asked the prince.

'There is,' said Trembling, speaking up in the closet; 'I'm here.'

'Oh! We have her for nothing but to put out the ashes,' said the sisters.

But the prince and the others wouldn't leave the house till they had seen her; so the two sisters had to open the door. When Trembling came out, the shoe was given to her, and it fitted exactly.

The prince of Emania looked at her and said, 'You are the woman the shoe fits, and you are the woman I took the shoe from.'

Then Trembling spoke up, and said, 'Do you stay here till I return.'

Then she went to the henwife's house. The old woman put on the cloak of darkness, got everything for her she had the first Sunday at church, and put her on the white mare in the same fashion. Then Trembling rode along the highway to the front of the house. All who saw her the first time said, 'This is the lady we saw at church.'

Then she went away a second time, and a second time came back on the black mare in the second dress which the henwife gave her. All who saw her the second Sunday said, 'That is the lady we saw at church.'

A third time she asked for a short absence, and soon came back on the third mare and in the third dress. All who saw her the third time said, 'That is the lady we saw at church.' Every man was satisfied, and knew that she was the woman.

Then all the princes and great men spoke up, and said to the son of the king of Emania, 'You'll have to fight now for her before we let her go with you.'

'I'm here before you, ready for combat,' answered the prince.

Then the son of the king of Lochlin stepped forth. The struggle began, and a terrible struggle it was. They fought for nine hours; and then the son of the king of Lochlin stopped, gave up his claim, and left the field. Next day the son of the king of Spain fought six hours, and yielded his claim. On the third day the son of the king of Nyerfói fought eight hours, and stopped. The fourth day the son of the king of Greece fought six hours, and stopped. On the fifth day no more strange princes wanted to fight; and all the sons of kings in Erin said they would not fight with a man of their own land, that the strangers had had their chance, and, as no others came to claim the woman, she belonged of right to the son of the king of Emania.

The marriage-day was fixed, and the invitations were sent out. The wedding lasted for a year and a day. When the wedding was over, the king's son brought home the bride, and when the time came a son was born. The young woman sent for her eldest sister, Fair, to be with her and care for her. One day, when Trembling was well, and when her husband was away hunting, the two sisters went out to walk; and when they came to the seaside, the eldest pushed the youngest sister in. A great whale came and swallowed her.

The eldest sister came home alone, and the husband asked, 'Where is your sister?'

'She has gone home to her father in Ballyshannon; now that I am well, I don't need her.'

'Well,' said the husband, looking at her, 'I'm in dread it's my wife that has gone.'

'Oh, no!' said she. 'It's my sister Fair that's gone.'

Since the sisters were very much alike, the prince was in doubt.

That night he put his sword between them, and said, 'If you are my wife, this sword will get warm; if not, it will stay cold.'

In the morning when he rose up, the sword was as cold as when he put it there.

It happened, when the two sisters were walking by the seashore, that a little cowboy was down by the water minding cattle, and saw Fair push Trembling into the sea; and next day, when the tide came in, he saw the whale swim up and throw her out on the sand. When she was on the sand she said to the cowboy, 'When you go home in the evening with the cows, tell the master that my sister Fair pushed me into the sea yesterday; that a whale swallowed me, and then threw me out, but will come again and swallow me with the coming of the next tide; then he'll go out with the tide, and come again with tomorrow's tide, and throw me again on the strand. The whale will cast me out three times. I'm under the enchantment of this whale, and cannot leave the beach or escape myself. Unless my husband saves me before I'm swallowed the fourth time, I shall be lost. He must come and shoot the whale with a silver bullet when he turns on the broad of his back. Under the breast-fin of the whale is a reddish-brown spot. My husband must hit him in that spot, for it is the only place in which he can be killed.'

When the cowboy got home, the eldest sister gave him a draught of oblivion, and he did not tell.

Next day he went again to the sea. The whale came and cast Trembling on shore again. She asked the boy, 'Did you tell the master what I told you to tell him?'

'I did not,' said he; 'I forgot.'

'How did you forget?' asked she.

'The woman of the house gave me a drink that made me forget.'

'Well, don't forget telling him this night; and if she gives you a drink, don't take it from her.'

As soon as the cowboy came home, the eldest sister offered him a drink. He refused to take it till he had delivered his message and told all to the master. The third day the prince went down with his gun and a silver bullet in it. He was not long down when the whale came and threw Trembling upon the beach as the two days before. She had no power to speak to her husband till he had killed the whale. Then the whale went out, turned over once on the broad of his back, and showed the spot for a moment only. That moment the prince fired. He had but the one chance, and a short one at that; but he took it, and hit the spot, and the whale, mad with pain, made the sea all around red with blood, and died.

That minute Trembling was able to speak, and went home with her husband, who sent word to her father what the eldest sister had done. The father came, and told him any death he chose to give her to give it. The prince told the father he would leave her life and death with himself. The father had her put out then on the sea in a barrel, with provisions in it for seven years.

In time Trembling had a second child, a daughter. The prince and she sent the cowboy to school, and trained him up as one of their own children, and said, 'If the little girl that is born to us now lives, no other man in the world will get her but him.'

The cowboy and the prince's daughter lived on till they were married. The mother said to her husband, 'You could not have saved me from the whale but for the little cowboy; on that account I don't grudge him my daughter.'

The son of the king of Emania and Trembling had fourteen children, and they lived happily till the two died of old age.

Jack and his Master

A poor woman had three sons. The eldest and second eldest were cunning clever fellows, but they called the youngest Jack the Fool, because they thought he was no better than a simpleton. The eldest got tired of staying at home, and said he'd go look for service. He stayed away a whole year, and then came back one day, dragging one foot after the other, and a poor wizened face on him, and he as cross as two sticks. When he was rested and got something to eat, he told them how he got service with the Gray Churl of the Townland of Mischance, and that the agreement was, whoever would first say he was sorry for his bargain, should get an inch wide of the skin of his back, from shoulder to hips, taken off. If it was the master, he should also pay double wages; if it was the servant, he should get no wages at all. 'But the thief,' says he, 'gave me so little to eat, and kept me so hard at work, that flesh and blood couldn't stand it; and when he asked me once, when I was in a passion, if I was sorry for my bargain, I was mad enough to say I was, and here I am disabled for life.'

Vexed enough were the poor mother and brothers; and the second eldest said on the spot he'd go and take service with the Gray Churl, and punish him by all the annoyance he'd give him till he'd make him say he was sorry for his agreement. 'Oh, won't I be glad to see the skin coming off the old villain's back!' said he. All they could say had no effect: he started off for the Townland of Mischance, and in a twelvemonth he was back just as miserable and helpless as his brother.

All the poor mother could say didn't prevent Jack the Fool from starting to see if he was able to regulate the Gray Churl. He agreed with him for a year for twenty pounds, and the terms were the same.

'Now, Jack,' said the Gray Churl, 'if you refuse to do anything you are able to do, you must lose a month's wages.'

'I'm satisfied,' said Jack; 'and if you stop me from doing a thing after telling me to do it, you are to give me an additional month's wages.'

'I am satisfied,' says the master.

'Or if you blame me for obeying your orders, you must give the same.'

'I am satisfied,' said the master again.

The first day that Jack served he was fed very poorly, and was worked to the saddleskirts. Next day he came in just before the dinner was sent up to the parlour. They were taking the goose off the spit, but well becomes Jack he whips a knife off the dresser, and cuts off one side of the breast, one leg and thigh, and one wing, and fell to. In came the master, and began to abuse him for his assurance. 'Oh, you know, master, you're to feed me, and wherever the goose goes won't have to be filled again till supper. Are you sorry for our agreement?'

The master was going to cry out he was, but he bethought himself in time. 'Oh no, not at all,' said he.

'That's well,' said Jack.

Next day Jack was to go clamp turf on the bog. They weren't sorry to have him away from the kitchen at dinner time. He didn't find his breakfast very heavy on his stomach; so he said to the mistress, 'I think, ma'am, it will be better for me to get my dinner now, and not lose time coming home from the bog.'

'That's true, Jack,' said she. So she brought out a good cake, and a print of butter, and a bottle of milk, thinking he'd take them away to the bog. But Jack kept his seat, and never drew rein till bread, butter, and milk went down the red lane.

'Now, mistress,' said he, 'I'll be earlier at my work tomorrow if I sleep comfortably on the sheltery side of a pile of dry peat on dry grass, and not be coming here and going back. So you may as well give me my supper, and be done with the day's trouble.' She gave him that, thinking he'd take it to the bog; but he fell to on the spot, and did not leave a scrap to tell tales on him; and the mistress was a little astonished.

He called to speak to the master in the haggard, and said he, 'What are servants asked to do in this country after aten their supper?'

'Nothing at all, but to go to bed.'

'Oh, very well, sir.' He went up on the stable-loft, stripped, and lay down, and someone that saw him told the master. He came up.

'Jack, you anointed scoundrel, what do you mean?'

'To go to sleep, master. The mistress, God bless her, is after giving me my breakfast, dinner, and supper, and yourself told me that bed was the next thing. Do you blame me, sir?'

'Yes, you rascal, I do.'

'Hand me out one pound thirteen and fourpence, if you please, sir.'

'One divel and thirteen imps, you tinker! What for?'

'Oh, I see, you've forgot your bargain. Are you sorry for it?'

'Oh, ya – no, I mean. I'll give you the money after your nap.'

Next morning early, Jack asked how he'd be employed that day. 'You are to be holding the plough in that fallow, outside the paddock.' The master went over about nine o'clock to see what kind of a ploughman was Jack, and what did he see but the little boy driving the bastes, and the sock and coulter of the plough skimming along the sod, and Jack pulling ding-dong again' the horses.

'What are you doing, you contrary thief?' said the master.

'An' ain't I strivin' to hold this divel of a plough, as you told me; but that ounkrawn of a boy keeps whipping on the bastes in spite of all I say; will you speak to him?'

'No, but I'll speak to you. Didn't you know, you bosthoon, that when I said "holding the plough", I meant reddening the ground.'

'Faith, an' if you did, I wish you had said so. Do you blame me for what I have done?'

The master caught himself in time, but he was so stomached, he said nothing.

'Go on and redden the ground now, you knave, as other ploughmen do.'

'An' are you sorry for our agreement?'

'Oh, not at all, not at all!'

Jack ploughed away like a good workman all the rest of the day.

In a day or two the master bade him go and mind the cows in a field that had half of it under young corn. 'Be sure, particularly,' said he, 'to keep Browney from the wheat; while she's out of mischief there's no fear of the rest.'

About noon, he went to see how Jack was doing his duty, and what did he find but Jack asleep with his face to the sod, Browney grazing near a thorn tree, one end of a long rope round her horns, and the other end round the tree, and the rest of the beasts all trampling and eating the green wheat. Down came the switch on Jack.

'Jack, you vagabone, do you see what the cows are at?'

'And do you blame me, master?'

'To be sure, you lazy sluggard, I do!'

'Hand me out one pound thirteen and fourpence, master. You said if I only kept Browney out of mischief, the rest would do no harm. There she is as harmless as a lamb. Are you sorry for hiring me, master?'

'To be – that is, not at all. I'll give you your money when you go to dinner. Now, understand me; don't let a cow go out of the field nor into the wheat the rest of the day.'

'Never fear, master!' and neither did he. But the churl would rather than a great deal he had not hired him.

The next day three heifers were missing, and the master bade Jack go in search of them.

'Where will I look for them?' said Jack.

'Oh, every place likely and unlikely for them all to be in.'

The churl was getting very exact in his words. When he was coming into the bawn at dinner-time, what work did he find Jack at but pulling armfuls of the thatch off the roof, and peeping into the holes he was making?

'What are you doing there, you rascal?'

'Sure, I'm looking for the heifers, poor things!'

'What would bring them there?'

'I don't think anything could bring them in it; but I looked first into the likely places, that is, the cowhouses, and the pastures, and the fields next 'em, and now I'm looking in the unlikeliest place I can think of. Maybe it's not pleasing to you it is.'

'And to be sure it isn't pleasing to me, you aggravating goose-cap!'

'Please, sir, hand me one pound thirteen and fourpence before you sit down to your dinner. I'm afraid it's sorrow that's on you for hiring me at all.'

'May the div – oh no; I'm not sorry. Will you begin, if you please, and put in the thatch again, just as if you were doing it for your mother's cabin?'

'Oh, faith I will, sir, with a heart and a half;' and by the time the farmer came out from his dinner, Jack had the roof better than it was before, for he made the boy give him new straw.

Says the master when he came out, 'Go, Jack, and look for the heifers, and bring them home.'

'And where will I look for 'em?'

'Go and search for them as if they were your own.' The heifers were all in the paddock before sunset.

Next morning, says the master, 'Jack, the path across the bog to the pasture is very bad; the sheep does be sinking in it every step; go and make the sheep's feet a good path.' About an hour after he came to the edge of the bog, and what did he find Jack at but sharpening a carving knife, and the sheep standing or grazing round.

'Is this the way you are mending the path, Jack?' said he.

'Everything must have a beginning, master,' said Jack, 'and a thing well begun is half done. I am sharpening the knife, and I'll have the feet off every sheep in the flock while you'd be blessing yourself.'

'Feet off my sheep, you anointed rogue! And what would you be taking their feet off for?'

'An' sure to mend the path as you told me. Says you, "Jack, make a path with the foot of the sheep." '

'Oh, you fool, I meant make good the path for the sheep's feet.'

'It's a pity you didn't say so, master. Hand me out one pound thirteen and fourpence if you don't like me to finish my job.'

'Divel do you good with your one pound thirteen and fourpence!'

'It's better pray than curse, master. Maybe you're sorry for your bargain?'

'And to be sure I am – not yet, anyway.'

The next night the master was going to a wedding; and says he to Jack, before he set out, 'I'll leave at midnight, and I wish you to come and be with me home, for fear I might be overtaken with the drink. If you're there before, you may throw a sheep's eye at me, and I'll be sure to see that they'll give you something for yourself.'

About eleven o'clock, while the master was in great spirits, he felt something clammy hit him on the cheek. It fell beside his tumbler, and when he looked at it what was it but the eye of a sheep. Well, he couldn't imagine who threw it at him, or why it was thrown at him. After a little he got a blow on the other cheek, and still it was by another sheep's eye. Well, he was very vexed, but he thought better to say nothing. In two minutes more, when he was opening his mouth to take a sup, another sheep's eye was slapped into it. He sputtered it out, and cried, 'Man o' the house, isn't it a great shame for you to have anyone in the room that would do such a nasty thing?'

'Master,' says Jack, 'don't blame the honest man. Sure it's only myself that was throwin' them sheep's eyes at you, to remind you I was here, and that I wanted to drink the bride and bridegroom's health. You know yourself bade me.'

'I know that you are a great rascal; and where did you get the eyes?'

'An' where would I get em' but in the heads of your own sheep? Would you have me meddle with the bastes of any neighbour, who might put me in the Stone Jug for it?'

'Sorrow on me that ever I had the bad luck to meet with you.'

'You're all witness,' said Jack, 'that my master says he is sorry for having met with me. My time is up. Master, hand me over double wages, and come into the next room, and lay yourself out like a man that has some decency in him, till I take a strip of skin an inch broad from your shoulder to your hip.'

Everyone shouted out against that; but, says Jack, 'You didn't hinder him when he took the same strips from the backs of my two brothers, and sent them home in that state, and penniless, to their poor mother.'

When the company heard the rights of the business, they were only too eager to see the job done. The master bawled and roared, but there was no help at hand. He was stripped to his hips, and laid on the floor in the next room, and Jack had the carving knife in his hand ready to begin.

'Now you cruel old villain,' said he, giving the knife a couple of scrapes along the floor, 'I'll make you an offer. Give me, along with my double wages, two hundred guineas to support my poor brothers, and I'll do without the strap.'

'No!' said he. 'I'd let you skin me from head to foot first.'

'Here goes then,' said Jack with a grin, but the first little scar he gave, Churl roared out, 'Stop your hand; I'll give the money.'

'Now, neighbours,' said Jack, 'you mustn't think worse of me than I deserve. I wouldn't have the heart to take an eye out of a rat itself; I got half a dozen of them from the butcher, and only used three of them.'

So all came again into the other room, and Jack was made sit down, and everybody drank his health, and he drank everybody's health at one offer. And six stout fellows saw himself and the master home, and waited in the parlour while he went up and brought down the two hundred guineas, and double wages for Jack himself. When he got home, he brought the summer along with him to the poor mother and the disabled brothers; and he was no more Jack the Fool in the people's mouths, but 'Skin Churl Jack'.

Andrew Coffey

My grandfather, Andrew Coffey, was known to the whole barony as a quiet, decent man. And if the whole barony knew him, he knew the whole barony, every inch, hill and dale, bog and pasture, field and covert. Fancy his surprise one evening, when he found himself in a part of the demesne he couldn't recognise a bit. He and his good horse were always stumbling up against some tree or stumbling down into some bog-hole that by rights didn't ought to be there. On the top of all this the rain came pelting down wherever there was a clearing, and the cold March wind tore through the trees. Glad he was then when he saw a light in the distance, and drawing near found a cabin, though for the life of him he couldn't think how it came there. However, in he walked, after tying up his horse, and right welcome was the brushwood fire blazing on the hearth. And there stood a chair right and tight, that seemed to say, 'Come, sit down in me.' There wasn't a soul else in the room. Well, he did sit, and got a little warm and cheered after his drenching. But all the while he was wondering and wondering.

'Andrew Coffey! Andrew Coffey!'

Good heavens! Who was calling him, and not a soul in sight? Look around as he might, indoors and out, he could find no creature with two legs or four, for his horse was gone.

'Andrew Coffey! Andrew Coffey! Tell me a story.'

It was louder this time, and it was nearer. And then what a thing to ask for! It was bad enough not to be let sit by the fire and dry oneself, without being bothered for a story.

'Andrew Coffey! Andrew Coffey! Tell me a story, or
it'll be the worse for you.'

My poor grandfather was so dumbfounded that he could only
stand and stare.

'Andrew Coffey! Andrew Coffey! I told you
it'd be the worse for you.'

And with that, out there bounced, from a cupboard that Andrew
Coffey had never noticed before, *a man*. And the man was in a
towering rage. But it wasn't that. And he carried as fine a
blackthorn as you'd wish to crack a man's head with. But it wasn't
that either. But when my grandfather clapped eyes on him, he
knew him for Patrick Rooney, and all the world knew *he'd* gone
overboard, fishing one night long years before.

Andrew Coffey would neither stop nor stay, but he took to his
heels and was out of the house as hard as he could. He ran and he
ran taking little thought of what was before till at last he ran up
against a big tree. And then he sat down to rest.

He hadn't sat for a moment when he heard voices.

'It's heavy he is, the vagabond.' 'Steady now, we'll rest when we
get under the big tree yonder.' Now that happened to be the tree
under which Andrew Coffey was sitting. At least he thought so,
for seeing a branch handy he swung himself up by it and was soon
snugly hidden away. Better see than be seen, thought he.

The rain had stopped and the wind fallen. The night was
blacker than ever, but Andrew Coffey could see four men, and
they were carrying between them a long box. Under the tree they
came, set the box down, opened it, and who should they bring out
but – Patrick Rooney. Never a word did he say, and he looked as
pale as old snow.

Well, one gathered brushwood, and another took out tinder
and flint, and soon they had a big fire roaring, and my grandfather
could see Patrick plainly enough. If he had kept still before, he
kept stiller now. Soon they had four poles up and a pole across,
right over the fire, for all the world like a spit, and on to the pole
they slung Patrick Rooney.

'He'll do well enough,' said one; 'but who's to mind him whilst we're away, who'll turn the fire, who'll see that he doesn't burn?'

With that Patrick opened his lips, 'Andrew Coffey,' said he.

'Andrew Coffey! Andrew Coffey! Andrew Coffey! Andrew Coffey!'

'I'm much obliged to you, gentlemen,' said Andrew Coffey, 'but indeed I know nothing about the business.'

'You'd better come down, Andrew Coffey,' said Patrick.

It was the second time he spoke, and Andrew Coffey decided he would come down. The four men went off and he was left all alone with Patrick.

Then he sat and he kept the fire even, and he kept the spit turning, and all the while Patrick looked at him.

Poor Andrew Coffey couldn't make it all out at all, at all, and he stared at Patrick and at the fire, and he thought of the little house in the wood, till he felt quite dazed.

'Ah, but it's burning me ye are!' says Patrick, very short and sharp.

'I'm sure I beg your pardon,' said my grandfather, 'but might I ask you a question?'

'If you want a crooked answer,' said Patrick. 'Turn away or it'll be the worse for you.'

But my grandfather couldn't get it out of his head; hadn't everybody, far and near, said Patrick had fallen overboard. There was enough to think about, and my grandfather did think.

'Andrew Coffey! Andrew Coffey! It's burning me ye are.'

Sorry enough my grandfather was, and he vowed he wouldn't do so again.

'You'd better not,' said Patrick, and he gave him a cock of his eye, and a grin of his teeth, that just sent a shiver down Andrew Coffey's back. Well it was odd, that here he should be in a thick wood he had never set eyes upon, turning Patrick Rooney upon a spit. You can't wonder at my grandfather thinking and thinking and not minding the fire.

'Andrew Coffey, Andrew Coffey, it's the death of you I'll be.'

And with that what did my grandfather see, but Patrick unslinging himself from the spit and his eyes glared and his teeth glistened.

It was neither stop nor stay my grandfather made, but out he ran into the night of the wood. It seemed to him there wasn't a stone but was for his stumbling, not a branch but beat his face, not a bramble but tore his skin. And wherever it was clear the rain pelted down and the cold March wind howled along.

Glad he was to see a light, and a minute after he was kneeling, dazed, drenched, and bedraggled by the hearth side. The brushwood flamed, and the brushwood crackled, and soon my grandfather began to feel a little warm and dry and easy in his mind.

'Andrew Coffey! Andrew Coffey!'

It's hard for a man to jump when he has been through all my grandfather had, but jump he did. And when he looked around, where should he find himself but in the very cabin he had first met Patrick in.

'Andrew Coffey, Andrew Coffey, tell me a story.'

'Is it a story you want?' said my grandfather as bold as may be, for he was just tired of being frightened. 'Well if you can tell me the rights of this one, I'll be thankful.'

And he told the tale of what had befallen him from first to last that night. The tale was long, and maybe Andrew Coffey was weary. It's asleep he must have fallen, for when he awoke he lay on the hillside under the open heavens, and his horse grazed at his side.

The Lad with the Goatskin

Long ago, a poor widow woman lived down near the iron forge, by Enniscorth, and she was so poor she had no clothes to put on her son; so she used to fix him in the ash-hole, near the fire, and pile the warm ashes about him; and according as he grew up, she sunk the pit deeper. At last, by hook or by crook, she got a goatskin, and fastened it round his waist, and he felt quite grand, and took a walk down the street. So says she to him next morning, 'Tom, you thief, you never done any good yet, and you six foot high, and past nineteen – take that rope and bring me a faggot from the wood.'

'Never say't twice, mother,' says Tom. 'Here goes.'

When he had it gathered and tied, what should come up but a big giant, nine foot high, and made a lick of a club at him. Well become Tom, he jumped a-one side, and picked up a ram-pike; and the first crack he gave the big fellow, he made him kiss the clod.

'If you have e'er a prayer,' says Tom, 'now's the time to say it, before I make fragments of you.'

'I have no prayers,' says the giant, 'but if you spare my life I'll give you that club; and as long as you keep from sin, you'll win every battle you ever fight with it.'

Tom made no bones about letting him off; and as soon as he got the club in his hands, he sat down on the bresna, and gave it a tap with the kippeen, and says, 'Faggot, I had great trouble gathering you, and run the risk of my life for you, the least you can do is to carry me home.' And sure enough, the wind o' the word was all it wanted. It went off through the wood, groaning and crackling, till it came to the widow's door.

Well, when the sticks were all burned, Tom was sent off again to pick more; and this time he had to fight with a giant that had two heads on him. Tom had a little more trouble with him – that's all; and the prayers he said, was to give Tom a fife, that nobody could help dancing when he was playing it. Begonies, he made the big faggot dance home, with himself sitting on it. The next giant was a beautiful boy with three heads on him. He had neither prayers nor catechism no more nor the others; and so he gave Tom a bottle of green ointment, that wouldn't let you be burned, nor scalded, nor wounded. 'And now,' says he, 'there's no more of us. You may come and gather sticks here till little Lunacy Day in Harvest, without giant or fairy-man to disturb you.'

Well, now, Tom was prouder nor ten paycocks, and used to take a walk down street in the heel of the evening; but some o' the little boys had no more manners than if they were Dublin jackeens, and put out their tongues at Tom's club and Tom's goatskin. He didn't like that at all, and it would be mean to give one of them a clout. At last, what should come through the town but a kind of a bellman, only it's a big bugle he had, and a huntsman's cap on his head, and a kind of a painted shirt. So this – he wasn't a bellman, and I don't know what to call him – bugleman, maybe, proclaimed that the king of Dublin's daughter was so melancholy that she didn't give a laugh for seven years, and that her father would grant her in marriage to whoever could make her laugh three times.

'That's the very thing for me to try,' says Tom; and so, without burning any more daylight, he kissed his mother, curled his club at the little boys, and off he set along the yalla highroad to the town of Dublin.

At last Tom came to one of the city gates, and the guards laughed and cursed at him instead of letting him in. Tom stood it all for a little time, but at last one of them – out of fun, as he said – drove his bayonet half an inch or so into his side. Tom done nothing but take the fellow by the scruff o' the neck and the waistband of his corduroys, and fling him into the canal. Some run to pull the fellow out, and others to let manners into the vulgarian with their swords and daggers; but a tap from his club sent them headlong into the moat or down on the stones, and they were soon begging him to stay his hands.

So at last one of them was glad enough to show Tom the way to the palace-yard; and there was the king, and the queen, and the princess, in a gallery, looking at all sorts of wrestling, and sword-playing, and long-dances, and mumming, all to please the princess; but not a smile came over her handsome face.

Well, they all stopped when they seen the young giant, with his boy's face, and long black hair, and his short curly beard – for his poor mother couldn't afford to buy razors – and his great strong arms, and bare legs, and no covering but the goatskin that reached from his waist to his knees. But an envious wizened bit of a fellow, with a red head, that wished to be married to the princess, and didn't like how she opened her eyes at Tom, came forward, and asked his business very snappishly.

'My business,' says Tom, says he, 'is to make the beautiful princess, God bless her, laugh three times.'

'Do you see all them merry fellows and skilful swordsmen,' says the other, 'that could eat you up with a grain of salt, and not a mother's soul of 'em ever got a laugh from her these seven years?'

So the fellows gathered round Tom, and the bad man aggravated him till he told them he didn't care a pinch o' snuff for the whole bilin' of 'em; let 'em come on, six at a time, and try what they could do.

The king, who was too far off to hear what they were saying, asked what did the stranger want.

'He wants,' says the red-headed fellow, 'to make hares of your best men.'

'Oh!' says the king. 'If that's the way, let one of 'em turn out and try his mettle.'

So one stood forward, with sword and pot-lid, and made a cut at Tom. He struck the fellow's elbow with the club, and up over their heads flew the sword, and down went the owner of it on the gravel from a thump he got on the helmet. Another took his place, and another, and another, and then half a dozen at once, and Tom sent swords, helmets, shields, and bodies, rolling over and over, and themselves bawling out that they were kilt, and disabled, and damaged, and rubbing their poor elbows and hips, and limping away. Tom contrived not to kill anyone; and the princess was so amused, that she let a great sweet laugh out of her that was heard over all the yard.

'King of Dublin,' says Tom, 'I've quarter your daughter.'

And the king didn't know whether he was glad or sorry, and all the blood in the princess's heart run into her cheeks.

So there was no more fighting that day, and Tom was invited to dine with the royal family. Next day, Redhead told Tom of a wolf, the size of a yearling heifer, that used to be serenading about the walls, and eating people and cattle; and said what a pleasure it would give the king to have it killed.

'With all my heart,' says Tom. 'Send a jackeen to show me where he lives, and we'll see how he behaves to a stranger.'

The princess was not well pleased, for Tom looked a different person with fine clothes and a nice green birredh over his long curly hair; and besides, he'd got one laugh out of her. However, the king gave his consent; and in an hour and a half the horrible wolf was walking into the palace-yard, and Tom a step or two behind, with his club on his shoulder, just as a shepherd would be walking after a pet lamb.

The king and queen and princess were safe up in their gallery, but the officers and people of the court that wor padrowling about the great bawn, when they saw the big baste coming in, gave themselves up, and began to make for doors and gates; and the wolf licked his chops, as if he was saying, 'Wouldn't I enjoy a breakfast off a couple of yez!'

The king shouted out, 'O Tom with the Goatskin, take away that terrible wolf, and you must have all my daughter.'

But Tom didn't mind him a bit. He pulled out his flute and began to play like vengeance; and dickens a man or boy in the yard but began shovelling away heel and toe, and the wolf himself was obliged to get on his hind legs and dance 'Tatther Jack Walsh,' along with the rest. A good deal of the people got inside, and shut the doors, the way the hairy fellow wouldn't pin them; but Tom kept playing, and the outsiders kept dancing and shouting, and the wolf kept dancing and roaring with the pain his legs were giving him; and all the time he had his eyes on Redhead, who was shut out along with the rest. Wherever Redhead went, the wolf followed, and kept one eye on him and the other on Tom, to see if he would give him leave to eat him. But Tom shook his head, and never stopped the tune, and Redhead never stopped dancing and bawling, and the wolf dancing and roaring, one leg up and the other down, and he ready to drop out of his standing from fair tiresomeness.

When the princess seen that there was no fear of anyone being kilt, she was so divarted by the stew that Redhead was in, that she gave another great laugh; and well become Tom, out he cried, 'King of Dublin, I have two halves of your daughter.'

'Oh, halves or alls,' says the king, 'put away that divel of a wolf, and we'll see about it.'

So Tom put his flute in his pocket, and says he to the baste that was sittin' on his currabingo ready to faint, 'Walk off to your mountain, my fine fellow, and live like a respectable baste; and if ever I find you come within seven miles of any town, I'll – '

He said no more, but spit in his fist, and gave a flourish of his club. It was all the poor divel of a wolf wanted: he put his tail between his legs, and took to his pumps without looking at man or mortal, and neither sun, moon, or stars ever saw him in sight of Dublin again.

At dinner everyone laughed but the foxy fellow; and sure enough he was laying out how he'd settle poor Tom next day.

'Well, to be sure!' says he. 'King of Dublin, you are in luck. There's the Danes moidhering us to no end. Deuce run to Lusk wid 'em! And if anyone can save us from 'em, it is this gentleman with the goatskin. There is a flail hangin' on the collar-beam in hell, and neither Dane nor devil can stand before it.'

'So,' says Tom to the king, 'will you let me have the other half of the princess if I bring you the flail?'

'No, no,' says the princess. 'I'd rather never be your wife than see you in that danger.'

But Redhead whispered and nudged Tom about how shabby it would look to reneague the adventure. So he asked which way he was to go, and Redhead directed him.

Well, he travelled and travelled, till he came in sight of the walls of hell; and, bedad, before he knocked at the gates, he rubbed himself over with the greenish ointment. When he knocked, a hundred little imps popped their heads out through the bars, and axed him what he wanted.

'I want to speak to the big divel of all,' says Tom. 'Open the gate.'

It wasn't long till the gate was thrune open, and the Ould Boy received Tom with bows and scrapes, and axed his business.

'My business isn't much,' says Tom. 'I only came for the loan of that flail that I see hanging on the collar-beam, for the king ofDublin to give a thrashing to the Danes.'

'Well,' says the other, 'the Danes is much better customers to me; but since you walked so far I won't refuse. Hand that flail,' says he to a young imp; and he winked the far-off eye at the same time. So, while some were barring the gates, the young devil climbed up, and took down the flail that had the handstaff and booltheen both made out of red-hot iron. The little vagabond was grinning to think how it would burn the hands o' Tom, but the dickens a burn it made on him, no more nor if it was a good oak sapling.

'Thankee,' says Tom. 'Now would you open the gate for a body, and I'll give you no more trouble.'

'Oh, tramp!' says Ould Nick. 'Is that the way? It is easier getting inside them gates than getting out again. Take that tool from him, and give him a dose of the oil of stirrup.'

So one fellow put out his claws to seize on the flail, but Tom gave him such a welt of it on the side of the head that he broke off one of his horns, and made him roar like a devil as he was. Well, they rushed at Tom, but he gave them, little and big, such a thrashing as they didn't forget for a while. At last says the ould thief of all, rubbing his elbow, 'Let the fool out; and woe to whoever lets him in again, great or small.'

So out marched Tom, and away with him, without minding the shouting and cursing they kept up at him from the tops of the walls; and when he got home to the big bawn of the palace, there never was such running and racing as to see himself and the flail. When he had his story told, he laid down the flail on the stone steps, and bid no one for their lives to touch it. If the king, and queen, and princess, made much of him before, they made ten times more of him now; but Redhead, the mean scruffhound, stole over, and thought to catch hold of the flail to make an end of him. His fingers hardly touched it, when he let a roar out of him as if heaven and earth were coming together, and kept flinging his arms about and dancing, that it was pitiful to look at him. Tom run at him as soon as he could rise, caught his hands in his own two, and rubbed them this way and that, and the burning pain left them before you could reckon one. Well the poor fellow, between the pain that was only just gone, and the comfort he was in, had the comicalest face that you ever see, it was such a mixtherum-gatherum of laughing and crying. Everybody burst out a laughing – the princess could not stop no more than the rest; and then says Tom, 'Now, ma'am, if there were fifty halves of you, I hope you'll give me them all.'

Well, the princess looked at her father, and by my word, she came over to Tom, and put her two delicate hands into his two rough ones, and I wish it was myself was in his shoes that day!

Tom would not bring the flail into the palace. You may be sure no other body went near it; and when the early risers were passing next morning, they found two long clefts in the stone, where it was after burning itself an opening downwards, nobody could tell how far. But a messenger came in at noon, and said that the Danes were so frightened when they heard of the flail coming into Dublin, that they got into their ships, and sailed away.

Well, I suppose, before they were married, Tom got some man, like Pat Mara of Tomenine, to learn him the 'principles of politeness', fluxions, gunnery and fortification, decimal fractions, practice, and the rule of three direct, the way he'd be able to keep up a conversation with the royal family. Whether he ever lost his time learning them sciences, I'm not sure, but it's as sure as fate that his mother never more saw any want till the end of her days.

The Fate of the Children of Lir

It happened that the five kings of Ireland met to determine who should have the head kingship over them, and King Lir of the Hill of the White Field expected surely he would be elected. When the nobles went into council together they chose for head king, Dearg, son of Daghda, because his father had been so great a druid and he was the eldest of his father's sons. But Lir left the assembly of the kings and went home to the Hill of the White Field. The other kings would have followed after Lir to give him wounds of spear and wounds of sword for not yielding obedience to the man to whom they had given the overlordship. But Dearg the king would not hear of it and said, 'Rather let us bind him to us by the bonds of kinship, so that peace may dwell in the land. Send over to him for wife the choice of the three maidens of the fairest form and best repute in Erin, the three daughters of Oilell of Aran, my own three bosom-nurslings.'

So the messengers brought word to Lir that Dearg the king would give him a foster-child of his foster-children. Lir thought well of it, and set out next day with fifty chariots from the Hill of the White Field. And he came to the Lake of the Red Eye near Killaloe. And when Lir saw the three daughters of Oilell, Dearg the king said to him, 'Take thy choice of the maidens, Lir.' 'I know not,' said Lir, 'which is the choicest of them all; but the eldest of them is the noblest, it is she I had best take.' 'If so,' said Dearg the king, 'Ove is the eldest, and she shall be given to thee, if thou willest.' So Lir and Ove were married and went back to the Hill of the White Field.

And after this there came to them twins, a son and a daughter, and they gave them for names Fingula and Aod. And two more sons came to them, Fiachra and Conn. When they came Ove died, and Lir mourned bitterly for her, and but for his great love for his children he would have died of his grief. And Dearg the king grieved for Lir and sent to him and said, 'We grieve for Ove for thy sake; but, that our friendship may not be rent asunder, I will give unto thee her sister, Oifa, for a wife.' So Lir agreed, and they were united, and he took her with him to his own house. And at first Oifa felt affection and honour for the children of Lir and her sister, and indeed everyone who saw the four children could not help giving them the love of his soul. Lir doted upon the children, and they always slept in beds in front of their father, who used to rise at early dawn every morning and lie down among his children. But thereupon the dart of jealousy passed into Oifa on account of this and she came to regard the children with hatred and enmity. One day her chariot was yoked for her and she took with her the four children of Lir in it. Fingula was not willing to go with her on the journey, for she had dreamed a dream in the night warning her against Oifa: but she was not to avoid her fate. And when the chariot came to the Lake of the Oaks, Oifa said to the people, 'Kill the four children of Lir and I will give you your own reward of every kind in the world.' But they refused and told her it was an evil thought she had. Then she would have raised a sword herself to kill and destroy the children, but her own womanhood and her weakness prevented her; so she drove the children of Lir into the lake to bathe, and they did as Oifa told them. As soon as they were upon the lake she struck them with a druid's wand of spells and wizardry and put them into the forms of four beautiful, perfectly white swans, and she sang this song over them:

'Out with you upon the wild waves, children of the king!
Henceforth your cries shall be with the flocks of birds.'

And Fingula answered:

'Thou witch! We know thee by thy right name!
Thou mayest drive us from wave to wave,
But sometimes we shall rest on the headlands;
We shall receive relief, but thou punishment.
Though our bodies may be upon the lake,
Our minds at least shall fly homewards.'

And again she spoke, 'Assign an end for the ruin and woe which thou hast brought upon us.'

Oifa laughed and said, 'Never shall ye be free until the woman from the south be united to the man from the north, until Lairgnen of Connaught wed Deoch of Munster; nor shall any have power to bring you out of these forms. Nine hundred years shall you wander over the lakes and streams of Erin. This only I will grant unto you: that you retain your own speech, and there shall be no music in the world equal to yours, the plaintive music you shall sing.' This she said because repentance seized her for the evil she had done.

And then she spake this lay:

'Away from me, ye children of Lir,
Henceforth the sport of the wild winds
Until Lairgnen and Deoch come together,
Until ye are on the north-west of Red Erin.

'A sword of treachery is through the heart of Lir,
Of Lir the mighty champion,
Yet though I have driven a sword.
My victory cuts me to the heart.'

The children of Lir

Then she turned her steeds and went on to the hall of Dearg the king. The nobles of the court asked her where were the children of Lir, and Oifa said, 'Lir will not trust them to Dearg the king.' But Dearg thought in his own mind that the woman had played some treachery upon them, and he accordingly sent messengers to the Hill of the White Field.

Lir asked the messengers, 'Wherefore are ye come?'

'To fetch thy children, Lir,' said they.

'Have they not reached you with Oifa?' said Lir.

'They have not,' said the messengers; 'and Oifa said it was you would not let the children go with her.'

Then was Lir melancholy and sad at heart, hearing these things, for he knew that Oifa had done wrong upon his children, and he set out towards the Lake of the Red Eye. And when the children of Lir saw him coming Fingula sang the lay:

> 'Welcome the cavalcade of steeds
> Approaching the Lake of the Red Eye,
> A company dread and magical
> Surely seek after us.
>
> 'Let us move to the shore, O Aod,
> Fiachra and comely Conn,
> No host under heaven can those horsemen be
> But King Lir with his mighty household.'

Now as she said this King Lir had come to the shores of the lake and heard the swans speaking with human voices. And he spake to the swans and asked them who they were. Fingula answered and said, 'We are thy own children, ruined by thy wife, sister of our own mother, through her ill mind and her jealousy.' 'For how long is the spell to be upon you?' said Lir. 'None can relieve us till the woman from the south and the man from the north come together, till Lairgnen of Connaught wed Deoch of Munster.'

Then Lir and his people raised their shouts of grief, crying, and lamentation, and they stayed by the shore of the lake listening to the wild music of the swans until the swans flew away, and King

Lir went on to the hall of Dearg the king. He told Dearg the king what Oifa had done to his children. And Dearg put his power upon Oifa and bade her say what shape on earth she would think the worst of all. She said it would be in the form of an air-demon. 'It is into that form I shall put you,' said Dearg the king, and he struck her with a druid's wand of spells and wizardry and put her into the form of an air-demon. And she flew away at once, and she is still an air-demon, and shall be so for ever.

But the children of Lir continued to delight the Milesian clans with the very sweet fairy music of their songs, so that no delight was ever heard in Erin to compare with their music until the time came appointed for the leaving the Lake of the Red Eye.

Then Fingula sang this parting lay:

> 'Farewell to thee, Dearg the king,
> Master of all druid's lore!
> Farewell to thee, our father dear,
> Lir of the Hill of the White Field!
>
> 'We go to pass the appointed time
> Away and apart from the haunts of men
> In the current of the Moyle,
> Our garb shall be bitter and briny,
>
> 'Until Deoch come to Lairgnen.
> So come, ye brothers of once ruddy cheeks;
> Let us depart from this Lake of the Red Eye,
> Let us separate in sorrow from the tribe that
> has loved us.'

And after they took to flight, flying highly, lightly, aerially till they reached the Moyle, between Erin and Albain.

The men of Erin were grieved at their leaving, and it was proclaimed throughout Erin that henceforth no swan should be killed. Then they stayed all solitary, all alone, filled with cold and grief and regret, until a thick tempest came upon them and Fingula said, 'Brothers, let us appoint a place to meet again if the power of the winds separate us.' And they said, 'Let us appoint to meet, O sister, at the Rock of the Seals.' Then the waves rose up and the thunder roared, the lightnings flashed, the sweeping tempest passed over the sea, so that the children of Lir were scattered from each other over the great sea. There came, how-ever, a placid calm after the great tempest and Fingula found herself alone, and she said this lay:

> 'Woe upon me that I am alive!
> My wings are frozen to my sides.
> O beloved three, O beloved three,
> Who hid under the shelter of my feathers,
> Until the dead come back to the living
> I and the three shall never meet again!'

And she flew to the Lake of the Seals and soon saw Conn coming towards her with heavy step and drenched feathers, and Fiachra also, cold and wet and faint, and no word could they tell, so cold and faint were they: but she nestled them under her wings and said, 'If Aod could come to us now our happiness would be complete.' But soon they saw Aod coming towards them with dry head and preened feathers. Fingula put him under the feathers of her breast, and Fiachra under her right wing, and Conn under her left, and they made this lay:

> 'Bad was our stepmother with us,
> She played her magic on us,
> Sending us north on the sea
> In the shapes of magical swans.

> 'Our bath upon the shore's ridge
> Is the foam of the brine-crested tide,
> Our share of the ale feast
> Is the brine of the blue-crested sea.'

One day they saw a splendid cavalcade of pure white steeds coming towards them, and when they came near they were the two sons of Dearg the king who had been seeking for them to give them news of Dearg the king and Lir their father. 'They are well,' they said, 'and live together happy in all except that ye are not with them, and for not knowing where ye have gone since the day ye left the Lake of the Red Eye.' 'Happy are not we,' said Fingula, and she sang this song:

> 'Happy this night the household of Lir,
> Abundant their meat and their wine.
> But the children of Lir – what is their lot?
> For bedclothes we have our feathers,
> And as for our food and our wine –
> The white sand and the bitter brine,
> Fiachra's bed and Conn's place
> Under the cover of my wings on the Moyle,
> Aod has the shelter of my breast,
> And so side by side we rest.'

So the sons of Dearg the king came to the hall of Lir and told the king the condition of his children.

Then the time came for the children of Lir to fulfil their lot, and they flew in the current of the Moyle to the Bay of Erris, and remained there till the time of their fate, and then they flew to the Hill of the White Field and found all desolate and empty, with nothing but unroofed green raths and forests of nettles – no house, no fire, no dwelling-place. The four came close together, and they raised three shouts of lamentation aloud, and Fingula sang this lay:

> 'Uchone! It is bitterness to my heart
> To see my father's place forlorn –
> No hounds, no packs of dogs,
> No women, and no valiant kings.
>
> 'No drinking-horns, no cups of wood,
> No drinking in its lightsome halls.
> Uchone! I see the state of this house
> That its lord our father lives no more.
>
> 'Much have we suffered in our wandering years,
> By winds buffeted, by cold frozen;
> Now has come the greatest of our pain –
> There lives no man who knoweth us in
>   the house where we were born.'

So the children of Lir flew away to the Glory Isle of Brandan the saint, and they settled upon the Lake of the Birds until the holy Patrick came to Erin and the holy Mac Howg came to Glory Isle.

And the first night he came to the island the children of Lir heard the voice of his bell ringing for matins, so that they started and leaped about in terror at hearing it; and her brothers left Fingula alone. 'What is it, beloved brothers?' said she. 'We know not what faint, fearful voice it is we have heard.' Then Fingula recited this lay:

'Listen to the cleric's bell,
Poise your wings and raise
Thanks to God for his coming,
Be grateful that you hear him,

'He shall free you from pain,
And bring you from the rocks and stones.
Ye comely children of Lir
Listen to the bell of the cleric.'

And Mac Howg came down to the brink of the shore and said to them, 'Are ye the children of Lir?' 'We are indeed,' said they. 'Thanks be to God!' said the saint. 'It is for your sakes I have come to this Isle beyond every other island in Erin. Come ye to land now and put your trust in me.' So they came to land, and he made for them chains of bright white silver, and put a chain between Aod and Fingula and a chain between Conn and Fiachra.

It happened at this time that Lairgnen was prince of Connaught and he was to wed Deoch the daughter of the king of Munster. She had heard the account of the birds and she became filled with love and affection for them, and she said she would not wed till she had the wondrous birds of Glory Isle. Lairgnen sent for them to the saint Mac Howg. But the saint would not give them, and both Lairgnen and Deoch went to Glory Isle. And Lairgnen went to seize the birds from the altar, but as soon as he had laid hands on them their feathery coats fell off, and the three sons of Lir became three withered bony old men, and Fingula, a lean withered old woman without blood or flesh. Lairgnen started at this and left the place hastily, but Fingula chanted this lay:

'Come and baptise us, O cleric,
Clear away our stains!
This day I see our grave –
Fiachra and Conn on each side,
And in my lap, between my two arms,
Place Aod, my beauteous brother.'

After this lay, the children of Lir were baptised. And they died, and were buried as Fingula had said, Fiachra and Conn on either side, and Aod before her face. A cairn was raised for them, and on it their names were written in runes. And that is the fate of the children of Lir.

Jack the Cunning Thief

There was a poor farmer who had three sons, and on the same day the three boys went to seek their fortune. The eldest two were sensible, industrious young men; the youngest never did much at home that was any use. He loved to be setting snares for rabbits and tracking hares in the snow, and inventing all sorts of funny tricks to annoy people at first and then set them laughing.

The three parted at crossroads, and Jack took the lonesomest. The day turned out rainy, and he was wet and weary, you may depend, at nightfall, when he came to a lonesome house a little off the road.

'What do you want?' said a blear-eyed old woman, that was sitting at the fire.

'My supper and a bed to be sure,' said he.

'You can't get it,' said she.

'What's to hinder me?' said he.

'The owners of the house is,' said she, 'six honest men that does be out mostly till three or four o'clock in the morning, and if they find you here they'll skin you alive at the very least.'

'Well, I think,' said Jack, 'that their very most couldn't be much worse. Come, give me something out of the cupboard, for here I'll stay. Skinning is not much worse than catching your death of cold in a ditch or under a tree such a night as this.'

Begonins she got afraid, and gave him a good supper; and when he was going to bed he said if she let any of the six honest men disturb him when they came home she'd sup sorrow for it. When he awoke in the morning, there were six ugly-looking spalpeens standing round his bed. He leaned on his elbow, and looked at them with great contempt.

'Who are you,' said the chief, 'and what's your business?'

'My name,' says he, 'is Master Thief, and my business just now is to find apprentices and workmen. If I find you any good, maybe I'll give you a few lessons.'

Bedad they were a little cowed, and says the head man, 'Well, get up, and after breakfast, we'll see who is to be the master, and who the journeyman.'

They were just done breakfast, when what should they see but a farmer driving a fine large goat to market. 'Will any of you,' says Jack, 'undertake to steal that goat from the owner before he gets out of the wood, and that without the smallest violence?'

'I couldn't do it,' says one; and 'I couldn't do it,' says another.

'I'm your master,' says Jack, 'and I'll do it.'

He slipped out, went through the trees to where there was a bend in the road, and laid down his right brogue in the very middle of it. Then he ran on to another bend, and laid down his left brogue and went and hid himself.

When the farmer sees the first brogue, he says to himself, 'That would be worth something if it had the fellow, but it is worth nothing by itself.'

He goes on till he comes to the second brogue.

'What a fool I was,' says he, 'not to pick up the other! I'll go back for it.'

So he tied the goat to a sapling in the hedge, and returned for the brogue. But Jack, who was behind a tree had it already on his foot, and when the man was beyond the bend he picked up the other and loosened the goat, and led him off through the wood.

Ochone! The poor man couldn't find the first brogue, and when he came back he couldn't find the second, nor neither his goat.

'*Mile mollacht!*' says he. 'What will I do after promising Johanna to buy her a shawl. I must only go and drive another beast to the market unknownst. I'd never hear the last of it if Joan found out what a fool I made of myself.'

The thieves were in great admiration at Jack, and wanted him to tell them how he had done the farmer, but he wouldn't tell them.

By and by, they see the poor man driving a fine fat wether the same way.

'Who'll steal that wether,' says Jack, 'before it's out of the wood, and no roughness used?'

'I couldn't,' says one; and 'I couldn't,' says another.

'I'll try,' says Jack. 'Give me a good rope.'

The poor farmer was jogging along and thinking of his misfortune, when he sees a man hanging from the bough of a tree. 'Lord save us!' says he. 'The corpse wasn't there an hour ago.' He went on about half a quarter of a mile, and there was another corpse again hanging over the road. 'God between us and harm,' said he, 'am I in my right senses?' There was another turn about the same distance, and just beyond it the third corpse was hanging. 'Oh, murdher!' said he. 'I'm beside myself. What would bring three hung men so near one another? I must be mad. I'll go back and see if the others are there still.'

He tied the wether to a sapling, and back he went. But when he was round the bend, down came the corpse, and loosened the wether, and drove it home through the wood to the robbers' house. You all may think how the poor farmer felt when he could find no one dead or alive going or coming, nor his wether, nor the rope that fastened him. 'Oh, misfortunate day!' cried he. 'What'll Joan say to me now? My morning gone, and the goat and wether lost! I must sell something to make the price of the shawl. Well, the fat bullock is in the nearest field. She won't see me taking it.'

Well, if the robbers were not surprised when Jack came into the bawn with the wether! 'If you do another trick like this,' said the captain, 'I'll resign the command to you.'

They soon saw the farmer going by again, driving a fat bullock this time.

'Who'll bring that fat bullock here,' says Jack, 'and use no violence?'

'I couldn't,' says one; and 'I couldn't,' says another.

'I'll try,' says Jack, and away he went into the wood.

The farmer was about the spot where he saw the first brogue, when he heard the bleating of a goat off at his right in the wood.

He cocked his ears, and the next thing he heard was the maaing of a sheep.

'Blood alive!' says he. 'Maybe these are my own that I lost.' There was more bleating and more maaing. 'There they are as sure as a gun,' says he, and he tied his bullock to a sapling that grew in the hedge, and away he went into the wood. When he got near the place where the cries came from, he heard them a little before him, and on he followed them. At last, when he was about half a mile from the spot where he tied the beast, the cries stopped altogether. After searching and searching till he was tired, he returned for his bullock; but there wasn't the ghost of a bullock there, nor anywhere else that he searched.

This time, when the thieves saw Jack and his prize coming into the bawn, they couldn't help shouting out, 'Jack must be our chief.' So there was nothing but feasting and drinking hand to fist the rest of the day. Before they went to bed, they showed Jack the cave where their money was hid, and all their disguises in another cave, and swore obedience to him.

One morning, when they were at breakfast, about a week after, said they to Jack, 'Will you mind the house for us today while we are at the fair of Mochurry? We hadn't a spree for ever so long: you must get your turn whenever you like.'

'Never say't twice,' says Jack, and off they went.

After they were gone says Jack to the wicked housekeeper, 'Do these fellows ever make you a present?'

'Ah, catch them at it! Indeed, and they don't, purshuin to 'em.'

'Well, come along with me, and I'll make you a rich woman.'

He took her to the treasure cave; and while she was in raptures, gazing at the heaps of gold and silver, Jack filled his pockets as full as they could hold, put more into a little bag, and walked out, locking the door on the old hag, and leaving the key in the lock. He then put on a rich suit of clothes, took the goat, and the wether, and the bullock, and drove them before him to the farmer's house.

Joan and her husband were at the door; and when they saw the animals, they clapped their hands and laughed for joy.

'Do you know who owns them bastes, neighbours?'

'Maybe we don't! Sure they're ours.'

'I found them straying in the wood. Is that bag with ten guineas in it that's hung round the goat's neck yours?'

'Faith, it isn't.'

'Well, you may as well keep it for a godsend! I don't want it.'

'Heaven be in your road, good gentleman!'

Jack travelled on till he came to his father's house in the dusk of the evening. He went in. 'God save all here!'

'God save you kindly, sir!'

'Could I have a night's lodging here?'

'Oh, sir, our place isn't fit for the likes of a gentleman such as yon.'

'Oh, *musha*, don't you know your own son?'

Well, they opened their eyes, and it was only a strife to see who'd have him in their arms first.

'But, Jack asthore, where did you get the fine clothes?'

'Oh, you may as well ask me where I got all that money?' said he, emptying his pockets on the table.

Well, they got in a great fright, but when he told them his adventures, they were easier in mind, and all went to bed in great content.

'Father,' says Jack, next morning, 'go over to the landlord, and tell him I wish to be married to his daughter.'

'Faith, I'm afraid he'd only set the dogs at me. If he asks me how you made your money, what'll I say?'

'Tell him I am a master thief, and that there is no one equal to me in the three kingdoms; that I am worth a thousand pounds, and all taken from the biggest rogues unhanged. Speak to him when the young lady is by.'

'It's a droll message you're sending me on. I'm afraid it won't end well.'

The old man came back in two hours.

'Well, what news?'

'Droll news, enough. The lady didn't seem a bit unwilling. I suppose it's not the first time you spoke to her; and the squire laughed, and said you would have to steal the goose off o' the spit in his kitchen next Sunday, and he'd see about it.'

'O! That won't be hard, anyway.'

Next Sunday, after the people came from early Mass, the squire and all his people were in the kitchen, and the goose turning before the fire. The kitchen door opened, and a miserable old beggar-man with a big wallet on his back put in his head.

'Would the mistress have anything for me when dinner is over, your honour?'

'To be sure. We have no room here for you just now; sit in the porch for a while.'

'God bless your honour's family, and yourself!'

Soon someone that was sitting near the window cried out, 'Oh, sir, there's a big hare scampering like the divil round the bawn. Will we run out and pin him?'

'Pin a hare indeed! Much chance you'd have; sit where you are.'

That hare made his escape into the garden, but Jack that was in the beggar's clothes soon let another out of the bag.

'Oh, master, there he is still pegging round. He can't make his escape. Let us have a chase. The hall door is locked on the inside, and Mr Jack can't get in.'

'Stay quiet, I tell you.'

In a few minutes he shouted out again that the hare was there still, but it was the third that Jack was just after giving its liberty. Well, by the laws, they couldn't be kept in any longer. Out pegged every mother's son of them, and the squire after them.

'Will I turn the spit, your honour, while they're catching the *hareyeen*?' says the beggar.

'Do, and don't let anyone in for your life.'

'Faith, an' I won't, you may depend on it.'

The third hare got away after the others, and when they all came back from the hunt, there was neither beggar nor goose in the kitchen.

'Purshuin' to you, Jack,' says the landlord, 'you've come over me this time.'

Well, while they were thinking of making out another dinner, a messenger came from Jack's father to beg that the squire, and the mistress, and the young lady would step across the fields, and take share of what God sent. There was no dirty mean pride about the family, and they walked over, and got a dinner with roast turkey, and roast beef, and their own roast goose; and the squire had like to burst his waistcoat with laughing at the trick, and Jack's good clothes and good manners did not take away any liking the young lady had for him already.

While they were taking their punch at the old oak table in the nice clean little parlour with the sanded floor, says the squire, 'You can't be sure of my daughter, Jack, unless you steal away my six horses from under the six men that will be watching them tomorrow night in the stable.'

'I'll do more than that,' says Jack, 'for a pleasant look from the young lady;' and the young lady's cheeks turned as red as fire.

Monday night the six horses were in their stalls, and a man on every horse, and a good glass of whiskey under every man's waistcoat, and the door was left wide open for Jack. They were merry enough for a long time, and joked and sung, and were pitying the poor fellow. But the small hours crept on, and the whiskey lost its power, and they began to shiver and wish it was morning. A miserable old colliach, with half a dozen bags round her, and a beard half an inch long on her chin came to the door.

'Ah, then, tendher-hearted Christians,' says she, 'would you let me in, and allow me a wisp of straw in the corner; the life will be froze out of me, if you don't give me shelter.'

Well, they didn't see any harm in that, and she made herself as snug as she could, and they soon saw her pull out a big black bottle, and take a sup. She coughed and smacked her lips, and seemed a little more comfortable, and the men couldn't take their eyes off her.

'Gorsoon,' says she, 'I'd offer you a drop of this, only you might think it too free-making.'

'Oh, hang all impedent pride,' says one, 'we'll take it, and thankee.'

So she gave them the bottle, and they passed it round, and the last man had the manners to leave half a glass in the bottom for the old woman. They all thanked her, and said it was the best drop ever passed their tongue.

'In throth, agras,' said she, 'it's myself that's glad to show how I value your kindness in giving me shelter; I'm not without another *buideal*, and you may pass it round while myself finishes what the dasent man left me.'

Well, what they drank out of the other bottle only gave them a relish for more, and by the time the last man got to the bottom, the first man was dead asleep in the saddle, for the second bottle had a sleepy posset mixed with the whiskey. The beggar woman lifted each man down, and laid him in the manger, or under the manger, snug and sausty, drew a stocking over every horse's hoof, and led them away without any noise to one of Jack's father's outhouses. The first thing the squire saw next morning was Jack riding up the avenue, and five horses stepping after the one he rode.

'Confound you, Jack!' says he. 'And confound the numskulls that let you outwit them!'

He went out to the stable, and didn't the poor fellows look very lewd o' themselves, when they could be woke up in earnest!

'After all,' says the squire, when they were sitting at breakfast, 'it was no great thing to outwit such ninnyhammers. I'll be riding out on the common from one to three today, and if you can outwit me of the beast I'll be riding, I'll say you deserve to be my son-in-law.'

'I'd do more than that,' says Jack, 'for the honour, if there was no love at all in the matter,' and the young lady held up her saucer before her face.

Well, the squire kept riding about and riding about till he was tired, and no sign of Jack. He was thinking of going home at last, when what should he see but one of his servants running from the house as if he was mad.

'Oh masther, masther,' says he, as far as he could be heard, 'fly home if you wish to see the poor mistress alive! I'm running for the surgeon. She fell down two flights of stairs, and her neck, or her hips, or both her arms are broke, and she's speechless, and it's a mercy if you find the breath in her. Fly as fast as the baste will carry you.'

'But hadn't you better take the horse? It's a mile and a half to the surgeon's.'

'Oh, anything you like, master. Oh, *Vuya*, *Vuya*! Misthless *alanna*, that I should ever see the day! And your purty body disfigured as it is!'

'Here, stop your noise, and be off like wildfire. 'Oh, my darling, my darling, isn't this a trial?'

He tore home like a fury, and wondered to see no stir outside, and when he flew into the hall, and from that to the parlour, his wife and daughter that were sewing at the table screeched out at the rush he made, and the wild look that was on his face.

'Oh, my darling!' said he, when he could speak. 'How's this? Are you hurt? Didn't you fall down the stairs? What happened at all? Tell me!'

'Why, nothing at all happened, thank God, since you rode out; where did you leave the horse?'

Well, no one could describe the state he was in for about a quarter of an hour, between joy for his wife and anger with Jack, and *sharoose* for being tricked. He saw the beast coming up the avenue, and a little gorsoon in the saddle with his feet in the stirrup leathers. The servant didn't make his appearance for a week; but what did he care with Jack's ten golden guineas in his pocket.

Jack didn't show his nose till next morning, and it was a queer reception he met.

'That was all foul play you gave,' says the squire. 'I'll never forgive you for the shock you gave me. But then I am so happy ever since, that I think I'll give you only one trial more. If you will take away the sheet from under my wife and myself tonight, the marriage may take place tomorrow.'

'We'll try,' says Jack, 'but if you keep my bride from me any longer, I'll steal her away if she was minded by fiery dragons.'

When the squire and his wife were in bed, and the moon shining in through the window, he saw a head rising over the sill to have a peep, and then bobbing down again.

'That's Jack,' says the squire; 'I'll astonish him a bit,' says the squire, pointing a gun at the lower pane.

'Oh Lord, my dear!' says the wife. 'Sure, you wouldn't shoot the brave fellow?'

'Indeed, an' I wouldn't for a kingdom; there's nothing but powder in it.'

Up went the head, bang went the gun, down dropped the body, and a great souse was heard on the gravel walk.

'Oh, Lord,' says the lady, 'poor Jack is killed or disabled for life.'

'I hope not,' says the squire, and down the stairs he ran. He never minded to shut the door, but opened the gate and ran into the garden. His wife heard his voice at the room door, before he could be under the window and back, as she thought.

'Wife, wife,' says he from the door, 'the sheet, the sheet! He is not killed, I hope, but he is bleeding like a pig. I must wipe it away as well as I can, and get someone to carry him in with me.' She pulled it off the bed, and threw it to him. Down he ran like lightning, and he had hardly time to be in the garden, when he was back, and this time he came back in his shirt, as he went out.

'High hanging to you, Jack,' says he, 'for an arrant rogue!'

'Arrant rogue?' says she. 'Isn't the poor fellow all cut and bruised?'

'I didn't much care if he was. What do you think was bobbing up and down at the window, and sossed down so heavy on the walk? A man's clothes stuffed with straw, and a couple of stones.'

'And what did you want with the sheet just now, to wipe his blood if he was only a man of straw?'

'Sheet, woman! I wanted no sheet.'

'Well, whether you wanted it or not, I threw it to you, and you standing outside o' the door.'

'Oh, Jack, Jack, you terrible tinker!' says the squire. 'There's no use in striving with you. We must do without the sheet for one night. We'll have the marriage tomorrow to get ourselves out of trouble.'

So married they were, and Jack turned out a real good husband. And the squire and his lady were never tired of praising their son-in-law, 'Jack the Cunning Thief'.

Paddy O'Kelly and the Weasel

A long time ago there was once a man of the name of Paddy O'Kelly, living near Tuam, in the county Galway. He rose up one morning early, and he did not know what time of day it was, for there was fine light coming from the moon. He wanted to go to the fair of Cauher-na-mart to sell a *sturk* of an ass that he had.

He had not gone more than three miles of the road when a great darkness came on, and a shower began falling. He saw a large house among trees about five hundred yards in from the road, and he said to himself that he would go to that house till the shower would be over. When he got to the house he found the door open before him, and in with him. He saw a large room to his left, and a fine fire in the grate. He sat down on a stool that was beside the wall, and began falling asleep, when he saw a big weasel coming to the fire with something yellow in his mouth, which it dropped on the hearth-stone, and then it went away. She soon came back again with the same thing in her mouth, and he saw that it was a guinea she had. She dropped it on the hearth-stone, and went away again. She was coming and going, until there was a great heap of guineas on the hearth. But at last, when she got her gone, Paddy rose up, thrust all the gold she had gathered into his pockets, and out with him.

He had not gone far till he heard the weasel coming after him, and she screeching as loud as a bagpipes. She went before Paddy and got on the road, and she was twisting herself back and forwards, and trying to get a hold of his throat. Paddy had a good oak stick, and he kept her from him, until two men came up who were going to the same fair, and one of them had a good dog, and it routed the weasel into a hole in the wall.

Paddy went to the fair, and instead of coming home with the money he got for his old ass, as he thought would be the way with him in the morning, he went and bought a horse with some of the money he took from the weasel, and he came home riding. When he came to the place where the dog had routed the weasel into the hole in the wall, she came out before him, gave a leap, and caught the horse by the throat. The horse made off, and Paddy could not stop him, till at last he gave a leap into a big drain that was full up of water and black mud, and he was drowning and choking as fast as he could, until men who were coming from Galway came up and drove away the weasel.

Paddy brought the horse home with him, and put him into the cow's byre and fell asleep.

Next morning, the day on the morrow, Paddy rose up early, and went out to give his horse hay and oats. When he got to the door he saw the weasel coming out of the byre and she covered with blood.

'My seven thousand curses on you,' said Paddy, 'but I'm afraid you've done harm.'

He went in and found the horse, a pair of milch cows, and two calves dead. He came out and set a dog he had after the weasel. The dog got a hold of her, and she got a hold of the dog. The dog was a good one, but he was forced to loose his hold of her before Paddy could come up. He kept his eye on her, however, all through, until he saw her creeping into a little hovel that was on the brink of a lake. Paddy came running, and when he got to the little hut he gave the dog a shake to rouse him up and put anger on him, and then he sent him in. When the dog went in he began barking. Paddy went in after him, and saw an old hag in the corner. He asked her if she saw a weasel coming in there.

'I did not,' said she. 'I'm all destroyed with a plague of sickness, and if you don't go out quick, you'll catch it from me.'

While Paddy and the hag were talking, the dog kept moving in all the time, till at last he gave a leap and caught the hag by the throat. She screeched and said, 'Paddy Kelly, take off your dog, and I'll make you a rich man.'

Paddy made the dog loose his hold, and said, 'Tell me who you are, or why did you kill my horse and my cows?'

'And why did you bring away my gold that I was gathering for five hundred years throughout the hills and hollows of the world?'

'I thought you were a weasel,' said Paddy, 'or I wouldn't touch your gold; and another thing,' says he, 'if you're for five hundred years in this world, it's time for you to go to rest now.'

'I committed a great crime in my youth,' said the hag, 'and now I am to be released from my sufferings if you can pay twenty pounds for a hundred and three-score masses for me.'

'Where's the money?' said Paddy.

'Go and dig under a bush that's over a little well in the corner of that field there without, and you'll get a pot filled with gold. Pay the twenty pounds for the masses, and yourself shall have the rest. When you'll lift the flag off the pot, you'll see a big black dog coming out; but don't be afraid before him; he is a son of mine. When you get the gold, buy the house in which you saw me at first. You'll get it cheap, for it has the name of there being a ghost in it. My son will be down in the cellar. He'll do you no harm, but he'll be a good friend to you. I shall be dead a month from this day, and when you get me dead, put a coal under this little hut and burn it. Don't tell a living soul anything about me – and the luck will be on you.'

'What is your name?' said Paddy.

'Mary Kerwan,' said the hag.

Paddy went home, and when the darkness of the night came on, he took with him a spade and went to the bush that was in the corner of the field, and began digging. It was not long till he found the pot, and when he took the flag off of it a big black dog leaped out, and off and away with him, and Paddy's dog after him.

Paddy brought home the gold, and hid it in the cowhouse. About a month after that he went to the fair of Galway, and bought a pair of cows, a horse, and a dozen sheep. The neighbours did not know where he had got all the money; they said that he had a share with the good people.

One day Paddy dressed himself, and went to the gentleman who owned the large house where he first saw the weasel, and asked to buy the house of him, and the land that was round about.

'You can have the house without paying any rent at all; but there is a ghost in it, and I wouldn't like you to go to live in it without my telling you, but I couldn't part with the land without getting a hundred pounds more than you have to offer me.'

'Perhaps I have as much as you have, yourself,' said Paddy. 'I'll be here tomorrow with the money, if you're ready to give me possession.'

'I'll be ready,' said the gentleman.

Paddy went home and told his wife that he had bought a large house and a holding of land.

'Where did you get the money?' says his wife.

'Isn't it all one to you where I got it?' says Paddy.

The day on the morrow Paddy went to the gentleman, gave him the money, and got possession of the house and land; and the gentleman left him the furniture and everything that was in the house, into the bargain.

Paddy remained in the house that night, and when darkness came he went down to the cellar, and he saw a little man with his two legs spread on a barrel.

'God save you, honest man,' says he to Paddy.

'The same to you,' says Paddy.

'Don't be afraid of me, at all,' says the little man. 'I'll be a friend to you, if you are able to keep a secret.'

'I am able, indeed; I kept your mother's secret, and I'll keep yours as well.'

'Maybe you're thirsty?' said the little man.

'I'm not free from it,' said Paddy.

The little man put a hand in his bosom and drew out a gold goblet. He gave it to Paddy, and said, 'Draw wine out of that barrel under me.'

Paddy drew the full up of the goblet, and handed it to the little man.

'Drink yourself first,' says he.

Paddy drank, drew another goblet, and handed it to the little man, and he drank it.

'Fill up and drink again,' said the little man. 'I have a mind to be merry tonight.'

The pair of them sat there drinking until they were half drunk. Then the little man gave a leap down to the floor, and said to Paddy, 'Don't you like music?'

'I do, surely,' said Paddy, 'and I'm a good dancer, too.'

'Lift up the big flag over there in the corner, and you'll get my pipes under it.'

Paddy lifted the flag, got the pipes, and gave them to the little man. He squeezed the pipes on him, and began playing melodious music. Paddy began dancing till he was tired. Then they had another drink, and the little man said, 'Do as my mother told you, and I'll show you great riches. You can bring your wife in here, but don't tell her that I'm there, and she won't see me. Any time at all that ale or wine are wanting, come here and draw. Farewell, now; go to sleep, and come again to me tomorrow night.'

Paddy went to bed, and it wasn't long till he fell asleep.

On the morning of the day on the morrow, Paddy went home, and brought his wife and children to the big house, and they were very comfortable. That night Paddy went down to the cellar; the little man welcomed him and asked him did he wish to dance?

'Not till I get a drink,' said Paddy.

'Drink your fill,' said the little man. 'That barrel will never be empty as long as you live.'

Paddy drank the full of the goblet, and gave a drink to the little man. Then the little man said to him, 'I am going to the Fortress of the Fairies tonight, to play music for the good people, and if you come with me you'll see fine fun. I'll give you a horse that you never saw the like of him before.'

'I'll go with you, and welcome,' said Paddy; 'but what excuse will I make to my wife?'

'I'll bring you away from her side without her knowing it, when you are both asleep together, and I'll bring you back to her the same way,' said the little man.

'I'm obedient,' says Paddy. 'We'll have another drink before I leave you.'

He drank drink after drink, till he was half drunk, and he went to bed with his wife.

When he awoke he found himself riding on a broom near Doon-na-shee, and the little man riding on another besom by his side. When they came as far as the green hill of the Doon, the little man said a couple of words that Paddy did not understand. The green hill opened, and the pair went into a fine chamber.

Paddy never saw before a gathering like that which was in the Doon. The whole place was full up of little people, men and women, young and old. They all welcomed little Donal – that was the name of the piper – and Paddy O'Kelly. The king and queen of the fairies came up to them, and said, 'We are all going on a visit tonight to Cnoc Matha, to the high king and queen of our people.'

They all rose up then and went out. There were horses ready for each one of them, and the *coash-t'ya bower* for the king and queen. The king and queen got into the coach, each man leaped on his own horse, and be certain that Paddy was not behind. The piper went out before them, and began playing them music, and then off and away with them. It was not long till they came to Cnoc Matha. The hill opened, and the king of the fairy host passed in.

Finvara and Nuala were there, the arch-king and queen of the fairy host of Connacht, and thousands of little persons. Finvara came up and said, 'We are going to play a hurling match tonight against the fairy host of Munster, and unless we beat them our fame is gone for ever. The match is to be fought out on Moytura, under Slieve Belgadaun.'

The Connacht host cried out, 'We are all ready, and we have no doubt but we'll beat them.'

'Out with ye all,' cried the high king; 'the men of the hill of Nephin will be on the ground before us.'

They all went out, and little Donal and twelve pipers more before them, playing melodious music. When they came to Moytura, the fairy host of Munster and the fairy men of the hill of Nephin were there before them. Now it is necessary for the fairy host to have two live men beside them when they are fighting or at a hurling match, and that was the reason that little Donal took Paddy O'Kelly with him. There was a man they called the '*Yellow Stongirya*', with the fairy host of Munster, from Ennis, in the County Clare.

It was not long till the two hosts took sides; the ball was thrown up between them, and the fun began in earnest.

They were hurling away, and the pipers playing music, until Paddy O'Kelly saw the host of Munster getting the strong hand, and he began helping the fairy host of Connacht. The *Stongirya* came up and he made at Paddy O'Kelly, but Paddy turned him head over heels. From hurling the two hosts began at fighting, but it was not long until the host of Connacht beat the other host. Then the host of Munster made flying beetles of themselves, and

they began eating every green thing that they came up to. They were destroying the country before them until they came as far as Cong. Then there rose up thousands of doves out of the hole, and they swallowed down the beetles. That hole has no other name until this day but Pull-na-gullam, the dove's hole.

When the fairy host of Connacht won their battle, they came back to Cnoc Matha joyous enough, and the king Finvara gave Paddy O'Kelly a purse of gold, and the little piper brought him home, and put him into bed beside his wife, and left him sleeping there.

A month went by after that without anything worth mentioning, until one

night Paddy went
down to the cellar,
and the little man
said to him, 'My
mother is dead;
burn the house
over her.'

'It is true for
you,' said Paddy.
'She told me that she hadn't but a month to be in the
world, and the month was up yesterday.'

On the next morning of the next day
Paddy went to the hut and he
found the hag dead. He put a coal
under the hut and burned it. He
came home and told the little
man that the hag was burnt. The
little man gave him a purse and
said to him, 'This purse will
never be empty as long as you
are alive. Now, you will never
see me more; but have a loving
remembrance of the weasel. She was the beginning and the prime
cause of your riches.' Then he went away and Paddy never saw
him again.

Paddy O'Kelly and his wife lived for years
after this in the large house, and when he died
he left great wealth behind him, and a large
family to spend it.

There now is the story for you, from the
first word to the last, as I heard it from my
grandmother.

The Vision of MacConglinney

Cathal, king of Munster, was a good king and a great warrior. But there came to dwell within him a lawless evil beast, that afflicted him with hunger that ceased not, and might not be satisfied, so that he would devour a pig, a cow, and a bull calf and three-score cakes of pure wheat, and a vat of new ale, for his breakfast, whilst as for his great feast, what he ate there passes account or reckoning. He was like this for three half-years, and during that time it was the ruin of Munster he was, and it is likely he would have ruined all Ireland in another half-year.

Now there lived in Armagh a famous young scholar and his name was Anier MacConglinney. He heard of the strange disease of King Cathal, and of the abundance of food and drink, of whitemeats, ale and mead, there were always to be found at the king's court. Thither then was he minded to go to try his own fortune, and to see of what help he could be to the king.

He arose early in the morning and tucked up his shirt and wrapped him in the folds of his white cloak. In his right hand he grasped his even-poised knotty staff, and going right-hand-wise round his home, he bade farewell to his tutors and started off.

He journeyed across all Ireland till he came to the house of Pichan. And there he stayed and told tales, and made all merry. But Pichan said, 'Though great thy mirth, son of learning, it does not make me glad.'

'And why?' asked MacConglinney.

'Knowest thou not, scholar, that Cathal is coming here tonight with all his host. And if the great host is troublesome, the king's first meal is more troublesome still; and troublesome though the first be, most troublesome of all is the great feast. Three things are wanted for this last: a bushel of oats, and a bushel of wild apples, and a bushel of flour cakes.'

'What reward would you give me if I shield you from the king from this hour to the same hour tomorrow?'

'A white sheep from every fold between Carn and Cork.'

'I will take that,' said MacConglinney.

Cathal, the king, came with the companies, and a host of horse of the Munster men. But Cathal did not let the thong of his shoe be half loosed before he began supplying his mouth with both hands from the apples round about him. Pichan and all the men of Munster looked on sadly and sorrowfully. Then rose MacConglinney, hastily and impatiently, and seized a stone, against which swords were used to be sharpened; this he thrust into his mouth and began grinding his teeth against the stone.

'What makes thee mad, son of learning?' asked Cathal.

'I grieve to see you eating alone,' said the scholar.

Then the king was ashamed and flung him the apples, and it is said that for three half-years he had not performed such an act of humanity.

'Grant me a further boon,' said MacConglinney.

'It is granted, on my troth,' said the king.

'Fast with me the whole night,' said the scholar.

And grievous though it was to the king, he did so, for he had passed his princely troth, and no king of Munster might transgress that.

In the morning MacConglinney called for juicy old bacon, and tender corned beef, honey in the comb, and English salt on a beautiful polished dish of white silver. A fire he lighted of oak wood without smoke, without fumes, without sparks.

And sticking spits into the portion of meat, he set to work to roast them. Then he shouted, 'Ropes and cords here.'

Ropes and cords were given to him, and the strongest of the warriors.

And they seized the king and bound him securely, and made him fast with knots and hooks and staples. When the king was thus fastened, MacConglinney sat himself down before him, and taking his knife out of his girdle, he carved the portion of meat that was on the spits, and every morsel he dipped in the honey, and, passing it in front of the king's mouth, put it in his own.

When the king saw that he was getting nothing, and he had been fasting for twenty-four hours, he roared and bellowed, and commanded the killing of the scholar. But that was not done for him.

'Listen, king of Munster,' said MacConglinney, 'a vision appeared to me last night, and I will relate it to you.'

He then began his vision, and as he related it he put morsel after morsel past Cathal's mouth into his own.

> 'A lake of new milk I beheld
> In the midst of a fair plain,
> Therein a well-appointed house,
> Thatched with butter.
> Puddings fresh boiled,
> Such were its thatch-rods,
> Its two soft door posts of custard,
> Its beds of glorious bacon.
> Cheeses were the palisades,
> Sausages the rafters.
> Truly 'twas a rich filled house,
> In which was great store of good feed.

'Such was the vision I beheld, and a voice sounded into my ears. "Go now, thither, MacConglinney, for you have no power of eating in you." "What must I do," said I, for the sight of that had made me greedy. Then the voice bade me go to the hermitage of the Wizard Doctor, and there I should find appetite for all kinds of savoury tender sweet food, acceptable to the body.

'There in the harbour of the lake before me I saw a juicy little coracle of beef; its thwarts were of curds, its prow of lard; its stern of butter; its oars were flitches of venison. Then I rowed across the wide expanse of the New Milk Lake, through seas of broth, past river mouths of meat, over swelling boisterous waves of butter milk, by perpetual pools of savoury lard, by islands of cheese, by headlands of old curds, until I reached the firm level land between Butter Mount and Milk Lake, in the land of O'Early-eating, in front of the hermitage of the Wizard Doctor.

'Marvellous, indeed, was the hermitage. Around it were seven-score hundred smooth stakes of old bacon, and instead of thorns above the top of every stake was fixed juicy lard. There was a gate of cream, whereon was a bolt of sausage. And there I saw the doorkeeper, Bacon Lad, son of Butterkins, son of Lardipole, with his smooth sandals of old bacon, his legging of pot-meat round his shins, his tunic of corned beef, his girdle of salmon skin round him, his hood of flummery about him, his steed of bacon under him, with its four legs of custard, its four hoofs of oaten bread, its ears of curds, its two eyes of honey in its head; in his hand a whip, the cords whereof were four-and-twenty fair white puddings, and every juicy drop that fell from each of these puddings would have made a meal for an ordinary man.

'On going in I beheld the Wizard Doctor with his two gloves of rump steak on his hands, setting order the house, which was hung all round with tripe, from roof to floor.

'I went into the kitchen, and there I saw the Wizard Doctor's son, with his fishing hook of lard in his hand, and the line was made of marrow, and he was angling in a lake of whey. Now he would bring up a flitch of ham, and now a fillet of corned beef. And as he was angling, he fell in, and was drowned.

'As I set my foot across the threshold into the house, I saw a pure white bed of butter, on which I sat down, but I sank down into it up to the tips of my hair. Hard work had the eight strongest men in the house to pull me out by the top of the crown of my head.

'Then I was taken into the Wizard Doctor. "What aileth thee?" said he.

'My wish would be, that all the many wonderful viands of the world were before me, that I might eat my fill and satisfy my greed. But alas! Great is the misfortune to me, who cannot obtain any of these.

' "On my word," said the Doctor, "the disease is grievous. But thou shall take home with thee a medicine to cure thy disease, and shalt be for ever healed therefrom."

' "What is that?" asked I.

' "When thou goest home tonight, warm thyself before a glowing red fire of oak, made up on a dry hearth, so that its embers may warm thee, its blaze may not burn thee, its smoke may not touch thee. And make for thyself thrice nine morsels, and every morsel as big as a heath fowl's egg, and in each morsel eight kinds of grain, wheat and barley, oats and rye, and therewith eight condiments, and to every condiment eight sauces. And when thou hast prepared thy food, take a drop of drink, a tiny drop, only as much as twenty men will drink, and let it be of thick milk, of yellow bubbling milk, of milk that will gurgle as it rushes down thy throat.

' "And when thou hast done this, whatever disease thou hast, shall be removed. Go now," said he, "in the name of cheese, and may the smooth juicy bacon protect thee, may yellow curdy cream protect, may the cauldron full of pottage protect thee." '

Now, as MacConglinney recited his vision, what with the pleasure of the recital and the recounting of these many pleasant viands, and the sweet savour of the honeyed morsels roasting on the spits, the lawless beast that dwelt within the king, came forth until it was licking its lips outside its head.

Then MacConglinney bent his hand with the two spits of food, and put them to the lips of the king, who longed to swallow them, wood, food, and all. So he took them an arm's length away from the king, and the lawless beast jumped from the throat of Cathal on to the spit. MacConglinney put the spit into the embers, and upset the cauldron of the royal house over the spit. The house was emptied, so that not the value of a cockchafer's leg was left in it, and four huge fires were kindled here and there in it. When the house was a tower of red flame and a huge blaze, the lawless beast sprang to the rooftree of the palace, and from thence he vanished, and was seen no more.

As for the king, a bed was prepared for him on a downy quilt, and musicians and singers entertained him going from noon till twilight. And when he awoke, this is what he bestowed upon the scholar – a cow from every farm, and a sheep from every house in Munster. Moreover, that so long as he lived, he should carve the king's food, and sit at his right hand.

Thus was Cathal, king of Munster, cured of his craving, and MacConglinney honoured.

Dream of Owen O'Mulready

There was a man long ago living near Ballaghadereen named Owen O'Mulready, who was a workman for the gentleman of the place, and was a prosperous, quiet, contented man. There was no one but himself and his wife Margaret, and they had a nice little house and enough potatoes in the year, in addition to their share of wages, from their master. There wasn't a want or anxiety on Owen, except one desire, and that was to have a dream – for he had never had one.

One day when he was digging potatoes, his master – James Taafe – came out to his ridge, and they began talking, as was the custom with them. The talk fell on dreams, and said Owen that he would like better than anything if he could only have one.

'You'll have one tonight,' says his master, 'if you do as I tell you.'

'Musha, I'll do it, and welcome,' says Owen.

'Now,' says his master, 'when you go home tonight, draw the fire from the hearth, put it out, make your bed in its place and sleep there tonight, and you'll get your enough of dreaming before the morning.'

Owen promised to do this. When, however, he began to draw the fire out, Margaret thought that he had lost his senses, so he explained everything James Taafe had said to him, had his own way, and they went to lie down together on the hearth.

Not long was Owen asleep when there came a knock at the door.

'Get up, Owen O'Mulready, and go with a letter from the master to America.'

Owen got up, and put his feet into his boots, saying to himself, 'It's late you come, messenger.'

He took the letter, and he went forward and never tarried till he came to the foot of Sliabh Charn, where he met a cowboy, and he herding cows.

'The blessing of God be with you, Owen O'Mulready,' says the boy.

'The blessing of God and Mary be with you, my boy,' says Owen. 'Everyone knows me, and I don't know anyone at all.'

'Where are you going this time of night?' says the boy.

'I'm going to America, with a letter from the master; is this the right road?' says Owen.

'It is; keep straight to the west; but how are you going to get over the water?' says the boy.

'Time enough to think of that when I get to it,' replied Owen.

He went on the road again, till he came to the brink of the sea; there he saw a crane standing on one foot on the shore.

'The blessing of God be with you, Owen O'Mulready,' says the crane.

'The blessing of God and Mary be with you, Mrs Crane,' says Owen. 'Everybody knows me, and I don't know anyone.'

'What are you doing here?'

Owen told her his business, and that he didn't know how he'd get over the water.

'Leave your two feet on my two wings, and sit on my back, and I'll take you to the other side,' says the crane.

'What would I do if tiredness should come on you before we got over?' says Owen.

'Don't be afraid, I won't be tired or wearied till I fly over.'

Then Owen went on the back of the crane, and she arose over the sea and went forward, but she hadn't flown more than half-way, when she cried out, 'Owen O'Mulready get off me; I'm tired.'

'That you may be seven times worse this day twelve months, you rogue of a crane,' says Owen. 'I can't get off you now, so don't ask me.'

'I don't care,' replied the crane, 'if you'll rise off me a while till I'll take a rest.'

With that they saw threshers over their heads, and Owen shouted, 'Och! Thresher, thresher, leave down your flail at me, that I may give the crane a rest!'

The thresher left down the flail, but when Owen took a hold with his two hands, the crane went from him laughing and mocking.

'My share of misfortunes go with you!' said Owen. 'It's you've left me in a fix hanging between the heavens and the water in the middle of the great sea.'

It wasn't long till the thresher shouted to him to leave go the flail.

'I won't let it go,' said Owen. 'Shan't I be drowned?'

'If you don't let it go, I'll cut the whang.'

'I don't care,' says Owen; 'I have the flail;' and with that he looked away from him, and what should he see but a boat a long way off.

'O sailor dear, sailor, come, come; perhaps you'll take my lot of bones,' said Owen.

'Are we under you now?' says the sailor.

'Not yet, not yet,' says Owen.

'Fling down one of your shoes, till we see the way it falls,' says the captain.

Owen shook one foot, and down fell the shoe.

'Uill, uill, puil, uil liu – who is killing me?' came a scream from Margaret in the bed. 'Where are you, Owen?'

'I didn't know whether 'twas you were in it, Margaret.'

'Indeed, then it is,' says she, 'who else would it be?'

She got up and lit the candle. She found Owen half-way up the chimney, climbing by the hands on the crook, and he black with soot! He had one shoe on, but the point of the other struck Margaret, and 'twas that which awoke her.

Owen came down off the crook and washed himself, and from that out there was no envy on him ever to have a dream again.

Morraha

Morraha rose in the morning and washed his hands and face, and said his prayers, and ate his food; and he asked God to prosper the day for him. So he went down to the brink of the sea, and he saw a currach, short and green, coming towards him; and in it there was but one youthful champion, and he was playing hurly from prow to stern of the currach. He had a hurl of gold and a ball of silver; and he stopped not till the currach was in on the shore; and he drew her up on the green grass, and put fastenings on her for a year and a day, whether he should be there all that time or should only be on land for an hour by the clock. And Morraha saluted the young man courteously; and the other saluted him in the same fashion, and asked him would he play a game of cards with him; and Morraha said that he had not the wherewithal; and the other answered that he was never without a candle or the making of it; and he put his hand in his pocket and drew out a table and two chairs and a pack of cards, and they sat down on the chairs and went to card-playing. The first game Morraha won, and the Slender Red Champion bade him make his claim; and he asked that the land above him should be filled with stock of sheep in the morning. It was well; and he played no second game, but home he went.

The next day Morraha went to the brink of the sea, and the young man came in the currach and asked him would he play cards; they played, and Morraha won. The young man bade him make his claim; and he asked that the land above should be filled with cattle in the morning. It was well; and he played no other game, but went home.

On the third morning Morraha went to the brink of the sea, and he saw the young man coming. He drew up his boat on the shore and asked him would he play cards. They played, and Morraha won the game; and the young man bade him give his claim. And he said he would have a castle and a wife, the finest and fairest in the world; and they were his. It was well; and the Red Champion went away.

On the fourth day his wife asked him how he had found her. And he told her. 'And I am going out,' said he, 'to play again today.'

'I forbid you to go again to him. If you have won so much, you will lose more; have no more to do with him.'

But he went against her will, and he saw the currach coming; and the Red Champion was driving his balls from end to end of the currach; he had balls of silver and a hurl of gold, and he stopped not till he drew his boat on the shore, and made her fast for a year and a day. Morraha and he saluted each other; and he asked Morraha if he would play a game of cards, and they played, and he won. Morraha said to him, 'Give your claim now.'

Said he, 'You will hear it too soon. I lay on you bonds of the art of the druid, not to sleep two nights in one house, nor finish a second meal at the one table, till you bring me the sword of light and news of the death of Anshgayliacht.'

He went home to his wife and sat down in a chair, and gave a groan, and the chair broke in pieces.

'That is the groan of the son of a king under spells,' said his wife; 'and you had better have taken my counsel than that the spells should be on you.'

He told her he had to bring news of the death of Anshgayliacht and the sword of light to the Slender Red Champion.

'Go out,' said she, 'in the morning of the morrow, and take the bridle in the window, and shake it; and whatever beast, handsome or ugly, puts its head in it, take that one with you. Do not speak a word to her till she speaks to you; and take with you three pint bottles of ale and three sixpenny loaves, and do the thing she tells you; and when she runs to my father's land, on a height above the castle, she will shake herself, and the bells will ring, and my father will say, "Brown Allree is in the land. And if the son of a king or queen is there, bring him to me on your shoulders; but if it is the son of a poor man, let him come no further." '

He rose in the morning, and took the bridle that was in the window, and went out and shook it; and Brown Allree came and put her head in it. He took the three loaves and three bottles of ale, and went riding; and when he was riding she bent her head down to take hold of her feet with her mouth, in hopes he would speak in ignorance; but he spoke not a word during the time, and the mare at last spoke to him, and told him to dismount and give her her dinner. He gave her the sixpenny loaf toasted, and a bottle of ale to drink.

'Sit up now riding, and take good heed of yourself: there are three miles of fire I have to clear at a leap.'

She cleared the three miles of fire at a leap, and asked if he were still riding, and he said he was. Then they went on, and she told him to dismount and give her a meal; and he did so, and gave her a sixpenny loaf and a bottle; she consumed them and said to him there were before them three miles of hill covered with steel thistles, and that she must clear it. She cleared the hill with a leap, and she asked him if he were still riding, and he said he was. They went on, and she went not far before she told him to give her a meal, and he gave her the bread and the bottleful. She went over three miles of sea with a leap, and she came then to the land of the king of France; she went up on a height above the castle, and she shook herself and neighed, and the bells rang; and the king said that it was Brown Allree was in the land.

'Go out,' said he; 'and if it is the son of a king or queen, carry him in on your shoulders; if it is not, leave him there.'

They went out; and the stars of the son of a king were on his breast; they lifted him high on their shoulders and bore him into the king. They passed the night cheerfully, playing and drinking, with sport and with diversion, till the whiteness of the day came upon the morrow morning.

Then the young king told the cause of his journey, and he asked the queen to give him counsel and good luck, and she told him everything he was to do.

'Go now,' said she, 'and take with you the best mare in the stable, and go to the door of Rough Niall of the Speckled Rock, and knock, and call on him to give you news of the death of

Anshgayliacht and the sword of light: and let the horse's back be to the door, and apply the spurs, and away with you.'

In the morning he did so, and he took the best horse from the stable and rode to the door of Niall, and turned the horse's back to the door, and demanded news of the death of Anshgayliacht and the sword of light; then he applied the spurs, and away with him. Niall followed him hard, and, as he was passing the gate, cut the horse in two. His wife was there with a dish of puddings and flesh, and she threw it in his eyes and blinded him, and said, 'Fool! Whatever kind of man it is that's mocking you, isn't that a fine condition you have got your father's horse into?'

On the morning of the next day Morraha rose, and took another horse from the stable, and went again to the door of Niall, and knocked and demanded news of the death of Anshgayliacht and the sword of light, and applied the spurs to the horse and away with him. Niall followed, and as Morraha was passing, the gate cut the horse in two and took half the saddle with him; but his wife met him and threw flesh in his eyes and blinded him.

On the third day, Morraha went again to the door of Niall; and Niall followed him, and as he was passing the gate, cut away the saddle from under him and the clothes from his back. Then his wife said to Niall, 'The fool that's mocking you is out yonder in the little currach, going home; and take good heed to yourself, and don't sleep one wink for three days.'

For three days the little currach kept in sight, but then Niall's wife came to him and said, 'Sleep as much as you want now. He is gone.'

He went to sleep, and there was heavy sleep on him, and Morraha went in and took hold of the sword that was on the bed at his head. And the sword thought to draw itself out of the hand of Morraha; but it failed. Then it gave a cry, and it wakened Niall, and Niall said it was a rude and rough thing to come into his house like that; and said Morraha to him, 'Leave your much talking, or I will cut the head off you. Tell me the news of the death of Anshgayliacht.'

'Oh, you can have my head.'

'But your head is no good to me; tell me the story.'

'Oh,' said Niall's wife, 'you must get the story.'

'Well,' said Niall, 'let us sit down together till I tell the story. I thought no one would ever get it; but now it will be heard by all.'

The Story

When I was growing up, my mother taught me the language of the birds; and when I got married, I used to be listening to their conversation; and I would be laughing; and my wife would be asking me what was the reason of my laughing, but I did not like to tell her, as women are always asking questions. We went out walking one fine morning, and the birds were arguing with one another. One of them said to another, 'Why should you be comparing yourself with me, when there is not a king nor knight that does not come to look at my tree?'

'What advantage has your tree over mine, on which there are three rods of magic mastery growing?'

When I heard them arguing, and knew that the rods were there, I began to laugh.

'Oh,' asked my wife, 'why are you always laughing? I believe it is at myself you are jesting, and I'll walk with you no more.'

'Oh, it is not about you I am laughing. It is because I understand the language of the birds.'

Then I had to tell her what the birds were saying to one another; and she was greatly delighted, and she asked me to go home, and she gave orders to the cook to have breakfast ready at six o'clock in the morning. I did not know why she was going out early, and breakfast was ready in the morning at the hour she appointed. She asked me to go out walking. I went with her. She went to the tree, and asked me to cut a rod for her.

'Oh, I will not cut it. Are we not better without it?'

'I will not leave this until I get the rod, to see if there is any good in it.'

I cut the rod and gave it to her. She turned from me and struck a blow on a stone, and changed it; and she struck a second blow on me, and made of me a black raven, and she went home and left me after her. I thought she would come back; she did not come, and I

had to go into a tree till morning.
In the morning, at six o'clock,
there was a bellman out,
proclaiming that everyone
who killed a raven would
get a fourpenny-bit. At
last you could not find
man or boy without a
gun, nor, if you were to
walk three miles, a raven
that was not killed. I
had to make a nest in
the top of the parlour
chimney, and hide
myself all day till
night came, and go
out to pick up a bit
to support me, till I
spent a month. Here
she is herself to say if
it is a lie I am telling.

'It is not,' said she.

Then I saw her out walking. I went up to her, and I thought she
would turn me back to my own shape, and she struck me with the
rod and made of me an old white horse, and she ordered me to be
put to a cart with a man, to draw stones from morning till night. I
was worse off then. She spread abroad a report that I had died
suddenly in my bed, and prepared a coffin, and waked and buried
me. Then she had no trouble. But when I got tired I began to kill
everyone who came near me, and I used to go into the haggard
every night and destroy the stacks of corn; and when a man came
near me in the morning I would follow him till I broke his bones.
Everyone got afraid of me. When she saw I was doing mischief
she came to meet me, and I thought she would change me. And
she did change me, and made a fox of me. When I saw she was
doing me every sort of damage I went away from her. I knew there
was a badger's hole in the garden, and I went there till night came,

and I made great slaughter among the geese and ducks. There she is herself to say if I am telling a lie.

'Oh! You are telling nothing but the truth, only less than the truth.'

When she had enough of my killing the fowl she came out into the garden, for she knew I was in the badger's hole. She came to me and made me a wolf. I had to be off, and go to an island, where no one at all would see me, and now and then I used to be killing sheep, for there were not many of them, and I was afraid of being seen and hunted; and so I passed a year, till a shepherd saw me among the sheep and a pursuit was made after me. And when the dogs came near me there was no place for me to escape to from them; but I recognised the sign of the king among the men, and I made for him, and the king cried out to stop the hounds. I took a leap upon the front of the king's saddle, and the woman behind cried out, 'My king and my lord, kill him, or he will kill you!'

'Oh! He will not kill me. He knew me; he must be pardoned.'

The king took me home with him, and gave orders I should be well cared for. I was so wise, when I got food, I would not eat one morsel until I got a knife and fork. The man told the king, and the king came to see if it was true, and I got a knife and fork, and I took the knife in one paw and the fork in the other, and I bowed to the king. The king gave orders to bring him drink, and it came; and the king filled a glass of wine and gave it to me.

I took hold of it in my paw and drank it, and thanked the king.

'On my honour,' said he, 'it is some king or other has lost him, when he came on the island; and I will keep him, as he is trained; and perhaps he will serve us yet.'

And this is the sort of king he was – a king who had not a child living. Eight sons were born to him and three daughters, and they were stolen the same night they were born. No matter what guard was placed over them, the child would be gone in the morning. A twelfth child now came to the queen, and the king took me with him to watch the baby. The women were not satisfied with me.

'Oh,' said the king, 'what was all your watching ever good for? One that was born to me I have not; I will leave this one in the dog's care, and he will not let it go.'

A coupling was put between me and the cradle, and when everyone went to sleep I was watching till the person woke who attended in the daytime; but I was there only two nights; when it was near the day, I saw a hand coming down through the chimney, and the hand was so big that it took round the child altogether, and thought to take him away. I caught hold of the hand above the wrist, and as I was fastened to the cradle, I did not let go my hold till I cut the hand from the wrist, and there was a howl from the person without. I laid the hand in the cradle with the child, and as I was tired I fell asleep; and when I awoke, I had neither child nor hand; and I began to howl, and the king heard me, and he cried out that something was wrong with me, and he sent servants to see what was the matter with me, and when the messenger came he saw me covered with blood, and he could not see the child; and he went to the king and told him the child was not to be got. The king came and saw the cradle coloured with the blood, and he cried out, 'Where has the child gone?' and everyone said it was the dog had eaten it.

The king said, 'It is not: loose him, and he will get the pursuit himself.'

When I was loosed, I found the scent of the blood till I came to a door of the room in which the child was. I went back to the king and took hold of him, and went back again and began to tear at the door. The king followed me and asked for the key. The servant said it was in the room of the stranger woman. The king caused search to be made for her, and she was not to be found. 'I will break the door,' said the king, 'as I can't get the key.' The king broke the door, and I went in, and went to the trunk, and the king asked for a key to unlock it. He got no key, and he broke the lock. When he opened the trunk, the child and the hand were stretched side by side, and the child was asleep. The king took the hand and ordered a woman to come for the child, and he showed the hand to everyone in the house. But the stranger woman was gone, and she did not see the king – and here she is herself to say if I am telling lies of her.

'Oh, it's nothing but the truth you have!'

Morraha

The king did not allow me to be tied any more. He said there was nothing so much to wonder at as that I cut the hand off, as I was tied.

The child was growing till he was a year old. He was beginning to walk, and no one cared for him more than I did. He was growing till he was three, and he was running out every minute; so the king ordered a silver chain to be put between me and the child, that he might not go away from me. I was out with him in the garden every day, and the king was as proud as the world of the child. He would be watching him everywhere we went, till the child grew so wise that he would loose the chain and get off. But one day that he loosed it I failed to find him; and I ran into the house and searched the house, but there was no getting him for me. The king cried to go out and find the child, that had got loose from the dog. They went searching for him, but could not find him. When they failed altogether to find him, there remained no more favour with the king towards me, and everyone disliked me, and I grew weak, for I did not get a morsel to eat half the time.

When summer came, I said I would try and go home to my own country. I went away one fine morning, and I went swimming, and God helped me till I came home. I went into the garden, for I knew there was a place in the garden where I could hide myself, for fear my wife should see me. In the morning I saw her out walking, and the child with her, held by the hand. I pushed out to see the child, and as he was looking about him everywhere, he saw me and called out, 'I see my shaggy papa. Oh!' said he. 'Oh, my heart's love, my shaggy papa, come here till I see you!'

I was afraid the woman would see me, as she was asking the child where he saw me, and he said I was up in a tree; and the more the child called me, the more I hid myself. The woman took the child home with her, but I knew he would be up early in the morning.

I went to the parlour-window, and the child was within, and he playing. When he saw me he cried out, 'Oh! My heart's love, come here till I see you, shaggy papa.' I broke the window and went in, and he began to kiss me. I saw the rod in front of the chimney, and I jumped up at the rod and knocked it down. 'Oh! My heart's love, no one would give me the pretty rod,' said he. I hoped he would strike me with the rod, but he did not. When I saw the time was short I raised my paw, and I gave him a scratch below the knee. 'Oh! You naughty, dirty, shaggy papa, you have hurt me so much, I'll give you a blow of the rod.' He struck me a light blow, and so I came back to my own shape again. When he saw a man standing before him he gave a cry, and I took him up in my arms. The servants heard the child. A maid came into see what was the matter with him. When she saw me she gave a cry out of her, and she said, 'Oh, if the master isn't come to life again!'

Another came in, and said it was he really. When the mistress heard of it, she came to see with her own eyes, for she would not believe I was there; and when she saw me she said she'd drown herself. But I said to her, 'If you yourself will keep the secret, no living man will ever get the story from me until I lose my head.' Here she is herself to say if I am telling the truth. 'Oh, it's nothing but truth you are telling.'

When I saw I was in a man's shape, I said I would take the child back to his father and mother, as I knew the grief they were in after him. I got a ship, and took the child with me; and as I journeyed I came to land on an island, and I saw not a living soul on it, only a castle dark and gloomy. I went into see was there anyone in it. There was no one but an old hag, tall and frightful, and she asked me, 'What sort of person are you?' I heard someone groaning in another room, and I said I was a doctor, and I asked her what ailed the person who was groaning.

'Oh,' said she, 'it is my son, whose hand has been bitten from his wrist by a dog.'

I knew then that it was he who had taken the child from me, and I said I would cure him if I got a good reward.

'I have nothing; but there are eight young lads and three young women, as handsome as anyone ever laid eyes on, and if you cure him I will give you them.'

'Tell me first in what place his hand was cut from him?'

'Oh, it was out in another country, twelve years ago.'

'Show me the way, that I may see him.'

She brought me into a room, so that I saw him, and his arm was swelled up to the shoulder. He asked me if I would cure him; and I said I would cure him if he would give me the reward his mother promised.

'Oh, I will give it; but cure me.'

'Well, bring them out to me.'

The hag brought them out of the room. I said I should burn the flesh that was on his arm. When I looked on him he was howling with pain. I said that I would not leave him in pain long. The wretch had only one eye in his forehead. I took a bar of iron, and put it in the fire till it was red, and I said to the hag, 'He will be howling at first, but will fall asleep presently, and do not wake him till he has slept as much as he wants. I will close the door when I am going out.' I took the bar with me, and I stood over him, and I turned it across through his eye as far as I could. He began to bellow, and tried to catch me, but I was out and away, having closed the door. The hag asked me, 'Why is he bellowing?'

'Oh, he will be quiet presently, and will sleep for a good while, and I'll come again to have a look at him; but bring me out the young men and the young women.'

I took them with me, and I said to her, 'Tell me where you got them.'

'My son brought them with him, and they are all the children of one king.'

I was well satisfied, and I had no wish for delay to get myself free from the hag, so I took them on board the ship, and the child I had myself. I thought the king might leave me the child I nursed myself; but when I came to land, and all those young people with me, the king and queen were out walking. The king was very aged, and the queen aged likewise. When I came to converse with them, and the twelve with me, the king and queen began to cry. I asked, 'Why are you crying?'

'It is for good cause I am crying. As many children as these I should have, and now I am withered, grey, at the end of my life, and I have not one at all.'

I told him all I went through, and I gave him the child in his hand, and 'These are your other children who were stolen from you, whom I am giving to you safe. They are gently reared.'

When the king heard who they were he smothered them with kisses and drowned them with tears, and dried them with fine cloths silken and the hair of his own head, and so also did their mother, and great was his welcome for me, as it was I who found them all. The king said to me, 'I will give you the last child, as it is you who have earned him best; but you must come to my court every year, and the child with you, and I will share with you my possessions.

'I have enough of my own, and after my death I will leave it to the child.'

I spent a time, till my visit was over, and I told the king all the troubles I went through, only I said nothing about my wife. And now you have the story.

And now when you go home, and the Slender Red Champion asks you for news of the death of Anshgayliacht and for the sword of light, tell him the way in which his brother was killed, and say you have the sword; and he will ask the sword from you. Say you to him, 'If I promised to bring it to you, I did not promise to bring it for you;' and then throw the sword into the air and it will come back to me.

He went home, and he told the story of the death of Anshgayliacht to the Slender Red Champion, 'And here,' said he, 'is the sword.' The Slender Red Champion asked for the sword; but he said, 'If I promised to bring it to you, I did not promise to bring it for you;' and he threw it into the air and it returned to Blue Niall.

The Story of the McAndrew Family

A long time ago, in the County Mayo, there lived a rich man of the name of McAndrew. He owned cows and horses without number, not to mention ducks and geese and pigs; and his land extended as far as the eye could reach on the four sides of you.

McAndrew was a lucky man, the neighbours all said; but as for himself, when he looked on his seven big sons growing up like weeds and with scarcely any more sense, he felt sore enough, for of all the stupid omadhauns the seven McAndrew brothers were the stupidest.

When the youngest grew to be a man, the father built a house for each of them, and gave every one a piece of land and a few cows, hoping to make men of them before he died, for, as the old man said, 'While God spares my life, I'll be able to have an eye to them, and maybe they will learn from experience.'

The seven young McAndrews were happy enough. Their fields were green, their cows were fat and sleek, and they thought they would never see a poor day.

All went well for a time, and the day of the fair of Killalla was as fine a day as ever shone in Ireland, when the whole seven got ready to be off, bright and early, in the morning.

Each one of them drove before him three fine cows, and a finer herd, when they were all together, was never seen in the country far or near.

Now, there was a smart farmer, named O'Toole, whose fields were nearing on the McAndrews', and he had many a time set his heart on the fine cattle belonging to his easy-going neighbours ; so when he saw them passing with their twenty-one cows he went out and hailed them.

'Where are ye going to, this fine morning?'

'It's to the fair of Killalla we're going, to sell these fine cows our father gave us,' they all answered together.

'And are ye going to sell cows that the evil eye has long been set on? Oh, Con and Shamus, I would never belave it of ye, even if that spalpeen of a Pat would do such a thing; anyone would think that the spirit of the good mother that bore ye would stretch out a hand and kape ye from committing such a mortal sin.'

This O'Toole said to the three eldest, who stood trembling, while the four younger ones stuck their knuckles into their eyes and began to cry.

'Oh, indade, Mr O'Toole, we never knew that the cows were under the evil eye. How did ye find it out? Oh, sorra the day when such a fine lot of cattle should go to the bad,' answered Con.

'Indade ye may well ask it, whin it's meself that was always a good neighbour and kept watch on auld Judy, the witch, when she used to stand over there laughing at the ravens flying over the cows. Do ye mind the time yer father spoke ugly to her down by the cross-roads? She never forgot it, and now yer twenty-one fine cows will never be worth the hides on their backs.'

'Worra, worra, worra,' roared the seven McAndrews, so loud that pretty Katie O'Toole bobbed her head out of the window, and the hindermost cows began to caper like mad.

'The spell has come upon them!' cried Shamus. 'Oh! What'll we do? What'll we do?'

'Hould yer whist, man alive,' said O'Toole. 'I'm a good neighbour, as I said before, so to give ye a lift in the world I'll take the risk on meself and buy the cows from ye for the price of their hides. Sure no harm can be done to the hides for making leather, so I'll give ye a shilling apiece, and that's better than nothing. Twenty-one bright shillings going to the fair may make yer fortune.'

It seemed neck or nothing with the McAndrews, and they accepted the offer, thanking O'Toole for his generosity, and helped him drive the cows into his field. Then they set off for the fair.

They had never been in a fair before, and when they saw the fine sights they forgot all about the cows, and only remembered that they had each a shilling to spend.

Everyone knew the McAndrews, and soon a crowd gathered round them, praising their fine looks and telling them what a fine father they had to give them so much money, so that the seven omadhauns lost their heads entirely, and treated right and left until there wasn't a farthing left of the twenty-one shillings. Then they staggered home a little the worse for the fine whiskey they drank with the boys.

It was a sorry day for old McAndrew when his seven sons came home without a penny of the price of their twenty-one fine cows, and he vowed he'd never give them any more.

So one day passed with another, and the seven young McAndrews were as happy as could be until the fine old father fell sick and died.

The eldest son came in for all the father had, so he felt like a lord. To see him strut and swagger was a sight to make a grum growdy laugh.

One day, to show how fine he could be, he dressed in his best, and with a purse filled with gold pieces started off for the market town.

When he got there, in he walked to a public house, and called for the best of everything, and to make a fine fellow of himself he tripled the price of everything to the landlord. As soon as he got through his eye suddenly caught sight of a little keg, all gilded over to look like gold, that hung outside the door for a sign. Con had never heeded it before, and he asked the landlord what it was.

Now the landlord, like many another, had it in mind that he might as well get all he could out of a McAndrew, and he answered quickly, 'You stupid omadhaun, don't you know what that is? It's a mare's egg.'

'And will a foal come out of it?'

'Of course; what a question to ask a dacent man!'

'I niver saw one before,' said the amazed McAndrew.

'Well, ye see one now, Con, and take a good look at it.'

'Will ye sell it?'

'Och, Con McAndrew, do ye think I want to sell that fine egg afther kaping it so long hung up there before the sun – when it is ready to hatch out a foal that will be worth twenty good guineas to me?'

'I'll give ye twenty guineas for it,' answered Con.

'Thin it's a bargain,' said the landlord; and he took down the keg and handed it to Con, who handed out the twenty guineas, all the money he had.

'Be careful of it, and carry it as aisy as ye can, and when ye get home hang it up in the sun.'

Con promised, and set off home with his prize.

Near the rise of a hill he met his brothers.

'What have ye, Con?'

'The most wonderful thing in the world – a mare's egg.'

'Faith, what is it like?' asked Pat, taking it from Con.

'Go aisy, can't ye? It's very careful ye have to be.'

But the brothers took no heed to Con, and before one could say, 'whist', away rolled the keg down the hill, while all seven ran after it; but before anyone could catch it, it rolled into a clump of bushes, and in an instant out hopped a hare.

'Bedad, there's the foal,' cried Con, and all seven gave chase; but there was no use trying to catch a hare.

'That's the foinest foal that ever was, if he was five year old the devil himself could not catch him,' Con said; and with that the seven omadhauns gave up the chase and went quietly home.

As I said before, everyone had it in mind to get all he could out of the McAndrews.

Everyone said, 'One man might as well have it as another, for they're bound to spend every penny they have.'

So their money dwindled away; then a fine horse would go for a few bits of glass they took for precious stones, and by and by a couple of pigs or a pair of fine geese for a bit of ribbon to tie on a hat; and at last their land began to go.

One day Shamus was sitting by his fire-place warming himself, and to make a good fire he threw on a big heap of turf so that by and by it got roaring hot, and instead of feeling chilly as he had before, Shamus got as hot as a spare rib on a spit. Just then in came his youngest brother.

'That's a great fire ye have here, Shamus.'

'It is, indade, and too near it is to me; run like a good boy to Giblin, the mason, and see if he can't move the chimney to the other side of the room.'

The youngest McAndrew did as he was bid, and soon in came Giblin, the mason.

'Ye're in a sad plight, Shamus, roasting alive; what can I do for ye?'

'Can ye move the chimney over beyant?'

'Faith, I can, but ye will have to move a bit; just go out for a walk with yer brother, and the job will be done when ye come back.'

Shamus did as he was bid, and Giblin took the chair the omadhaun was sitting on and moved it away from the fire, and then sat down for a quiet laugh for himself and to consider on the price he'd charge for the job.

When Shamus came back, Giblin led him to the chair, saying, 'Now, isn't that a great deal better?'

'Ye're a fine man, Giblin, and ye did it without making a bit of dirt; what'll I give ye for so fine a job?'

'If ye wouldn't mind, I'd like the meadow field nearing on mine. It's little enough for a job like that.'

'It's yours and welcome, Giblin;' and without another word the deed was drawn.

That was the finest of the McAndrew fields, and the only pasture land left to Shamus.

It was not long before it came about that first one and then another lost the house he lived in, until all had to live together in the father's old place.

O'Toole and Giblin had encroached field by field, and there was nothing left but the old house and a strip of garden that none of them knew how to till.

It was hard times for the seven McAndrews, but they were happy and contented as long as they had enough to eat, and that they had surely, for the wives of the men who got away all their fine lands and cattle, had sore hearts when they saw their men enriched at the expense of the omadhauns, and every day, unbeknown to their husbands, they carried them meat and drink.

O'Toole and Giblin now had their avaricious eyes set on the house and garden, and they were on the watch for a chance to clutch them, when luck, or something worse, threw the chance in the way of O'Toole.

He was returning from town one day just in the cool of the afternoon, when he spied the seven brothers by the roadside, sitting in a circle facing each other.

'What may ye be doing here instead of earning yer salt, ye seven big sturks?'

'We're in a bad fix, Mr O'Toole,' answered Pat. 'We can't get up.'

'What's to hinder ye from getting up? I'd like to know.'

'Don't ye see our feet are all here together in the middle, and not for the life of us can we each tell our own. You see if one of us gets up he don't know what pair of feet to take with him.'

O'Toole was never so ready to laugh before in his life, but he thought, 'Now's me chance to get the house and garden before Giblin, the mason, comes round;' so he looked very grave and said, 'I suppose it is hard to tell one man's feet from another's when they're all there in a heap, but I think I can help you as I have many a time before. It would be a sorry day for ye if ye did not have me for a neighbour. What will ye give me if I help you find yer feet?'

'Anything, anything we have, so that we can get up from here,' answered the whole seven together.

'Will ye give me the house and garden?'

'Indade we will; what good is a house and garden, if we have to sit here all the rest of our lives?'

'Then it's a bargain,' said O'Toole; and with that he went over to the side of the road and pulled a good stout rod. Then he commenced to belabour the poor McAndrews over the heads, feet, shoulders, and any place he could get in a stroke, until with screeches of pain they all jumped up, everyone finding his own feet, and away they ran.

So O'Toole got the last of the property of the McAndrews, and there was nothing left for them but to go and beg.

The Greek Princess and the Young Gardener

There was once a king, but I didn't hear what country he was over, and he had one very beautiful daughter. Well, he was getting old and sickly, and the doctors found out that the finest medicine in the world for him was the apples of a tree that grew in the orchard just under his window. So you may be sure he had the tree well minded, and used to get the apples counted from the time they were the size of small marbles. One harvest, just as they were beginning to turn ripe, the king was awakened one night by the flapping of wings outside in the orchard; and when he looked out, what did he see but a bird among the branches of his tree. Its feathers were so bright that they made a light all round them, and the minute it saw the king in his nightcap and nightshirt it picked off an apple, and flew away. 'Oh, botheration to that thief of a gardener!' says the king, 'This is a nice way he's watching my precious fruit.'

He didn't sleep a wink the rest of the night; and as soon as anyone was stirring in the palace, he sent for the gardener, and abused him for his neglect.

'Please your majesty,' says he, 'not another apple you shall lose! My three sons are the best shots at the bow and arrow in the kingdom, and they and myself will watch in turn every night.'

When the night came, the gardener's eldest son took his post in the garden, with his bow strung and his arrow between his fingers, and watched, and watched. But at the dead hour, the king, that was wide awake, heard the flapping of wings, and ran to the window. There was the bright bird in the tree, and the boy fast asleep, sitting with his back to the wall, and his bow on his lap.

'Rise, you lazy thief!' says the king. 'There's the bird again, botheration to her!'

Up jumped the poor fellow; but while he was fumbling with the arrow and the string, away was the bird with the nicest apple on the tree. Well, to be sure, how the king fumed and fretted, and how he abused the gardener and the boy, and what a twenty-four hours he spent till midnight came again!

He had his eye this time on the second son of the gardener; but though he was up and lively enough when the clock began to strike twelve, it wasn't done with the last bang when he saw him stretched like one dead on the long grass, and saw the bright bird again, and heard the flap of her wings, and saw her carry away the third apple. The poor fellow woke with the roar the king let at him, and even was in time enough to let fly an arrow after the bird. He did not hit her, you may depend; and though the king was mad enough, he saw the poor fellows were under *pishtrogues*, and could not help it.

Well, he had some hopes out of the youngest, for he was a brave, active young fellow, that had everybody's good word. There he was ready, and there was the king watching him, and talking to him at the first stroke of twelve. At the last clang, the brightness coming before the bird lighted up the wall and the trees, and the rushing of the wings was heard as it flew into the branches; but at the same instant the crack of the arrow on her side might be heard a quarter of a mile off. Down came the arrow and a large bright feather along with it, and away was the bird, with a screech that was enough to break the drum of your ear. She hadn't time to carry off an apple; and bedad, when the feather was thrown up into the king's room it was heavier than lead, and turned out to be the finest beaten gold.

Well, there was great *cooramuch* made about the youngest boy next day, and he watched night after night for a week, but not a mite of a bird or bird's feather was to be seen, and then the king told him to go home and sleep. Everyone admired the beauty of the gold feather beyond anything, but the king was fairly bewitched. He was turning it round and round, and rubbing it against his forehead and his nose the live-long day; and at last he proclaimed that he'd give his daughter and half his kingdom to whoever would bring him the bird with the gold feathers, dead or alive.

The gardener's eldest son had great conceit of himself, and

away he went to look for the bird. In the afternoon he sat down under a tree to rest himself, and eat a bit of bread and cold meat that he had in his wallet, when up comes as fine a looking fox as you'd see in the burrow of Munfin. 'Musha, sir,' says he, 'would you spare a bit of that meat to a poor body that's hungry?'

'Well,' says the other, 'you must have the divil's own assurance, you common robber, to ask me such a question. Here's the answer,' and he let fly at the *moddhereen rua*.

The arrow scraped from his side up over his back, as if he was made of hammered iron, and stuck in a tree a couple of perches off.

'Foul play,' says the fox; 'but I respect your young brother, and will give a bit of advice. At nightfall you'll come into a village. One side of the street you'll see a large room lighted up, and filled with young men and women, dancing and drinking. The other side you'll see a house with no light, only from the fire in the front room, and no one near it but a man and his wife, and their child. Take a fool's advice, and get lodging there.' With that he curled his tail over his crupper, and trotted off.

The boy found things as the fox said, but *begonies* he chose the dancing and drinking, and there we'll leave him. In a week's time, when they got tired at home waiting for him, the second son said he'd try his fortune, and off he set. He was just as ill-natured and foolish as his brother, and the same thing happened to him. Well, when a week was over, away went the youngest of all, and as sure as the hearth-money, he sat under the same tree, and pulled out his bread and meat, and the same fox came up and saluted him. Well, the young fellow shared his dinner with the *moddhereen*, and he wasn't long beating about the bush, but told the other he knew all about his business.

'I'll help you,' says he, 'if I find you're biddable. So just at nightfall you'll come into a village . . . Goodbye till tomorrow.'

It was just as the fox said, but the boy took care not to go near dancer, drinker, fiddler or piper. He got welcome in the quiet house to supper and bed, and was on his journey next morning before the sun was the height of the trees.

He wasn't gone a quarter of a mile when he saw the fox coming out of a wood that was by the roadside.

'Good-morrow, fox,' says one.

'Good-morrow, sir,' says the other.

'Have you any notion how far you have to travel till you find the golden bird?'

'Dickens a notion have I – how could I?'

'Well, I have. She's in the king of Spain's palace, and that's a good two hundred miles off.'

'Oh, dear! We'll be a week going.'

'No, we won't. Sit down on my tail, and we'll soon make the road short.'

'Tail, indeed! That 'ud be the droll saddle, my poor *moddhereen*.'

'Do as I tell you, or I'll leave you to yourself.'

Well, rather than vex him he sat down on the tail that was spread out level like a wing, and away they went like thought. They overtook the wind that was before them, and the wind that came after didn't overtake them. In the afternoon, they stopped in a wood near the king of Spain's palace, and there they stayed till nightfall.

'Now,' says the fox, 'I'll go before you to make the minds of the guards easy, and you'll have nothing to do but go from lighted hall to another lighted hall till you find the golden bird in the last. If you have a head on you, you'll bring himself and his cage outside the door, and no one then can lay hands on him or you. If you haven't a head I can't help you, nor no one else.' So he went over to the gates.

In a quarter of an hour the boy followed, and in the first hall he passed he saw a score of armed guards standing upright, but all dead asleep. In the next he saw a dozen, and in the next half a dozen, and in the next three, and in the room beyond that there was no guard at all, nor lamp, nor candle, but it was as bright as day; for there was the golden bird in a common wood and wire cage, and on the table were the three apples turned into solid gold.

On the same table was the most lovely golden cage eye ever beheld, and it entered the boy's head that it would be a thousand pities not to put the precious bird into it, the common cage was so unfit for her. Maybe he thought of the money it was worth; anyhow he made the exchange, and he had soon good reason to be sorry for it. The instant the shoulder of the bird's wing touched the golden wires, he let such a *squawk* out of him as was enough to break all the panes of glass in the windows, and at the same minute the three men, and the half-dozen, and the dozen, and the score men, woke up and clattered their swords and spears, and surrounded the poor boy, and jibed, and cursed, and swore at home, till he didn't know whether it's his foot or head he was standing on. They called the king, and told him what happened, and he put on a very grim face. 'It's on a gibbet you ought to be this moment,' says he, 'but I'll give you a chance of your life, and of the golden bird, too. I lay you under prohibitions, and restrictions, and death, and destruction, to go and bring me the king of Morocco's bay filly that outruns the wind, and leaps over the walls of castle-bawns. When you fetch her into the bawn of this palace, you must get the golden bird, and liberty to go where you please.'

Out passed the boy, very downhearted, but as he went along, who should come out of a brake but the fox again.

'Ah, my friend,' says he, 'I was right when I suspected you hadn't a head on you; but I won't rub your hair again' the grain. Get on my tail again, and when we come to the king of Morocco's palace, we'll see what we can do.'

So away they went like thought. The wind that was before them they would overtake; the wind that was behind them would not overtake them.

Well, the nightfall came on them in a wood near the palace, and says the fox, 'I'll go and make things easy for you at the stables, and when you are leading out the filly, don't let her touch the door, nor doorposts, nor anything but the ground, and that with her hoofs; and if you haven't a head on you once you are in the stable, you'll be worse off than before.'

So the boy delayed for a quarter of an hour, and then he went into the big bawn of the palace. There were two rows of armed men reaching from the gate to the stable, and every man was in the depth of deep sleep, and through them went the boy till he got into the stable. There was the filly, as handsome a beast as ever stretched leg, and there was one stableboy with a currycomb in his hand, and another with a bridle, and another with a sieve of oats, and another with an armful of hay, and all as if they were cut out of stone. The filly was the only live thing in the place except himself. She had a common wood and leather saddle on her back, but a golden saddle with the nicest work on it was hung from the post, and he thought it the greatest pity not to put it in place of the other. Well, I believe there was some *pishrogues* over it for a saddle; anyhow, he took off the other, and put the gold one in its place.

Out came a squeal from the filly's throat when she felt the strange article, that might be heard from Tombrick to Bunclody, and all as ready were the armed men and the stableboys to run and surround the *omadhan* of a boy, and the king of Morocco was soon there along with the rest, with a face on him as black as the sole of your foot. After he stood enjoying the abuse the poor boy got from everybody for some time, he says to him, 'You deserve high hanging for your impudence, but I'll give you a chance for your life and the filly, too. I lay on you all sorts of prohibitions, and restrictions, and death, and destruction, to go bring me Princess Golden Locks, the king of Greece's daughter. When you deliver her into my hand, you may have the "daughter of the wind", and welcome. Come in and take your supper and your rest, and be off at the flight of night.'

The poor boy was down in the mouth, you may suppose, as he was walking away next morning, and very much ashamed when the fox looked up in his face after coming out of the wood.

'What a thing it is,' says he, 'not to have a head when a body wants it worst; and here we have a fine long journey before us to the king of Greece's palace. The worse luck now, the same always. Here, get on my tail, and we'll be making the road shorter.'

So he sat on the fox's tail, and swift as thought they went. The wind that was before them they would overtake it, the wind that was behind them would not overtake them, and in the evening they were eating their bread and cold meat in the wood near the castle.

'Now,' says the fox, when they were done, 'I'll go before you to make things easy. Follow me in a quarter of an hour. Don't let Princess Golden Locks touch the jambs of the doors with her hands, or hair, or clothes, and if you're asked any favour, mind how you answer. Once she's outside the door, no one can take her from you.'

Into the palace walked the boy at the proper time, and there were the score, and the dozen, and the half-dozen, and the three guards all standing up or leaning on their arms, and all dead asleep, and in the farthest room of all was the Princess Golden Locks, as lovely as Venus herself. She was asleep in one chair, and her father, the king of Greece, in another. He stood before her for ever so long with the love sinking deeper into his heart every minute, till at last he went down on one knee, and took her darling white hand in his hand, and kissed it.

When she opened her eyes, she was a little frightened, but I believe not very angry, for the boy, as I call him, was a fine handsome young fellow, and all the respect and love that ever you could think of was in his face. She asked him what he wanted, and he stammered, and blushed, and began his story six times, before she understood it.

'And would you give me up to that ugly black king of Morocco?' says she.

'I am obliged to do so,' says he, 'by prohibitions, and restrictions, and death, and destruction, but I'll have his life and free you, or lose my own. If I can't get you for my wife, my days on the earth will be short.'

'Well,' says she, 'let me take leave of my father at any rate.'

'Ah, I can't do that,' says he, 'or they'd all waken, and myself would be put to death, or sent to some task worse than any I got yet.'

But she asked leave at any rate to kiss the old man; that wouldn't waken him, and then she'd go. How could he refuse her, and his heart tied up in every curl of her hair? But, bedad, the moment her lips touched her father's, he let a cry, and everyone of the score, the dozen guards woke up, and clashed their arms, and were going to make *gibbets* of the foolish boy.

But the king ordered them to hold their hands, till he'd be *insensed* of what it was all about, and when he heard the boy's story he gave him a chance for his life.

'There is,' says he, 'a great heap of clay in front of the palace, that won't let the sun shine on the walls in the middle of summer. Everyone that ever worked at it found two shovelfuls added to it for every one they threw away. Remove it, and I'll let my daughter go with you. If you're the man I suspect you to be, I think she'll be in no danger of being wife to that yellow *Molott*.'

Early next morning was the boy tackled to his work, and for every shovelful he flung away two came back on him, and at last he could hardly get out of the heap that gathered round him. Well, the poor fellow scrambled out some way, and sat down on a sod, and he'd have cried only for the shame of it. He began at it in ever so many places, and one was still worse than the other, and in the heel of the evening, when he was sitting with his head between his hands, who should be standing before him but the fox.

'Well, my poor fellow,' says he, 'you're low enough. Go in: I won't say anything to add to your trouble. Take your supper and your rest: tomorrow will be a new day.'

'How is the work going off?' says the king, when they were at supper.

The Greek princess

'Faith, your majesty,' says the poor boy, 'it's not going off, but coming on it is. I suppose you'll have the trouble of digging me out at sunset tomorrow, and waking me.'

'I hope not,' says the princess, with a smile on her kind face; and the boy was as happy as anything the rest of the evening.

He was wakened up next morning with voices shouting, and bugles blowing, and drums beating, and such a hullibulloo he never heard in his life before. He ran out to see what was the matter, and there, where the heap of clay was the evening before, were soldiers, and servants, and lords, and ladies, dancing like mad for joy that it was gone.

'Ah, my poor fox!' says he to himself. 'This is your work.'

Well, there was little delay about his return. The king was going to send a great retinue with the princess and himself, but he wouldn't let him take the trouble.

'I have a friend,' says he, 'that will bring us both to the king of Morocco's palace in a day, devil fly away with him!'

There was great crying when she was parting from her father.

'Ah!' says he, 'what a lonesome life I'll have now! Your poor brother in the power of that wicked witch, and kept away from us, and now you taken from me in my old age!'

Well, they both were walking on through the wood, and he telling her how much he loved her; out walked the fox from behind a brake, and in a short time he and she were sitting on the brush, and holding one another fast for fear of slipping off, and away they went like thought. The wind that was before them they would overtake it, and in the evening he and she were in the big bawn of the king of Morocco's castle.

'Well,' says he to the boy, 'you've done your duty well; bring out the bay filly. I'd give the full of the bawn of such fillies, if I had them, for this handsome princess. Get on your steed, and here is a good purse of guineas for the road.'

'Thank you,' says he. 'I suppose you'll let me shake hands with the princess before I start.'

'Yes, indeed, and welcome.'

Well, he was some little time about the handshaking, and before it was over he had her fixed snug behind him; and while you could count three, he, and she, and the filly were through all the guards, and a hundred perches away. On they went, and next morning they were in the wood near the king of Spain's palace, and there was the fox before them.

'Leave your princess here with me,' says he, 'and go get the golden bird and the three apples. If you don't bring us back the filly along with the bird, I must carry you both home myself.'

Well, when the king of Spain saw the boy and the filly in the bawn, he made the golden bird, and the golden cage, and the golden apples be brought out and handed to him, and was very thankful and very glad of his prize. But the boy could not part with the nice beast without petting it and rubbing it; and while no one was expecting such a thing, he was up on its back, and through the guards, and a hundred perches away, and he wasn't long till he came to where he left his princess and the fox.

They hurried away till they were safe out of the king of Spain's land, and then they went on easier; and if I was to tell you all the loving things they said to one another, the story wouldn't be over till morning. When they were passing the village of the dance house, they found his two brothers begging, and they brought them along. When they came to where the fox appeared first, he begged the young man to cut off his head and his tail. He would not do it for him; he shivered at the very thought, but the eldest brother was ready enough. The head and tail vanished with the blows, and the body changed into the finest young man you could see, and who was he but the princess's brother that was bewitched. Whatever joy they had before, they had twice as much now, and when they arrived at the palace bonfires were set blazing, oxes roasting, and puncheons of wine put out in the lawn.

The young prince of Greece was married to the king's daughter, and the prince's sister to the gardener's son. He and she went a shorter way back to her father's house, with many attendants, and the king was so glad of the golden bird and the golden apples, that he had sent a waggon full of gold and a waggon full of silver along with them.

Smallhead and the King's Sons

Long ago there lived in Erin a woman who married a man of high degree and had one daughter. Soon after the birth of the daughter the husband died.

The woman was not long a widow when she married a second time, and had two daughters. These two daughters hated their half-sister, thought she was not so wise as another, and nick-named her Smallhead. When the elder of the two sisters was fourteen years old their father died. The mother was in great grief then, and began to pine away. She used to sit at home in the corner and never left the house. Smallhead was kind to her mother, and the mother was fonder of her eldest daughter than of the other two, who were ashamed of her.

At last the two sisters made up in their minds to kill their mother. One day, while their half-sister was gone, they put the mother in a pot, boiled her, and threw the bones outside. When Smallhead came home there was no sign of the mother.

'Where is my mother?' asked she of the other two.

'She went out somewhere. How should we know where she is?'

'Oh, wicked girls! You have killed my mother,' said Smallhead.

Smallhead wouldn't leave the house now at all, and the sisters were very angry.

'No man will marry either one of us,' said they, 'if he sees our fool of a sister.'

Since they could not drive Smallhead from the house they made up their minds to go away themselves. One fine morning they left home unknown to their half-sister and travelled on many miles. When Smallhead discovered that her sisters were gone she hurried after them and never stopped till she came up with the two. They had to go home with her that day, but they scolded her bitterly.

The two settled then to kill Smallhead, so one day they took twenty needles and scattered them outside in a pile of straw. 'We are going to that hill beyond,' said they, 'to stay till evening, and if you have not all the needles that are in that straw outside gathered and on the tables before us, we'll have your life.'

Away they went to the hill. Smallhead sat down, and was crying bitterly when a short grey cat walked in and spoke to her.

'Why do you cry and lament so?' asked the cat.

'My sisters abuse me and beat me,' answered Smallhead. 'This morning they said they would kill me in the evening unless I had all the needles in the straw outside gathered before them.'

'Sit down here,' said the cat, 'and dry your tears.'

The cat soon found the twenty needles and brought them to Smallhead. 'Stop there now,' said the cat, 'and listen to what I tell you. I am your mother; your sisters killed me and destroyed my body, but don't harm them; do them good, do the best you can for them, save them: obey my words and it will be better for you in the end.'

The cat went away for herself, and the sisters came home in the evening. The needles were on the table before them. Oh, but they were vexed and angry when they saw the twenty needles, and they said someone was helping their sister!

One night when Smallhead was in bed and asleep they started

away again, resolved this time never to return. Smallhead slept till morning. When she saw that the sisters were gone she followed, traced them from place to place, inquired here and there day after day, till one evening some person told her that they were in the house of an old hag, a terrible enchantress, who had one son and three daughters: that the house was a bad place to be in, for the old hag had more power of witchcraft than anyone and was very wicked.

Smallhead hurried away to save her sisters, and facing the house knocked at the door, and asked lodgings for God's sake.

'Oh, then,' said the hag, 'it is hard to refuse anyone lodgings, and besides on such a wild, stormy night. I wonder if you are anything to the young ladies who came the way this evening?'

The two sisters heard this and were angry enough that Smallhead was in it, but they said nothing, not wishing the old hag to know their relationship. After supper the hag told the three strangers to sleep in a room on the right side of the house. When her own daughters were going to bed Smallhead saw her tie a ribbon around the neck of each one of them, and heard her say, 'Do you sleep in the left-hand bed.' Smallhead hurried and said to her sisters, 'Come quickly, or I'll tell the woman who you are.'

They took the bed in the left-hand room and were in it before the hag's daughters came.

'Oh,' said the daughers, 'the other bed is as good.' So they took the bed in the right-hand room. When Smallhead knew that the hag's daughters were asleep she rose, took the ribbons off their necks, and put them on her sister's necks and on her own. She lay awake and watched them. After a while she heard the hag say to her son, 'Go, now, and kill the three girls; they have the clothes and money.'

'You have killed enough in your life and so let these go,' said the son.

But the old woman would not listen. The boy rose up, fearing his mother, and taking a long knife, went to the right-hand room and cut the throats of the three girls without ribbons. He went to bed then for himself, and when Smallhead found that the old hag was asleep she roused her sisters, told what had happened, made them dress quickly and follow her. Believe me, they were willing and glad to follow her this time.

The three travelled briskly and came soon to a bridge, called at that time 'The Bridge of Blood'. Whoever had killed a person could not cross the bridge. When the three girls came to the bridge the two sisters stopped: they could not go a step further. Smallhead ran across and went back again.

'If I did not know that you killed our mother,' said she, 'I might know it now, for this is the Bridge of Blood.'

She carried one sister over the bridge on her back and then the other. Hardly was this done when the hag was at the bridge.

'Bad luck to you, Smallhead!' said she. 'I did not know that it was you that was in it last evening. You have killed my three daughters.'

'It wasn't I that killed them, but yourself,' said Smallhead.

The old hag could not cross the bridge, so she began to curse, and she put every curse on Smallhead that she could remember. The sisters travelled on till they came to a king's castle. They heard that two servants were needed in the castle.

'Go now,' said Smallhead to the two sisters, 'and ask for service. Be faithful and do well. You can never go back by the road you came.'

The two found employment at the king's castle. Smallhead took lodgings in the house of a blacksmith near by.

'I should be glad to find a place as kitchen-maid in the castle,' said Smallhead to the blacksmith's wife.

'I will go to the castle and find a place for you if I can,' said the woman.

The blacksmith's wife found a place for Smallhead as kitchen-maid in the castle, and she went there next day.

'I must be careful,' thought Smallhead, 'and do my best. I am in a strange place. My two sisters are here in the king's castle. Who knows, we may have great fortune yet.'

She dressed neatly and was cheerful. Everyone liked her, liked her better than her sisters, though they were beautiful. The king had two sons, one at home and the other abroad. Smallhead thought to herself one day, 'It is time for the son who is here in the

THE BRIDGE OF BLOOD

castle to marry. I will speak to him the first time I can.' One day she saw him alone in the garden, went up to him, and said, 'Why are you not getting married, it is high time for you?'

He only laughed and thought she was too bold, but then thinking that she was a simple-minded girl who wished to be pleasant, he said, 'I will tell you the reason: My grandfather bound my father by an oath never to let his oldest son marry until he could get the Sword of Light, and I am afraid that I shall be long without marrying.'

'Do you know where the Sword of Light is, or who has it?' asked Smallhead.

'I do,' said the king's son. 'An old hag who has great power and enchantment, and she lives a long distance from this, beyond the Bridge of Blood. I cannot go there myself, I cannot cross the bridge, for I have killed men in battle. Even if I could cross the bridge I would not go, for many is the king's son that hag has destroyed or enchanted.'

'Suppose some person were to bring the Sword of Light, and that person a woman, would you marry her?'

'I would, indeed,' said the king's son.

'If you promise to marry my elder sister I will strive to bring the Sword of Light.'

'I will promise most willingly,' said the king's son.

Next morning early, Smallhead set out on her journey. Calling at the first shop she bought a stone weight of salt, and went on her way, never stopping or resting till she reached the hag's house at nightfall. She climbed to the gable, looked down, and saw the son making a great pot of stirabout for his mother, and she hurrying him. 'I am as hungry as a hawk!' cried she.

Whenever the boy looked away, Smallhead dropped salt down, dropped it when he was not looking, dropped it till she had the whole stone of salt in the stirabout. The old hag waited and waited till at last she cried out, 'Bring the stirabout. I am starving! Bring the pot. I will eat from the pot. Give the milk here as well.'

The boy brought the stirabout and the milk, the old woman began to eat, but the first taste she got she spat out and screamed, 'You put salt in the pot in place of meal!'

'I did not, mother.'

'You did, and it's a mean trick that you played on me. Throw this stirabout to the pig outside and go for water to the well in the field.'

'I cannot go,' said the boy, 'the night is too dark; I might fall into the well.'

'You must go and bring the water; I cannot live till morning without eating.'

'I am as hungry as yourself,' said the boy, 'but how can I go to the well without a light? I will not go unless you give me a light.'

'If I give you the Sword of Light there is no knowing who may follow you; maybe that devil of a Smallhead is outside.'

But sooner than fast till morning the old hag gave the Sword of Light to her son, warning him to take good care of it. He took the Sword of Light and went out. As he saw no one when he came to the well he left the sword on the top of the steps going down to the water, so as to have good light. He had not gone down many steps when Smallhead had the sword, and away she ran over hills, dales, and valleys towards the Bridge of Blood.

The boy shouted and screamed with all his might. Out ran the hag. 'Where is the sword?' cried she.

'Someone took it from the step.'

Off rushed the hag, following the light, but she didn't come near Smallhead till she was over the bridge.

'Give me the Sword of Light, or bad luck to you,' cried the hag.

'Indeed, then, I will not; I will keep it, and bad luck to yourself,' answered Smallhead.

On the following morning she walked up to the king's son and said, 'I have the Sword of Light; now will you marry my sister?'

'I will,' said he.

The king's son married Smallhead's sister and got the Sword of Light. Smallhead stayed no longer in the kitchen – the sister didn't care to have her in kitchen or parlour.

The king's second son came home. He was not long in the castle when Smallhead said to herself, 'Maybe he will marry my second sister.'

She saw him one day in the garden and went towards him; he

said something, she answered, then asked, 'Is it not time for you to be getting married like your brother?'

'When my grandfather was dying,' said the young man, 'he bound my father not to let his second son marry till he had the Black Book. This book used to shine and give brighter light than ever the Sword of Light did, and I suppose it does yet. The old hag beyond the Bridge of Blood has the book, and no one dares to go near her, for many is the king's son killed or enchanted by that woman.'

'Would you marry my second sister if you were to get the Black Book?'

'I would, indeed; I would marry any woman if I got the Black Book with her. The Sword of Light and the Black Book were in our family till my grandfather's time, then they were stolen by that cursed old hag.'

'I will have the book,' said Smallhead, 'or die in the trial to get it.'

Knowing that stirabout was the main food of the hag, Smallhead settled in her mind to play another trick. Taking a bag she scraped the chimney, gathered about a stone of soot, and took it with her. The night was dark and rainy. When she reached the hag's house, she climbed up the gable to the chimney and found that the son was making stirabout for his mother. She dropped the soot down by degrees till at last the whole stone of soot was in the pot; then she scraped around the top of the chimney till a lump of soot fell on the boy's hand.

'Oh, mother,' said he, 'the night is wet and soft, the soot is falling.'

'Cover the pot,' said the hag. 'Be quick with that stirabout, I am starving.'

The boy took the pot to his mother.

'Bad luck to you,' cried the hag the moment she tasted the stirabout, 'this is full of soot; throw it out to the pig.'

'If I throw it out there is no water inside to make more, and I'll not go in the dark and rain to the well.'

'You must go!' screamed she.

'I'll not stir a foot out of this unless I get a light,' said the boy.

'Is it the book you are thinking of, you fool, to take it and lose it as you did the sword? Smallhead is watching you.'

'How could Smallhead, the creature, be outside all the time? If you have no use for the water you can do without it.'

Sooner than stop fasting till morning, the hag gave her son the book, saying, 'Do not put this down or let it from your hand till you come in, or I'll have your life.'

The boy took the book and went to the well. Smallhead followed him carefully. He took the book down into the well with him, and when he was stooping to dip water she snatched the book and pushed him into the well, where he came very near drowning.

Smallhead was far away when the boy recovered, and began to scream and shout to his mother. She came in a hurry, and finding that the book was gone, fell into such a rage that she thrust a knife into her son's heart and ran after Smallhead, who had crossed the bridge before the hag could come up with her.

When the old woman saw Smallhead on the other side of the bridge facing her and dancing with delight, she screamed, 'You took the Sword of Light and the Black Book, and your two sisters are married. Oh, then, bad luck to you. I will put my curse on you wherever you go. You have all my children killed, and I a poor, feeble, old woman.'

'Bad luck to yourself,' said Smallhead. 'I am not afraid of a curse from the likes of you. If you had lived an honest life you wouldn't be as you are today.'

'Now, Smallhead,' said the old hag, 'you have me robbed of everything, and my children destroyed. Your two sisters are well married. Your fortune began with my ruin. Come, now, and take care of me in my old age. I'll take my curse from you, and you will have good luck. I bind myself never to harm a hair of your head.'

Smallhead thought awhile, promised to do this, and said, 'If you harm me, or try to harm me, it will be the worse for yourself.'

The old hag was satisfied and went home. Smallhead went to the castle and was received with great joy. Next morning she found the king's son in the garden, and said, 'If you marry my sister tomorrow, you will have the Black Book.'

'I will marry her gladly,' said the king's son.

Next day the marriage was celebrated and the king's son got the book. Smallhead remained in the castle about a week, then she left good health with her sisters and went to the hag's house. The old woman was glad to see her and showed the girl her work. All Smallhead had to do was to wait on the hag and feed a large pig that she had.

'I am fatting that pig,' said the hag; 'he is seven years old now, and the longer you keep a pig the harder his meat is: we'll keep this pig a while longer, and then we'll kill and eat him.'

Smallhead did her work; the old hag taught her some things, and Smallhead learned herself far more than the hag dreamt of. The girl fed the pig three times a day, never thinking that he could be anything but a pig. The hag had sent word to a sister that she had in the Eastern World, bidding her come and they would kill the pig and have a great feast. The sister came, and one day when the hag was going to walk with her sister she said to Smallhead, 'Give the pig plenty of meal today; this is the last food he'll have; give him his fill.'

The pig had his own mind and knew what was coming. He put his nose under the pot and threw it on Smallhead's toes, and she barefoot. With that she ran into the house for a stick, and seeing a rod on the edge of the loft, snatched it and hit the pig.

That moment the pig was a splendid young man.

Smallhead was amazed.

'Never fear,' said the young man, 'I am the son of a king that the old hag hated, the king of Munster. She stole me from my father seven years ago and enchanted me – made a pig of me.'

Smallhead told the king's son, then, how the hag had treated her. 'I must make a pig of you again,' said she, 'for the hag is coming. Be patient and I'll save you, if you promise to marry me.'

'I promise you,' said the king's son.

With that she struck him, and he was a pig again. She put the switch in its place and was at her work when the two sisters came. The pig ate his meal now with a good heart, for he felt sure of rescue.

'Who is that girl you have in the house, and where did you find her?' asked the sister.

'All my children died of the plague, and I took this girl to help me. She is a very good servant.'

At night the hag slept in one room, her sister in another, and Smallhead in a third. When the two sisters were sleeping soundly Smallhead rose, stole the hag's magic book, and then took the rod. She went next to where the pig was, and with one blow of the rod made a man of him.

With the help of the magic book Smallhead made two doves of herself and the king's son, and they took flight through the air and flew on without stopping. Next morning the hag called Smallhead, but she did not come. She hurried out to see the pig. The pig was gone. She ran to her book. Not a sign of it.

'Oh!' cried she. 'That villain of a Smallhead has robbed me. She has stolen my book, made a man of the pig, and taken him away with her.'

What could she do but tell her whole story to the sister. 'Go you,' said she, 'and follow them. You have more enchantment than Smallhead has.'

'How am I to know them?' asked the sister.

'Bring the first two strange things that you find; they will turn themselves into something wonderful.'

The sister then made a hawk of herself and flew away as swiftly as any March wind.

'Look behind,' said Smallhead to the king's son some hours later; 'see what is coming.'

'I see nothing,' said he, 'but a hawk coming swiftly.'

'That is the hag's sister. She has three times more enchantment than the hag herself. But fly down on the ditch and be picking yourself as doves do in rainy weather, and maybe she'll pass without seeing us.'

The hawk saw the doves, but thinking them nothing wonderful, flew on till evening, and then went back to her sister.

'Did you see anything wonderful?'

'I did not; I saw only two doves, and they picking themselves.'

'You fool, those doves were Smallhead and the king's son. Off with you in the morning and don't let me see you again without the two with you.'

Away went the hawk a second time, and swiftly as Smallhead and the king's son flew, the hawk was gaining on them. Seeing this Smallhead and the king's son dropped down into a large village, and, it being market-day, they made two heather brooms of themselves. The two brooms began to sweep the road without anyone holding them, and swept toward each other. This was a great wonder. Crowds gathered at once around the two brooms.

The old hag flying over in the form of a hawk saw this and thinking that it must be Smallhead and the king's son were in it, came down, turned into a woman, and said to herself, 'I'll have those two brooms.'

She pushed forward so quickly through the crowd that she came near knocking down a man standing before her. The man was vexed.

'You cursed old hag!' cried he. 'Do you want to knock us down?' With that he gave her a blow and drove her against another man, that man gave her a push that sent her spinning against a third man, and so on till between them all they came near putting the life out of her, and pushed her away from the brooms. A woman in the crowd called out then, 'It would be nothing but right to knock the head off that old hag, and she trying to push us away from the mercy of God, for it was God who sent the brooms to sweep the road for us.'

'True for you,' said another woman. With that the people were as angry as angry could be, and were ready to kill the hag. They were going to take the head off the hag when she made a hawk of herself and flew away, vowing never to do another stroke of work for her sister. She might do her own work or let it alone.

When the hawk disappeared the two heather brooms rose and turned into doves. The people felt sure when they saw the doves that the brooms were a blessing from heaven, and it was the old hag that drove them away.

On the following day Smallhead and the king's son saw his father's castle, and the two came down not too far from it in their own forms. Smallhead was a very beautiful woman now, and why not? She had the magic and didn't spare it. She made herself as beautiful as ever she could: the like of her was not to be seen in that kingdom or the next one.

The king's son was in love with her that minute, and did not wish to part with her, but she would not go with him.

'When you are at your father's castle,' said Smallhead, 'all will be overjoyed to see you, and the king will give a great feast in your honour. If you kiss anyone or let any living thing kiss you, you'll forget me for ever.'

'I will not let even my own mother kiss me,' said he.

The king's son went to the castle. All were overjoyed; they had thought him dead, had not seen him for seven years. He would let no one come near to kiss him. 'I am bound by oath to kiss no one,' said he to his mother. At that moment an old greyhound came in, and with one spring was on his shoulder licking his face: all that the king's son had gone through in seven years was forgotten in one moment.

Smallhead went toward a forge near the castle. The smith had a wife far younger than himself, and a stepdaughter. They were no beauties. In the rear of the forge was a well and a tree growing over it. 'I will go up in that tree,' thought Smallhead. 'and spend the night in it.' She went up and sat just over the well. She was not long in the tree when the moon came out high above the hill tops and shone on the well. The blacksmith's stepdaughter, coming for water, looked down in the well, saw the face of the woman above in the tree, thought it her own face, and cried, 'Oh, then, to have me bringing water to a smith, and I such a beauty. I'll never bring another drop to him.' With that she cast the pail in the ditch and ran off to find a king's son to marry.

When she was not coming with the water, and the blacksmith waiting to wash after his day's work in the forge, he sent the mother. The mother had nothing but a pot to get the water in, so off she went with that, and coming to the well saw the beautiful face in the water.

'Oh, you black, swarthy villain of a smith,' cried she, 'bad luck to the hour that I met you, and I such a beauty. I'll never draw another drop of water for the life of you!'

She threw the pot down, broke it, and hurried away to find some king's son.

When neither mother nor daughter came back with water the smith himself went to see what was keeping them. He saw the pail in the ditch, and, catching it, went to the well; looking down, he saw the beautiful face of a woman in the water. Being a man, he knew that it was not his own face that was in it, so he looked up, and there in the tree saw a woman. He spoke to her and said, 'I know now why my wife and her daughter did not bring water. They saw your face in the well, and, thinking themselves too good for me, ran away. You must come now and keep the house till I find them.'

'I will help you,' said Smallhead. She came down, went to the smith's house, and showed the road that the women took. The smith hurried after them, and found the two in a village ten miles away. He explained their own folly to them, and they came home.

The mother and daughter washed fine linen for the castle. Smallhead saw them ironing one day, and said, 'Sit down: I will iron for you.'

She caught the iron, and in an hour had the work of the day done.

The women were delighted. In the evening the daughter took the linen to the housekeeper at the castle.

'Who ironed this linen?' asked the housekeeper.

'My mother and I.'

'Indeed, then, you did not. You can't do the like of that work, and tell me who did it.'

The girl was in dread now and answered, 'It is a woman who is stopping with us who did the ironing.'

The housekeeper went to the queen and showed her the linen.

'Send that woman to the castle,' said the queen.

Smallhead went: the queen welcomed her, wondered at her beauty; put her over all the maids in the castle. Smallhead could do anything; everybody was fond of her. The king's son never knew that he had seen her before, and she lived in the castle a year; what the queen told her she did.

The king had made a match for his son with the daughter of the king of Ulster. There was a great feast in the castle in honour of the young couple; the marriage was to be a week later. The bride's father brought many of his people who were versed in all kinds of tricks and enchantment.

The king knew that Smallhead could do many things, for neither the queen nor himself had asked her to do a thing that she did not do in a twinkle.

'Now,' said the king to the queen, 'I think she can do something that his people cannot do.' He summoned Smallhead and asked, 'Can you amuse the strangers?'

'I can if you wish me to do so.'

When the time came and the Ulster men had shown their best tricks, Smallhead came forward and raised the window, which was forty feet from the ground. She had a small ball of thread in her hand; she tied one end of the thread to the window, threw the ball out and over a wall near the castle; then she passed out the window, walked on the thread and kept time to music from players that no man could see. She came in; all cheered her and were greatly delighted.

'I can do that,' said the king of Ulster's daughter, and sprang out on the string; but as she did, she fell and broke her neck on the stones below. There were cries, there was lamentation, and, in place of a marriage, a funeral.

The king's son was angry and grieved and wanted to drive Smallhead from the castle in some way.

'She is not to blame,' said the king of Munster, who did nothing but praise her.

Another year passed: the king got the daughter of the king of Connacht for his son. There was a great feast before the wedding day, and as the Connacht people are full of enchantment and witchcraft, the king of Munster called Smallhead and said, 'Now show the best trick of any.'

'I will,' said Smallhead.

When the feast was over and the Connacht men had shown their tricks the king of Munster called Smallhead.

She stood before the company, threw two grains of wheat on the floor, and spoke some magic words. There was a hen and a cock there before her of beautiful plumage; she threw a grain of wheat between them; the hen sprang to eat the wheat, the cock gave her a blow of his bill, the hen drew back, looked at him, and said, 'Bad luck to you, you wouldn't do the like of that when I was serving the old hag and you her pig, and I made a man of you and gave you back your own form.'

The king's son looked at her and thought, 'There must be something in this.'

Smallhead threw a second grain. The cock pecked the hen again. 'Oh,' said the hen, 'you would not do that the day the hag's sister was hunting us, and we two doves.'

The king's son was still more astonished.

She threw a third grain. The cock struck the hen, and she said, 'You would not do that to me the day I made two heather brooms out of you and myself.' She threw a fourth grain. The cock pecked the hen a fourth time. 'You would not do that the day you promised not to let any living thing kiss you or kiss anyone yourself but me – but then you let the hound kiss you and you forgot me.'

The king's son made one bound forward, embraced and kissed Smallhead, and told the king his whole story from beginning to end.

'This is my wife,' said he; 'I'll marry no other woman.'

'Whose wife will my daughter be?' asked the king of Connacht.

'Oh, she will be the wife of the man who will marry her,' said the king of Munster, 'my son gave his word to this woman before he saw your daughter, and he must keep it.'

So Smallhead married the king of Munster's son.

The Legend of Knockgrafton

There was once a poor man who lived in the fertile glen of Aherlow, at the foot of the gloomy Galtee mountains, and he had a great hump on his back: he looked just as if his body had been rolled up and placed upon his shoulders; and his head was pressed down with the weight so much that his chin, when he was sitting, used to rest upon his knees for support. The country people were rather shy of meeting him in any lonesome place, for though, poor creature, he was as harmless and as inoffensive as a newborn infant, yet his deformity was so great that he scarcely appeared to be a human creature, and some ill-minded persons had set strange stories about him afloat. He was said to have a great knowledge of herbs and charms; but certain it was that he had a mighty skilful hand in plaiting straw and rushes into hats and baskets, which was the way he made his livelihood.

Lusmore, for that was the nickname put upon him by reason of his always wearing a sprig of the fairy cap, or lusmore (the foxglove), in his little straw hat, would ever get a higher penny for his plaited work than anyone else, and perhaps that was the reason why someone, out of envy, had circulated the strange stories about him. Be that as it may, it happened that he was returning one evening from the pretty town of Cahir towards Cappagh, and as little Lusmore walked very slowly, on account of the great hump upon his back, it was quite dark when he came to the old moat of Knockgrafton, which stood on the right-hand side of his road. Tired and weary was he, and noways comfortable in his own mind at thinking how much farther he had to travel, and that he should be walking all the night; so he sat down under the moat to rest himself, and began looking mournfully enough upon the moon.

Presently there rose a wild strain of unearthly melody upon the ear of little Lusmore; he listened, and he thought that he had never heard such ravishing music before. It was like the sound of many voices, each mingling and blending with the other so strangely that they seemed to be one, though all singing different strains, and the words of the song were these –

Da Luan, Da Mort, Da Luan, Da Mort, Da Luan, Da Mort;

when there would be a moment's pause, and then the round of melody went on again.

Lusmore listened attentively, scarcely drawing his breath lest he might lose the slightest note. He now plainly perceived that the singing was within the moat; and though at first it had charmed him so much, he began to get tired of hearing the same round sung over and over so often without any change; so availing himself of the pause when the *Da Luan, Da Mort*, had been sung three times, he took up the tune, and raised it with the words *augus Da Cadine*, and then went on singing with the voices inside of the moat, *Da Luan, Da Mort*, finishing the melody, when the pause again came, with *augus Da Cadine*.

The fairies within Knockgrafton, for the song was a fairy melody, when they heard this addition to the tune, were so much delighted that, with instant resolve, it was determined to bring the mortal among them, whose musical skill so far exceeded theirs, and little Lusmore was conveyed into their company with the eddying speed of a whirlwind.

Glorious to behold was the sight that burst upon him as he came down through the moat, twirling round and round, with the lightness of a straw, to the sweetest music that kept time to his motion. The greatest honour was then paid him, for he was put above all the musicians, and he had servants tending upon him, and everything to his heart's content, and a hearty welcome to all; and, in short, he was made as much of as if he had been the first man in the land.

Presently Lusmore saw a great consultation going forward among the fairies, and, notwithstanding all their civility, he felt very much frightened, until one stepping out from the rest came up to him and said:

> 'Lusmore! Lusmore!
> Doubt not, nor deplore,
> For the hump which you bore
> On your back is no more;
> Look down on the floor,
> And view it, Lusmore!'

When these words were said, poor little Lusmore felt himself so light, and so happy, that he thought he could have bounded at one jump over the moon, like the cow in the history of the cat and the fiddle; and he saw, with inexpressible pleasure, his hump tumble down upon the ground from his shoulders. He then tried to lift up his head, and he did so with becoming caution, fearing that he might knock it against the ceiling of the grand hall, where he was; he looked round and round again with greatest wonder and delight upon everything, which appeared more and more beautiful; and, overpowered at beholding such a resplendent scene, his head grew dizzy, and his eyesight became dim. At last he fell into a sound sleep, and when he awoke he found that it was broad daylight, the sun shining brightly, and the birds singing sweetly; and that he was lying just at the foot of the moat of Knockgrafton, with the cows and sheep grazing peacefully round about him. The first thing Lusmore did, after saying his prayers, was to put his hand behind to feel for his hump, but no sign of one was there on his back, and he looked at himself with great pride, for he had now become a well-shaped dapper little fellow, and more than that, found himself in a full suit of new clothes, which he concluded the fairies had made for him.

Towards Cappagh he went, stepping out as lightly, and springing up at every step as if he had been all his life a dancing-master. Not a creature who met Lusmore knew him without his hump, and he had a great work to persuade everyone that he was the same man – in truth he was not, so far as outward appearance went.

Of course it was not long before the story of Lusmore's hump got about, and a great wonder was made of it. Through the country, for miles round, it was the talk of everyone, high and low.

One morning, as Lusmore was sitting contented enough, at his cabin door, up came an old woman to him, and asked him if he could direct her to Cappagh.

'I need give you no directions, my good woman,' said Lusmore, 'for this is Cappagh; and whom may you want here?'

'I have come,' said the woman, 'out of Decie's country, in the county of Waterford looking after one Lusmore, who, I have heard tell, had his hump taken off by the fairies; for there is a son of a gossip of mine who has got a hump on him that will be his death; and maybe if he could use the same charm as Lusmore, the hump may be taken off him. And now I have told you the reason of my coming so far: 'tis to find out about this charm, if I can.'

Lusmore, who was ever a good-natured little fellow, told the woman all the particulars, how he had raised the tune for the fairies at Knockgrafton, how his hump had been removed from his shoulders, and how he had got a new suit of clothes into the bargain.

The woman thanked him very much, and then went away quite happy and easy in her own mind. When she came back to her gossip's house, in the county of Waterford, she told her every-thing that Lusmore had said, and they put the little hump-backed man, who was a peevish and cunning creature from his birth, upon a car, and took him all the way across the country. It was a long journey, but they did not care for that, so the hump was taken from off him; and they brought him, just at nightfall, and left him under the old moat of Knockgrafton.

Jack Madden, for that was the humpy man's name, had not been sitting there long when he heard the tune going on within the moat much sweeter than before; for the fairies were singing it the way Lusmore had settled their music for them, and the song was going on; *Da Luan, Da Mort, Da Luan, Da Mort, Da Luan, Da Mort, augus Da Cadine*, without ever stopping. Jack Madden, who was in a great hurry to get quit of his hump, never thought of waiting until the fairies had done, or watching for a fit opportunity to raise the tune higher again than Lusmore had; so having heard them sing it over seven times without stopping, out he bawls, never minding the time or the humour of the tune, or how he could bring his words in properly, *augus Da Cadine, augus Da Hena*, thinking that if one day was good, two were better; and that if Lusmore had one new suit of clothes given him, he should have two.

No sooner had the words passed his lips than he was taken up and whisked into the moat with prodigious force; and the fairies came crowding round about him with great anger, screeching, and screaming, and roaring out, 'Who spoiled our tune? Who spoiled our tune?' and one stepped up to him, above all the rest, and said,

'Jack Madden! Jack Madden!
Your words came so bad in
The tune we felt glad in –
This castle you're had in,
That your life we may sadden;
Here's two humps for Jack Madden!'

And twenty of the strongest fairies brought Lusmore's hump and put it down upon poor Jack's back, over his own, where it became fixed as firmly as if it was nailed on with twelve-penny nails, by the best carpenter that ever drove one. Out of their castle they then kicked him; and, in the morning, when Jack Madden's mother and her gossip came to look after their little man, they found him half dead, lying at the foot of the moat, with the other hump upon his back. Well to be sure, how they did look at each other! But they were afraid to say anything, lest a hump might be put upon their own shoulders. Home they brought the unlucky Jack Madden with them, as downcast in their hearts and their looks as ever two gossips were; and what through the weight of his other hump, and the long journey, he died soon after, leaving they say his heavy curse to anyone who would go to listen to fairy tunes again.

How Cormac Mac Art went to Faery

Cormac, son of Art, son of Conn of the Hundred Battles, was high king of Ireland, and held his court at Tara. One day he saw a youth upon the green having in his hand a glittering fairy branch with nine apples of red. And whensoever the branch was shaken, wounded men and women enfeebled by illness would be lulled to sleep by the sound of the very sweet fairy music which those apples uttered, nor could anyone upon earth bear in mind any want, woe, or weariness of soul when that branch was shaken for him.

'Is that branch thy own?' said Cormac.

'It is indeed mine.'

'Wouldst thou sell it? And what wouldst thou require for it?'

'Will you give me what I ask?' said the youth.

The king promised, and the youth then claimed his wife, his daughter, and his son. Sorrowful of heart was the king, heaviness of heart filled his wife and children when they learned that they must part from him. But Cormac shook the branch amongst them, and when they heard the soft sweet music of the branch they forgot all care and sorrow and went forth to meet the youth, and he and they took their departure and were seen no more. Loud cries of weeping and mourning were made throughout Erin when this was known : but Cormac shook the branch so that there was no longer any grief or heaviness of heart upon anyone.

After a year Cormac said, 'It is a year today since my wife, my son, and my daughter were taken from me. I will follow them by the same path that they took.'

Cormac went off, and a dark magical mist rose about him, and he chanced to come upon a wonderful marvellous plain. Many horsemen were there, busy thatching a house with the feathers of foreign birds; when one side was thatched they would go and seek more, and when they returned not a feather was on the roof. Cormac gazed at them for a while and then went forward.

Again, he saw a youth dragging up trees to make a fire; but before he could find a second tree the first one would be burnt, and it seemed to Cormac that his labour would never end.

Cormac journeyed onwards until he saw three immense wells on the border of the plain, and on each well was a head. From out the mouth of the first head there flowed two streams, into it there flowed one; the second head had a stream flowing out of and another stream into its mouth, whilst three streams were flowing from the mouth of the third head. Great wonder seized Cormac, and he said, 'I will stay and gaze upon these wells, for I should find no man to tell me your story.' With that he set onwards till he came to a house in the middle of a field. He entered and greeted the inmates. There sat within a tall couple clad in many-hued garments, and they greeted the king, and bade him welcome for the night.

Then the wife bade her husband seek food, and he arose and returned with a huge wild boar upon his back and a log in his hand. He cast down the swine and the log upon the floor, and said, 'There is meat; cook it for yourselves.'

'How can I do that?' said Cormac.

'I will teach you,' said the youth. 'Split this great log, make four pieces of it, and make four quarters of the hog; put a log under each quarter; tell a true story, and the meat will be cooked.'

'Tell the first story yourself,' said Cormac.

'Seven pigs I have of the same kind as the one I brought, and I could feed the world with them. For if a pig is killed I have but to put its bones into the stye again, and it will be found alive the next morning.'

The story was true, and a quarter of the pig was cooked.

Then Cormac begged the woman of the house to tell a story.

'I have seven white cows, and they fill seven cauldrons with milk every day, and I give my word that they yield as much milk as would satisfy the men of the whole world if they were out on yonder plain drinking it.'

That story was true, and a second quarter of the pig was cooked.

Cormac was bidden now to tell a story for his quarter, and he told how he was upon a search for his wife, his son and his daughter that had been borne away from him a year before by a youth with a fairy branch.

'If what thou sayest be true,' said the man of the house, 'thou art indeed Cormac, son of Art, son of Conn of the Hundred Battles.'

'Truly I am,' quoth Cormac.

That story was true, and a quarter of the pig was cooked.

'Eat thy meal now,' said the man of the house.

'I never ate before,' said Cormac, 'having only two people in my company.'

'Wouldst thou eat it with three others?'

'If they were dear to me, I would,' said Cormac.

Then the door opened, and there entered the wife and children of Cormac: great was his joy and his exultation.

Then Manannan mac Lir, lord of the fairy cavalcade, appeared before him in his own true form, and said thus, 'I it was, Cormac, who bore away these three from thee. I it was who gave thee this branch, all that I might bring thee here. Eat now and drink.'

'I would do so,' said Cormac, 'could I learn the meaning of the wonders I saw today.'

'Thou shalt learn them,' said Manannan. 'The horsemen thatching the roof with feathers are a likeness of people who go forth into the world to seek riches and fortune; when they return their houses are bare, and so they go on for ever. The young man dragging up the trees to make a fire is a likeness of those who labour for others: much trouble they have, but they never warm themselves at the fire. The three heads in the wells are three kinds of men. Some there are who give freely when they get freely; some who give freely though they get little; some who get much and give little, and they are the worst of the three, Cormac,' said Manannan.

After that Cormac and his wife and his children sat down, and a tablecloth was spread before them.

'That is a very precious thing before thee,' said Manannan, 'there is no food however delicate that shall be asked of it but it shall be had without doubt.'

'That is well,' quoth Cormac.

After that Manannan thrust his hand into his girdle and brought out a goblet and set it upon his palm. 'This cup has this virtue, said he, 'that when a false story is told before it, it makes four pieces of it, and when a true story is related it is made whole again.'

'Those are very precious things you have, Manannan,' said the king.

'They shall all be thine,' said Manannan, 'the goblet, the branch and the tablecloth.'

Then they ate their meal, and that meal was good, for they could not think of any meat but they got it upon the tablecloth, nor of any drink but they got it in the cup. Great thanks did they give to Manannan.

When they had eaten their meal a couch was prepared for them and they lay down to slumber and sweet sleep.

Where they rose on the morrow morn was in Tara of the kings, and by their side were tablecloth, cup, and branch.

Thus did Cormac fare at the court of Manannan, and this is how he got the fairy branch.

Author's notes to the stories

Connla and the Fairy Maiden

Source: From the old Irish 'Echtra Condla chaim maic Cuind Chetchathaig' of the *Leabhar na h-Uidhre* (Book of the Dun Cow), which must have been written before 1106, when its scribe Maelori (Servant of Mary) was murdered.

Guleesh

Source: From Dr Douglas Hyde's *Beside the Fire*, pp. 104–28, where it is a translation from the same author's *Leabhar Sgeulaighteachta*. Dr Hyde got it from one Shamus O'Hart, a gamekeeper of French-park. One is curious to know how far the very beautiful landscapes in the story are due to Dr Hyde, who confesses to have only taken notes. I have omitted a journey to Rome.

The Field of Boliauns

Source: T. Crofton Croker's *Fairy Legends of the South of Ireland*, edited by Wright, pp. 135–9. In the original the gnome is a cluricaune, but as a friend of Mr Batten's had heard the tale told of a lepracaun, I have adopted the better known title.

The Horned Women

Source: Lady Wilde's *Ancient Legends*, the first story.

Hudden and Dudden and Donald O'Neary

Source: From oral tradition, by Mr D. W. Logie, taken down by Mr Alfred Nutt.

The Story of Deirdre

Source: *Celtic Magazine*, xiii, pp. 69, *seq*. I have abridged somewhat, made the sons of Fergus all faithful instead of two traitors, and omitted an incident in the house of the wild men called here 'strangers'. The original Gaelic was given in the *Transactions of the*

Inverness Gaelic Society for 1887, pp. 241, *seq.*, by Mr Carmichael. I have inserted Deirdre's 'Lament' from the *Book of Leinster*.

Munachar and Manachar

Source: I have combined the Irish version given by Dr Hyde in his *Leabhar Sgeulaighteachta*, and translated by him for Mr Yeats' *Irish Folk and Fairy Tales*, and the Scotch version given in Gaelic and English by Campbell, No. viii.

King O'Toole and His Goose

Source: S. Lover's *Stories and Legends of the Irish Peasantry*.

Jack and his Comrades

Source: Kennedy's *Legendary Fictions of the Irish Celts*.

The Shee an Gannon and the Gruagach Gaire

Source: Curtin, *Myths and Folklore of Ireland*, pp. 114, *seq*. I have shortened the earlier part of the tale and introduced into the latter a few touches from Campbell's story of 'Fionn's Enchantment', in *Revue Celtique*, t. i, pp. 193, *seq.*

The Storyteller at Fault

Source: Griffin's *Tales from a Jury-Room*, combined with Campbell, No. xvii, *c*, 'The Slim Swarthy Champion'.

A Legend of Knockmany

Source: W. Carleton, *Traits and Stories of the Irish Peasantry*.

Fair, Brown and Trembling

Source: Curtin, *Myths and Folklore of Ireland*, pp. 78, *seq.*

Jack and his Master

Source: Kennedy, *Fireside Stories of Ireland*, pp. 74–80, 'Shan an Omadhan and his Master'.

Andrew Coffey

Source: From Mr D. W. Logie, written down by Mr Alfred Nutt.

The Lad with the Goatskin

Source: Kennedy, *Legendary Fictions*, pp. 23–31, the adventures of 'Gilla na Chreck an Gour'.

The Fate of the Children of Lir

Source: Abridged from the text and translation published by the Society for the Preservation of the Irish Language in 1883.

Jack the Cunning Thief

Sources: Kennedy, *Stories of Ireland*, pp. 38–46; Campbell, *West Highland Tales*, i, pp. 320, *seq*., 'The Shifty Lad'; Dasent, *Popular Tales from the Norse*, pp. 232–51, 'Master Thief'.

Paddy O'Kelly and the Weasel

Source: Hyde, *Beside the Fire*, pp. 73–91.

The Vision of MacConglinney

Source: Kindly condensed by Mr Alfred Nutt from Professor Meyer's edition of *The Vision* published in book form in 1892. This contains two versions, a longer one from a fourteenth-century manuscript, *Lebhar Breac or Speckled Book*, and a shorter one from a sixteenth-century manuscript in the Library of Trinity College, Dublin.

Dream of Owen O'Mulready

Source: Kindly translated by Mr Leland L. Duncan from *Gaelic Journal*, vol. iv, pp. 57, *seq*.

Morraha

Sources: The second story in Mr W. Larminie's *West Irish Folktales*, pp. 10–30. The framework was collected from P. McGrale of Achill Island, Co. Mayo. The story itself was from Terence Davis of Rendyle, Co. Galway.

The Story of the McAndrew Family

Source: Supplied by Mrs Gale, now in the United States, from the recitation of her mother who left Ireland over fifty years ago.

The Greek Princess and the Young Gardener

Source: Kennedy, *Fireside Stories*, pp. 47–56.

Smallhead and the King's Sons

Source: Mr Curtin's 'Hero Tales of Ireland', contributed to the *New York Sun*.

The Legend of Knockgrafton

Source: Croker, *Fairy Legends of the South of Ireland*.

How Cormac Mac Art went to Faery

Source: Kindly condensed by Mr Alfred Nutt from an English version by Mr S. H. O'Grady in *Ossianic Society's Publications*, vol. iii. The story existed in some form in the early eleventh century.